TOUCH YOUR DEFENSES

Touch Your Defenses

A life in stories.

JEFF SYKES

Indy Pub

First paperback edition September 2024

Book design by Chris M. Ballenger
www.chrisballenger.com

ISBN 979-8-3302-3401-1 (paperback edition)

Printed and bound by Ingram Spark

Published by Jeff Sykes
www.jeffsykes.com

Contents

It Comes Back to You

Blake was seven when he began to realize the world was bigger than the parts he knew about. His family lived in a suburban apartment complex carved from pasture-land astride a busy thoroughfare.

Most of what he knew was Andy and Barney just before the six o'clock news, a few cartoons on Saturday morning—Scooby Doo, Muhammad Ali—and whatever tunes came dancing from car windows passing by his stoop at 4B near the back of Countryside Villa.

It was a Saturday in late August, just after lunch, when he stepped out to see what the afternoon might hold. Blake looked across the playground equipment that became less interesting each day and saw Mandy coming from the sliding glass door. Blonde hair hung below a blue ball cap she pulled down tight but Blake could see her overbite and her pouty mouth as she walked across the playground. He grabbed his bike and headed over.

Mandy kicked at the dirt. Her legs hung from the swing set, her shoulders drooped. Blake noticed the ball glove under her right arm.

"Wanna play catch?" he asked.

Mandy sniffled. "No. I want to be watching the Yankees game on our new cable TV but my mom says I have to be outside."

"What's cable TV?" Blake asked.

"You know, they run a wire to your house. You pay for it and they plug one end into your TV set. Then you can watch movies and Yankees games and cartoons from Atlanta on Turner."

"We don't have that," Blake said, looking back toward 4B.

"You have to pay for it," she said. "Our parents got a card in the mail or something. Ask your mom."

Blake looked down at his feet on the bike pedals, his shoelaces tucked into the Cugas because he'd yet to learn how to tie them. He wasn't going to ask his mom. She'd made it clear to him to stay out of 4B until she called him for supper. She seemed worn down as of late, ever since Elvis died it seemed most adults were in a sad state. Or maybe being an adult made people sad. Blake couldn't tell. Earlier in the week he'd come running home from the school bus—that's how he avoided danger—only to find his mom crying and holding his little sister, also crying. They sat in the apartment's darkness in late afternoon, curtains drawn. The girl slammed her fingers in the heavy apartment door after his mom rushed in from the car, forgetting her in the first flush of the king's death.

Mandy took the ball glove from under her arm and punched it a few times and caught sight of Blake's Cugas.

"You still ain't learned to tie your shoes?" She stood up. "Get off the bike. Let me help you."

Mandy knelt down and pulled the laces from the sides. Her long fingers tipped by dirty nails, elegant but strong. She weaved one lace around the other, placed a finger, wrapped them around and pulled the knot.

"There. Not so bad," she said. "You better learn how before Monday. I heard what Kyle said when we got off the bus yesterday."

Kyle and his brother Bryce, the Starnes twins, were the reason Blake ran home from the school bus each day. They lived in a building around a curve in the parking lot from 4B with their mom and sister. The twins teased Blake relentlessly when they weren't baiting him into a false sense of friendship only to turn on him with their cries of "attack, a-ttack, uh-tack!" as they tackled him to the ground and pummeled him in unison.

"It's 'cause I'm bigger than they are, my mom says. Plus they don't got no daddy around," Blake said. "I don't mind standing up to them but there's two of them and just one of me."

Blake knelt and stuck his other shoe out and Mandy finished and stood.

"Well, you learn to tie those shoes and that's one less thing they can tease you about. Plus you'll be able to run faster."

"My papaw told me not to run from them," Blake said. "He says only cowards run away and that he didn't run from them Chinamen in Korea and I shouldn't run now."

"But you run home from the bus stop everyday."

"Well I ain't running from them. I get off the bus first and run so they can't start no trouble," Blake said.

The swing set chains creaked a bit as Mandy got back up in the plastic saddle. Cardinals and Blue Jays whistled between the few trees the developers left standing. An uneasy peace broken when Blake heard quickened bike pedals coming around the corner of a nearby building.

"Attack, a-ttack, uh-tack!" Kyle Starnes cried as he led his brother in a rush toward the playground. The world seemed to pause an instant as Blake froze. Rear bicycle tires kicked up gravel and red clay as Kyle and Bryce slid to a halt on either side.

"How come you not running, Tuck? I thought you was a scaredy cat the way you run from the bus stop every-day," Kyle said.

"Who's Tuck?" Blake asked. "Why you calling me Tuck. You know my name."

"We gonna call you Tuck 'cause you can't tie your shoes so you tuck them in them Cugas your mom got at Pic'n Pay sissy boy."

"Aw come on Kyle, leave him alone," Mandy said. "You know he's bigger than you but there's two of you. That's not fair. Besides, Blake's a nice kid, he don't start trouble. Why can't y'all be friends? Sure would be more peaceful around here."

Kyle looked Blake up and down, noticed his neatly tied sneakers, and looked over to his brother.

"Maybe you're right. He does seem kind of tough maybe the way he fights us both at the same time," Kyle said. "Say, we was about to go exploring under this hole we found in the fence line. Y'all wanna come?"

Blake looked toward Mandy and she shrugged. "Nah, I gotta go back inside and see if my mom will let me watch the Yankees game now."

"How about you Blake? Not scared are you?" Kyle asked.

"Yeah Blake, come on. We'll play fair," Bryce added. "Besides, I get tired being around Kyle all day. Will be nice to have someone else around."

Blake headed toward the playground's edge, gently thinking about the danger the Starnes twins represented. He let out a huff and was about to step in front of a moving car had he not caught a hint of some bouncy music. The car rolled by and Blake heard "it will come back to you".

Man I love that song, he thought, reflecting on the times he'd heard it coming from speakers in his dad's car. "I seen your picture, I keep it with your letter," the man sang with a strange emphasis on each phrase's ending.

Blake looked both ways this time and followed behind Kyle as Bryce raced ahead, already heading between two apartment buildings toward the complex rear. The mist of the afternoon lifted and the August sun pushed in. Blake reached the fence as Bryce was clearing away debris.

"Do you think you can fit," Kyle asked his brother.

"Yeah, I think the two of us can, but not sure about Tuc.. I mean Blake. He is kinda big."

Bryce moved the last of the brush away and knelt by the hole. He pushed back some grass clumps and smoothed the red clay along the hole's bottom.

"Well see if you fit," Kyle said.

Bryce flattened himself on the earth and stuck his head and then his torso through the gap below the fence line. His feet disappeared just as they heard the dog and the man's voice.

"Get back, get back!" Kyle shouted.

"I told you boys to stay out of my field," they heard the man shout, unseen beyond the fence. Cornstalks rustled and the dog raced toward them. Bryce's head appeared in the hole as he struggled to get back. Blake and Kyle reached down as his shoulders appeared. They pulled Bryce up, his body covered in Carolina red clay, just as the dog's snout appeared below the fence. A german shepherd, its fangs flashed as drool dripped to the ground.

Bryce steadied himself and brushed debris from his chest and bottom.

The man reached the fence and banged on the wood a few times.

"Don't let me catch you in my field again," he shouted. "Y'all need to learn some damn respect for people's property." He banged the wooden slats a few more times.

"Stay out! You hear?"

The boys ran back to their bikes that rested near the back corner of an apartment building.

"Man that was close," Kyle said.

"Too close," Blake replied.

Bryce brushed himself off and caught his breath.

"Did you see the fangs and drool on that dog?" Bryce said. "I thought I was a goner."

The danger excited Blake and for a second his stomach felt loose. He grimaced.

Kyle noticed the funny look on Blake's face and was about to say something but a voice snarled from a window.

"You kids get lost," a man said from the dark. The boys hustled their bikes to the sidewalk, heading back toward 4B.

"I can't go home," Blake said. "And I don't wanna go that way. There was some kind of fight last night in that building next to us."

"Yeah, we saw. And our mom was talking about it on the phone," Kyle said. "She said your mom helped the lady afterward."

"I heard her arguing with my dad about blood or something, cleaning it up," Blake said. "Then she made me go to bed."

The boys looked across the parking lot to the empty playground.

"Let's go to our place," Kyle said. "We can show you our dad's stuff."

Blake had been in their apartment once in the winter, briefly warming his hands and drinking hot chocolate on a snow day. Their dad was gone then too. Blake followed the twins across the blacktop and down the sidewalk away from 4B.

The curve ran toward the back of the complex and Blake looked out across the sloped pasture that ran down toward Minorcas Creek. Beyond the sagging barbed-wire fence the land rippled away in clumps until framed in by woods along the horizon.

The twins stood their bikes before the shrubs separating the building from a small patch of grass and then the sidewalk. Blake did the same and followed them up the stairs. The breezeway was dark and smelled of summer wet. Pungent meat smells wafted from one of the four units on the upper story.

Bryce opened the apartment door and Blake followed.

"Our mom's not here," Kyle said. "She had to work at her weekend job at K-Mart."

The front room was framed by a couch and two chairs. A floor-model television before the window, backlit from the fading afternoon sun. Pictures of the family, and the dad who was rarely there, sat atop the floor model and broke up the bare walls in clusters. Bryce went down the hall and into a room. Blake thought he heard muffled sounds.

Kyle noticed Blake's quizzical look.

"Don't worry none about that," he said. "Come see my dad's war stuff."

Blake followed him to the end of the hall and into the parent's bedroom. Kyle didn't turn on the light but walked to the far wall, itself decorated with photos of men in unbuttoned fatigues in a mountainous country-side with green hills beyond the helicopter's rotor blades.

"That's him," Kyle said, pointing to a thin man with a narrow face and a light black mustache. "He served three tours, but mom said he never really left in his mind. That's why he has to go away sometimes."

"Where does he go," Blake asked.

"She won't tell us," Kyle replied. "To get help, I think, from his aunt and uncle. I just know them as Aunt Dix and Uncle Umstead. Never met them. He goes for a few weeks and comes back. Sometimes he's happy. Mostly he drinks and yells and wakes up in the night thinking he's back over there."

"Where?"

"Some place called Vietnam," Kyle answered. "Kind of like your papaw in Korea, I think, except it never ended or we quit or something. My dad says we left people over there and that's why he can't get it out of his head."

Kyle showed Blake the medals atop the dresser. A bronze star with a red ribbon and a blue streak down the center. Another medal anchored a felt board propped up on a picture holder. This one round, the ribbon yellow with green and white stripes. The words "Vietnam service medal" curved around the circumference. A handful of colored uniform squares.

"This one's for marksmanship," Kyle said. He rubbed his finger across the ribbons and pushed the board back in place.

"They took his guns," Kyle said. "But here's his bayonet. Here's his field knife. His uniform's in the closet."

Kyle went to open the closet but Bryce stepped in.

"We better go," Bryce said.

Kyle pulled his hand from the closet door.

"Yeah, is she getting antsy," he asked.

"I think she might work loose soon," Bryce answered.

Kyle knew the twins had a sister but he'd never seen a dog or a cat. Maybe they got a new pet, he thought.

"Did you get a dog or something?"

"She's a dog alright, but she's not ours," Kyle said.

The boys stepped from the room and moved toward the apartment's front. Kyle stopped by the last door on the right.

Blake heard the muffled sounds again. Kyle opened the door and Blake could see their sister, who was about 12 if he remembered right, tied down to her bed with bits of rope, gunmetal belts around her wrists and ankles anchoring her to the bed frame. A t-shirt or towel tied loose around her mouth.

"My God," Blake said and he felt the knot in his stomach again, a pain or a pressure that demanded relief. He took off past Bryce as Kyle shut the door. Blake ran from the apartment. He bounded down the stairs to his bike and pushed it quickly down the sidewalk.

Blake stopped at the corner to catch his breath. His body felt strange. A weird energy coming from his chest. The birds seemed to speak to him and he felt a disconnect between his mind and the energy racing through his body. His chin quivered and he couldn't tell if he was excited or afraid. The girl had looked at him wild-eyed as she raised her head, her torso restricted by the sheet tight across her chest. Her arms flailed out wide, held down by military strap belts. He shook his head to clear the vision.

His breath came back to him as his wild heart slowed. Kyle was next to him.

"Sorry about that, Blake," he said. "I guess we should've kept that to ourselves."

"Why is she tied up?" Blake asked. "Is your mom punishing her?"

"Hardly," Kyle said. "She tries to be our mom when mom's not at home. We done told her to leave us alone. She won't listen. She tried to tell us we couldn't have another bowl of cereal and then she said we couldn't watch Wild, Wild, West. So we put her up."

Blake felt like running. He felt like running all the way back to 4B. To ask his mom for help. To keep him safe. To make him feel loved. But she'd told him not to come back until she called him for dinner. The sun moved lower in the sky as the cicadas began low in the distance.

Bryce was suddenly next to Blake and the twins had him boxed in.

"She's alright," Bryce said. "We didn't do nothing to her. She mouthed off to us from the other room so Kyle pretended he was hurt and called for her. She came down the hall and we jumped her from both sides of the kitchen."

Blake remembered the time earlier this summer when the boys asked him to swim in the deep end of the pool. There were few families around that evening and as they rocked the deep with cannonballs and jackknifes Blake had tried to come up from the water but the twins held him down. He fought and grasped for anything to hold onto but the twins' water slick limbs evaded his grasp. The twins held onto the concrete edge and continued to kick him below the surface.

Blake had been about to pass out, his mouth filling with chlorinated water, when a man scattered the twins and pulled him to safety.

Earlier that month the twins had pummeled him in the back of the school bus, Bryce giving him rib shots as Kyle held his hand over Blake's mouth.

An older girl named Tracy, a fifth grader with jet black skin and beads in her rope-braided hair, smacked Bryce across his face.

"Leave that boy alone," she said. "He ain't done shit to y'all."

She was bigger than the three boys put together and Kyle let go and put his hands up.

"Ok, Tracy. Ok," he said. "We're just teaching him to expect the unexpected."

Blake thought about these things and thought he should run home to 4B. Kyle took hold of his bike handle.

"Come on now Blake, she's ok. She'll work loose soon and then she'll tell mom and then we'll deny it," Kyle said. "That's just how it is at our house. Our dad's tied us up with those belts plenty of times for being bad. He says it's to 'teach us our place.'"

Blake didn't have anywhere else to go. He couldn't go home. Mandy was watching her Yankees game. The twins would tackle him if he ran. He knew the drill by now. If he sat here on his bike at the corner, maybe he'd be safe.

A station wagon came along the parking lot's curve. More music coming from the windows upon approach. A piercing guitar, gritty with a faint Hawaiian feel, the music rose and slid down in a rotor wash of notes.

"And when you smile for the camera, I know I love you better!"

"I'm sick of that song," Bryce said. "Yeah, it will come back to you," the boy sang. "What does it even mean?"

"I don't know," Blake said. "But I like the music. It makes me want to move around. It's groovy."

"Groovy my ass," Kyle said. "Our dad hates that song. He said so last time. He likes that Eagles band. Says that's real music. Sometimes after he fights my mom he drinks and they play some of their songs. One's about a to-kill-ya sunrise, he says, and the other's about a new kid coming around. Johnny come lately, he calls it."

"Kind of like you," Bryce said. "The new kid. That's why we like fighting with you. My dad says it's what boys do."

Blake's butt began to hurt from sitting still on the bike so long. He went to get off the bike.

"Where you going?" Kyle asked. "Why don't we go down to the creek? I don't think that old man owns it. See."

Kyle pointed to the distance where the wooden fence kept going straight along the back of the apartment row that included 4B. The fence ran straight down the field's slope, disappearing with the land's curve toward the creek bottom. The field across from the twins' apartment, wide and inviting.

"Alright, let's go," Blake said. Moving across the lot and to the field's edge would at least get him from between the twins. The boys walked their bikes amidst the cars and stopped along the barbed wire fence.

"We can leave our bikes here," Kyle said and the boys made their way through a gap in the wires. The field's dirt was lumpy and thick with ground cover. Blake felt free among the open land and his cares receded.

The group made their way toward the creek bottom and Blake's mind began to consider the rocks and logs and crawdads he might find in the thin flow of Minorcas Creek. He walked ahead of the twins and past a ravine when the air around him exploded.

"Attack! A-ttack! Uh-ttack," was all Blake heard as the rocks and clods of dirt knocked him off balance and he fell into the ravine. Kyle and Bryce stood over him, showering Blake with clumps of dirt pulled from the field. He tried to stand but the weird angle of the ravine's bottom made it hard to find footing. He rose to his hands and knees but the clip of a rock struck his head and he fell back.

Face down in the red dirt he put his hands over his head. Blake felt he could survive if he was still.

Bryce uttered guttural cries as he pulled clumps of earth, raised it over his head and slammed it down onto Blake's body, motionless in the cut.

Of a sudden, the twins stopped and jumped into the ravine. Kyle held Blakes' face into the red earth, wet now with the boy's blood.

"Blake! Blake!," he heard his mother calling in the distance.

"Shut up sissy boy," Kyle said. "Don't move."

"Don't you dare cry for your momma," Bryce demanded.

Blake felt the pressure holding his head recede.

"Oh, shit," Kyle said and the twins raced away toward the creek.

Blake gathered himself. His head throbbed and his face stung from the caked clay in his eyes and nostrils.

The boy rose, a survivor, and as he oriented himself he looked across the ravine's top, his height allowing him to see just across the grass.

In the distance, at the edge of the field he saw Mandy eating an apple.

His mother raced toward him, the twins' sister next to her with the loosened t-shirt still around her collar.

Ugly as Sin

Derrick was only outside because he wanted a cigarette and some fresh air and to walk off the third erection
Mary's bare thighs had given him during the Christmas
cantata's first act.

He slipped from his chair at the end of the balcony's
third row and was around the exit and to the steps before
Todd, his best friend who'd dated Mary for two months
now, looked up from where his fingers rested entwined
with Mary's, his wrist brushing against the charms dangling from her tennis bracelet.

There were a few older couples moving through the
vast concrete lobby at Reynolds Auditorium, but no
adults from the church leadership or those involved with
the youth group. So Derrick passed through the double
doors and into the freedom of a December night.

He followed the walkway around the auditorium's
side to avoid being detected once he lit the filtered
Camel, enjoying the pungent aroma as the smoke hit his
nostrils for the first time. He'd just flicked the match

onto the erect winter grass, frozen in place by a sudden cold snap of the type that visits central North Carolina before the often mild winters set in, when he saw two people coming down the walkway.

He turned back toward the front of the auditorium and caught sight of a crescent moon just below Orion's sword held in the distance.

"Derrick! What's going on?"

It was Jeff Pyrtle, another youth group member. Beside him Kevin Ballance, the pastor's eldest son. "Still smoking those things?" Jeff said. "I thought you'd made a prayer request last month for help to stop?"

Derrick pulled on the filter and inhaled the smoke before blowing it high into the vacant night.

"Kind of tough," he said. "What are you dudes doing out here?"

"We're heading back to the church," Kevin said. "Trey wants us to get the PA working in the gym so it will be ready for tomorrow."

The youth group had grown very large. Much larger than when Derrick first started at this church years earlier while still in fifth grade. His middle school group had maybe twenty kids but once he hit high school the youth group exploded and the church grew weekly until it became the largest, most visible church in town. Its prominent position at a major intersection across from Wake Forest University didn't hinder the progress.

The youth group had outgrown the classrooms, even the new areas of the church that spread out from the original building on both sides like angel wings.

Jeff turned to walk and Derrick followed him down the sidewalk leading to the parking lot. He would walk to the end and finish his cigarette and then turn back to look for Todd and Mary and see if they wanted to bail.

"Who's the new girl Todd's with?" Kevin asked him.

"Man is she ugly," Jeff said.

"Ugly as sin," Kevin replied.

Derrick was stunned as he pulled the Camel from his lips. But he was in no mood to argue and so he replied in a flat tone that masked his shock and anger.

"Her name's Mary. She lives in Buena Vista. I guess they met in class or something."

Derrick stopped walking. "I like her a lot. She's a nice person."

He turned without speaking and walked back toward the steps leading to the concert hall's entrance. Pausing at the base of the steps he looked back to Orion. Dots of light forming a pattern interpreted ages before. He liked to look at the stars and try to find his own patterns but none ever came. So he contented himself with the structure of the heavens.

He'd long ago grown tired of Christians. Their patterns bored him. But he liked the shape of any number of the girls he'd grown up with in the church. Girls turning to women all around him. Todd could have his pick of the bunch. It'd been that way since they first became friends six years earlier, meeting on a ball field, talking about sports during Sunday school, growing closer on sleepovers or day trips with their families.

Todd was his best friend. They'd been inseparable for years. Now that they each had their own car and their own job and their own pocket money and Todd even had an attractive girlfriend, their pair merely became three of a kind. Everyone knew they were like brothers, especially the pastor's son Kevin. He was a year younger but he'd played countless hours of basketball with them and spent an equal amount in church pews or classrooms talking game or girls. He knew what he was doing calling Mary ugly in front of Derrick. Todd would hit the roof.

Derrick had seen Mary around the high school halls before she began dating his best friend. She was a pretty girl with a sweet mouth, pursed lips like a ripe plum. She was small and thin and oh so feminine. Her dresses and dangling bracelets helped her cut a swath of womanhood among the girls at school still wearing jeans and tennis shoes.

She lived in one of those neighborhoods full of large homes near the university, while Todd lived in a small apartment complex next to a public housing project. Derrick's parents were divorced now and he lived with his mom in a small ranch just outside the city limits.

Derrick was surprised at the suddenness of Todd's fall for Mary. Overnight they'd gone from spending their afternoons finding a basketball game or getting a burger and fries to timing their freedom to Mary's whims.

But they'd not cast him off. Quite the opposite. Mary was engaging and Derrick enjoyed their conversations about music and friends or where they might go to school in less than two years. Todd's parents were very strict with his comings and goings. His dad was a deacon at the church and prone to making the loudest amen shouts at least once a Sunday.

Derrick didn't realize at first that he was Todd's cover story. But as the fall progressed and the routines became established he adjusted and played his role as protector of his friend's private time.

It amounted to little more than keeping up appearances at first, showing up as he'd done since getting a driver's license and taking Todd to the rec center or the Y to play basketball, chatting with Todd's mom about school and grades and the looming SATs, and then taking Todd to Mary's. He'd always try to leave, to give them space to be alone, but it was Mary who would beg him to stay.

Over the course of several weeks they had all grown very close. Mary only recently began to come to church with Todd, where he was even more popular than at school, and she'd caused quite the stir among the gossip chain. Derrick was the one left to field many questions about her, mostly from girls who attended other high schools across the city. Most were harmless questions about her name, where she lived, what she was like.

Kevin and Jeff were fully aware of this.

Back in the auditorium's lobby he looked for Todd and Mary and saw them coming from the balcony steps. Mary spotted him, waved her hand and smiled. She was far from ugly. Her dirty blond hair hugged her oval face and bounced with her stride. Her light pink makeup like pastel on the canvas of her brown skin.

She had a toothy grin, perhaps the one flaw he could account for, but the sparkle in her hazel eyes attracted his attention and her mouth was to die for. "How can anybody think she's ugly?" he thought. "What's ugly is all these fake people pretending to be holy, hiding their fears and hates behind a lie."

He must have looked disturbed as Todd and Mary approached.

"What's the matter babe?" she asked.

"Nothing, just bored."

"You look ready to fight somebody, man," Todd said. "Cheer up dude, it's Christmas."

"Yeah, you're right. It's just - I get bored with this scene lately. With this repetition."

"I know what you need," Mary said. "A girlfriend. Who do we know Todd?"

"Now, now, hold up," Derrick said. "I'm content enjoying your happiness for the moment."

"Just don't get too attached," Todd said.

"Now you two don't fight," Mary said. "We can just be happy together. Are you guys about ready to go back to my parent's house? Mom picked up a couple of movies for us at Blockbuster today."

Todd and Mary walked along in front of him on the way to the car. They had all come in Derrick's Oldsmobile and he thought about saying something to them about the insult as he reached to unlock the passenger door and let them into the spacious back seat. But he didn't want to spoil Mary's night, or cause trouble for his friend. He knew well that Todd would get angry if told what Jeff and Kevin had said.

He was silent on the short drive back to Mary's home, where they often spent an evening in the basement watching movies. Derrick had been able to buy a six pack of beer at the Shell station near the university. He easily passed for a college student because he was well over six feet tall. He'd bought beer there several times despite it being just a few months past his sixteenth birthday.

It was cold in the basement and Mary had asked Derrick to come sit on the couch with them. "You've got to keep this side warm," she said while lifting the edge of the quilt as he slid underneath.

Just as he got settled she asked him to hand her the beer can on the table in front of them. He leaned forward and took the can and handed it to her, their fingers touched for a moment and she glanced at him with those large hazel eyes before leaning back into Todd.

"Okay, babe, start it again," she said.

The movie was a teen romance about a poor girl and a rich guy and her poor friend who gets his feelings hurt when she no longer wants to pal around with him after school, opting instead for the rich guy's car and house parties. She ended up feeling slighted in her new scene and pouted in isolation from both suitors, until she forgives the rich guy, the poor friend absolves her and she disappears into a Hollywood ending with her Romeo. In a brief denouement, the poor friend is seen catching the eye of a cute blonde attracted to his sartorial panache.

Todd excused himself as the credits rolled to pass what remained of his two beers. As he rounded the corner, Mary leaned across Derrick to put her beer can on the end table. She lingered, with her erect nipple pressed into his forearm, before she withdrew. He shifted in discomfort as Mary adjusted the quilt, moving her hands below the downy thickness.

But she didn't stay still. She moved her hand across Derrick's leg until her fingers wrapped around his penis.

"What are you doing?" he gasped.

"Shh, babe. Be still. I just had to know if I was right. I see the way you look at me," she whispered. "You're a sweet boy, Derrick. Don't play seconds to anyone."

She kissed his cheek and pulled her hand away, straightening the quilt nice and flat this time. Todd came back in a moment and said he needed to get home.

"I'll wait outside," Derrick said. He shifted clumsily to hide the lingering excitement, covering it with his wadded jacket as he moved for the basement door.

"Bye, babe. See ya tomorrow maybe?"

"Yeah, have a good night. Thanks for the movie and stuff."

Outside he waited before starting the car, hoping the winter air would cool him off.

It did not.

Work it Out

It's dark in Big Red's place. The blinds are drawn tight and the only lamp has a thick orange shade that gives just enough light to make out the edges of the furniture and the markings on the Nintendo controller.

Not that Keith needs light to know which buttons to push to make Lawrence Taylor chase Dan Marino on the pixelated television resting on the makeshift counter. He's got that memorized. Muscle memory. Even if Big Red lights another pin joint Keith won't forget. He's dialed in. The kind of focus that worried his grandma back in Huntersville when she would try to entice him out of the arcade at the mall. Back then it was Ten Yard Fight, but his parents got him a Nintendo for Christmas two years ago, but he sold it for dope three months later.

But Big Red has Tecmo Bowl. And Keith has Lawrence Taylor, LT for short, and you can't block him. You can only hope to contain him.

"Damn, motherfucker, why don't you pick the Jets or some shit next time," Big Red says when Keith, um, LT that is, plants Dan Marino on the analog green turf once again. "That's it. You can't come in my house and pick the Giants. Ever. Or the 49ers for that matter."

Keith smirks and picks up the bottle of Coke on the end table. He doesn't mean to be a bad guest, but Tecmo Bowl is something he takes seriously. It's not like the classes he could give a fuck about or the job he goes to at the rec center checking professors and the occasional Howie into the racquetball courts. Those three hours drive him crazy. He's lucky there's no clock in the utility storage area where he puts up the portable table. But once he gets the four o'clock regulars signed in he goes out into the hall every five minutes to check the clock above the large glass window separating the courts from the corridor.

No, Tecmo Bowl is the shit. It's fast and requires strategy and if he gets just so high he enters a perfect state of equilibrium where his racing thoughts meet the frequency of his hand-eye coordination.

Big Red slams his controller into the couch as Keith steers Joe Morris into the vertical end zone. "Man, go home. Why you always down here beating me on my own game? You the only dude that can beat me at this shit."

"Cause I love you, Red. That's why," Keith says. "That and you are the only dude I know who has Tecmo, Straight Outta Compton and Fear of a Black Planet."

Big Red smirks and leans his head back. "You the craziest white dude I know. You probably shoulda been a brother."

"My grandma would have a fit."

"What's she got against black people?"

"I don't know. Never asked her. Just old I guess."

He knew but he wasn't saying. No point in going into all that. She wasn't going to change. Better just to change himself and keep his mouth shut when he was back home and she complained about "the blacks" and something she saw on the cable news.

Up on campus the next day he went through the motions. Yessir, 1066. Federal layer cake, yessir. Quid pro quo, yessir, sir. Four hours of that. In the hall of the law department, McInturff called out to him.

"Keith, man, do the lyrics for that Fuck the Police song. Everette here doesn't believe that you know them."

"Oh yeah? Well fuck Everette and fuck the police and I said it with authority, cause the niggas on the street is a majority of gangs, and to whoever I'm stepping, a motherfuckin' weapon is kept in ..."

"I told you," McInturff said to Everette, who stood there, mouth agape.

"How, better yet, why do you know that crap?" Everette said.

"Simple. It's just more interesting than Winger and a lot of those guys are more entertaining than your frat brothers," Keith said.

"Yeah, but these blacks won't help you get a job or get into law school."

"Maybe so," Keith said.

"And don't get caught around them when one gets drunk and decides to beat up a white boy. You'll find out who your friends are then real quick."

On Saturday morning Keith woke up and after milling around the apartment he walked halfway down the row to knock on Darryl's door. A withdrawn voice said "come in" and Keith was smacked at once with the gloomy darkness. Darryl sat on the couch and didn't move as Keith shut the door and took a seat.

"Damn, D, what happened to your face?" Keith said. He'd just observed Darryl's swollen cheek, eye of black and the way his lip's left side pressed against the swollen skin like an elongated balloon about to pop.

Darryl made a ruinous slurping noise and then pulled on the straw in his juice glass. He turned slowly, as if heavily medicated.

"I got my ass kicked by the frat boys at the Theta house across the field there," Darryl said. "Shawn wasn't here, he was working late at Lilly's, and so I walked over there about midnight. I was bored and just wanted to get out. I didn't see your car, so I kept going over to their house.

"Anyway, I had a beer and was mingling on the back deck. Your friend McInturff was there and that blonde dude Everette."

Darryl stopped to slurp again, and then spit in a can, pausing to wipe ruddy saliva from his inflated lip.

"They were telling nigger jokes and I was about to walk off. But then Everette told this crude joke about Indians, and, well I shouldn't have opened my mouth, but I did. I told them that I was part Cherokee and that I didn't appreciate their sense of humor."

Darryl wiped his lip, slurped, and then leaned gingerly back into the sofa.

"Somebody hit me from the side. Then I was on the ground and they were kicking me in the ribs and in the face. McInturff got them off me and helped me off the porch. I came in here and passed out." He spit again.

"I probably need to go to the fucking hospital for stitches. My lip won't stop bleeding."

Keith had a fat bag of weed on Tuesday and no one was around. He walked down to Big Red's place at the end of the row about two o'clock. They smoked a joint and Big Red made him choose between the Steelers and the Rams if he wanted to even dream about touching the Nintendo controller.

Big Red himself selected the Dolphins as always. The Dan Marino to Mark Clayton connection was his favorite. John was there and egged Keith on as Big Red ran up the score in the third quarter.

"He's kicking your ass big dog!" John laughed. "LT can't save you now." The EPMD tape ended.

"Put on that PE tape with 911 is a Joke," Keith said.

John passed around the eight inch plastic bong they kept under the end table. Chuck D got it going and as Big Red scored again the first song reached its crescendo in a frenzy of raw drums and amalgamated samples. Voices over the top in a counter beat to the main rhythm pulsated in Keith's ears. He listened, trying to make out the refrain.

"Get violent, let's get violent. Get violent, let's get violent." Over and over. Keith heard this clearly and said so to John.

"Man, you is crazy. The song is Brothers Gonna Work it Out and that's what they are saying," John replied. "Yo Red, this dude thinks they are saying let's get violent."

"Man you smoke too much weed, big dog," Red said. "Maybe you should check yourself."

One Night on Coward Knob

Crisp leaves crunch on the ridge line up to Coward Knob. My friends Jordan and Will rush ahead with Laurel. Kim is just in front of me and I watch her calf muscle flex with each step.

Jordan and Will fight to be first. I'm more concerned with maintaining my balance along the incline. Anticipation pulls me forward. Despite the burning fatigue I refuse to give in.

When Kim pulls up, I stop alongside her. She wipes her brow and moves strands of black hair behind her ear.

"Steeper than I remembered," she says.

Ahead of us the colors dance between the trees. Laurel has stopped as well, unable to keep up with the alpha males. Her red hair mingles with the breeze and she waves encouragement.

Soon we catch up to where Laurel waits.

"Those two never rest," she says. "I guess they assume you'll help us, Scott, if we need a push."

Kim stops and our eyes follow the two miniature figures up the mountainside. They remind me of celebratory figures printed on rainbow culture posters. Hands in the sky, hair flowing, wildly jumping. They approach the crest and Jordan disappears first.

"We should catch up," I say. "Don't want to miss the show."

Laurel reaches out for Kim's hand.

"Come on girl," she says. "You can make it."

She pulls Kim a few steps forward. Just before Laurel turns to beckon me on I adjust my camera bag and fall in.

"Hurry up, Scott! The light is perfect," Will calls from above. Deeper breaths, pushing myself. Soon I join them at the crest.

Laurel lights up as she reclines into Will's embrace. The April sun radiates across her face like a cherry blossom.

The dense forest gives way to a rock prominence some sixty yards across. It slopes for thirty feet in three varied sections before the rocks drop in steep gaps of air and the forest begins again. Low in the distance is the valley along Caney Fork Creek, which we came up to the trailhead off Tobacco Road. Cullowhee Mountain rises across the open space and the lustrous hills fade into blue.

No one speaks as five minds react to this beauty. Jordan wraps his slight arms around Kim. He whispers something into her ear and she turns to face him. They kiss softly and turn back to the late afternoon.

I take out the camera and move down the rock face so as not to attract attention. Just as I've moved a few degrees between the sun and the heat between Jordan and Kim I press the shutter. The weightless light bounces off Kim's high cheekbones. It plays along the strands of her hair that fall to where Jordan's chin rests on her right shoulder.

His blond hair is pulled into a ponytail. The sunlight reveals hints of gold and light green in his eyes. His childish smile, one of his many calming features, belies his devilish ways. He's not wearing his glasses today and so the thick soul patch below his mouth stands out. I'm able to get off one more shot before they realize what I'm about.

"Dude you have got to stop with that camera," Jordan says. "I'm beginning to think you got something going for my girl."

He's smiling as he moves past and guides Kim along the ribbed surface of the knob. Will is reclined on his elbows and forearms. Laurel sits between his legs with her red hair burning against his muscular frame.

"Get used to it Jordan because I think he's changing his major, isn't that so Scotty?" Will says. Kim and Jordan fold into the rock and I move around to get the sun behind my back.

Before they can protest I've captured a half-dozen more shots.

"I think so," I say. "It hit me sometime over spring break that I have so many attractive friends and I'm here in this beautiful place that maybe I need to spend my time making a visual record. Why waste all this time and beauty chasing a business degree?"

I put the camera in the bag and kneel beside Will and look back out across the spectacle.

"No eternal reward will forgive us now for wasting the dawn," I say, quoting Jim Morrison.

"But we came here to see the sunset," Laurel says, gesturing to the sky.

She means for me not to get caught up in a detailed conversation with Will. So I take a deep breath. I feel the first hint of the acid we each swallowed about an hour earlier. The first tint of amber begins to appear as the afternoon fades.

"I want to get just a few more photos of you guys as the light changes," I say and slide myself across the rock, moving like a spider on my hands and feet.

As I roll the film forward I look over to Jordan and Kim, still enthralled by the beauty of these mountains in spring. Before Jordan can notice I catch a few shots of their far off gaze, framing them in the late light. I catch a loose rock with my foot and slip. I barely catch myself with my right hand as I raise the camera with my left.

Jordan notices what I'm doing and gives me a dismissive glance.

He shifts Kim to the other side of his body and lowers his face toward me.

"If you're finished now we can smoke this bud."

Standing and capping the lens I say, "Yeah, I think that would be good."

We all move closer together and spend about ten minutes evaporating orange-haired buds into the cooling air.

A few clouds have crept through the sky. The mountains spread across the horizon. A sudden warm breeze wafts across the rock face. I notice a thin cloud floating parallel to the top of the hills with a stem sticking up at a 45 degree angle higher into the sky. It has the shape of a submarine I've seen in books about old wars.

Jordan wraps his arms tighter around Kim then points toward the horizon. I think about turning to say something but remember Laurel told me to be quiet.

And so I move my focus back to the now wine red sky. My cloud remains submerged in the light sea. Its bow takes shape with a raised tip, like a rhino horn cutting through the air. A beautiful apparition floating in the sky as the light fades.

Only the mountain tops remain, with the lower reaches dark and still. The sunset lifts through crimson to light rose and my cloud moves toward east's darkness. My eyes are adjusting when I hear movement behind me.

Laurel moves down to my level.

"It must be interesting," she says.

"What?"

"Whatever it is you've been staring at silently for 20 minutes," she says and rubs her hands together. She takes the light fleece jacket tied around her waist and slides it over her shoulders. "Having a good time?"

"So far yeah. You?"

"I decided not to drop after all. Will's mad at me."

He's walked over to Jordan and I think he motions for him to bring Kim over to us.

"He's mad that I won't trip with him. Upset that we won't ..." she hesitates. "You know ... be in the same frame of mind later."

She is sitting beside me now. I'm cross legged with my camera bag in my lap. The disappearance of light seems to have sucked what bit of warmth there was in the air but the heat remaining on the knob is comfortable.

Laurel's face is next to my shoulder. I know she's only one person but the fractals have started and I see several of her. Each one is outlined in black marker and the movement of her head and extended hands as she speaks is mechanical, robotic even, as if she's a video game with a glitch.

She's given the last two years of her life to Will but lately I've noticed an edge of tension between them. She's taken to voicing her fears to me.

"Things will be ok once his trip settles in," I say. "We've all been down this path before."

"Yeah but each time it is different you know."

There's sadness in her eyes that I've not noticed. I think she regrets coming out here with us. I think she regrets more than just that.

I'm wondering where Will is and why he's left Laurel here with me and so I look over and Jordan and Kim and Will have disappeared.

"What in the hell," I say.

"Huh?" Laurel asks.

"Where did they go?"

"I don't want to know," she says.

Movement at the edge of the woods. In the rising moonlight three bodies joined as one.

"What the fuck."

Laurel buries her face in my chest. My arm around her heaving body before I realize what's going down. Kim, Jordan and Will melt into one over by the tree line about fifty feet up the rock. This I did not expect. And the suddenness of it is the strange part. Laurel is crying. A whimper on my now damp chest. Not a wail but a muted suffering.

I caress her shoulder, finding the soft fleece and her nearness adds warmth to the suddenly cold night.

"Do you want to head back to the car?" I ask her. She raises her tear filled face to me. Her helplessness stirs my heart. I wipe away a stream of tears with my left thumb and lean down to softly kiss her cheek. Pulling her head closer to my chest I wrap my arms around her and hold her to me.

"He's leaving me Scotty. He's going back home and not coming back. He said it's over and he doesn't feel committed to me anymore."

"Don't cry Laurel," I say. "Come on. Let's get out of here."

I'm about half-way standing when the camera bag goes tumbling down the face of Coward Knob. I try to dive for it but only land on my chest as my chin splits open when it hits the granite. I hear the bag bounce a few times before a period of silence after which it lands along the slanted forest floor.

"I can't believe that just happened," I say and roll onto my back and begin to sit up. Laurel kneels beside me and a warm trickle covers my chin. I wipe at it but the sting in the middle lets me know I'm bleeding.

"Here," she says and hands me a small athletic towel. "Will has a few towels and an extra shirt in his bag."

Pressing the towel to my chin my mind is on that camera bag God knows how far down the mountain side. The calculation is how and when I am going to find it.

I'm working this over in my mind when I remember my friends have disappeared in the darkness up the hill. I recall seeing Jordan and Kim do this twice at parties. They've never approached me about it and honestly if they did I'm not sure I could.

I pull the towel back and touch my finger to my chin It's still bleeding.

I try not to look to where they are but
straight there anyway. Three peop'
etted by moonlight against the tree

"I cannot believe Will is doing th.
you out of here."

"What about your camera?"

"Nothing I can do tonight. Maybe I can get back out here in the morning and find it."

We walk gingerly to where the path down to the road opens up.

Walking back to the car I swear I can feel eyes following us. A creepy sensation glides up the back of my neck. What began as just another afternoon of rolling with it has turned into chaos. There is also sadness. There is a delirious sense of guilt. A sense that I deserved to have my camera smashed, my trip shattered.

We're making decent time down the back side of Coward Mountain despite the darkness. The rocks and trees I passed on the way up serve as a guide and a brace against the gravity of the earlier sunset.

Near the point where Kim and I paused to watch the race to the crest, I hear the dogs. I sense that our paths will cross. I hope we get to the car first, but I remember we came in Jordan's car. I only hope he left it unlocked.

We come to a broken elevation in the path and I make the slight drop over a fallen tree and around a boulder. Only the trunk of a small tree keeps me from falling. With my feet on level ground I turn back and step one foot toward Laurel.

Her step is uncertain and she begins to waver. Laurel omes to rest in my arms and I hold firm. I take a deep ath and can smell the sweetness of her hair. The full- of her body sends electricity across my chest. We together for a moment.

"I am glad you are my friend, Scott. You've been a great friend," she says and is now looking up to me. Her eyes are brilliant in the night air. I hear the dogs again, less faint than before, and she hears them this time. "What is that?"

"I'm not sure," I say. "A pack of dogs I think. We'd better get to the car."

The path makes itself apparent in the darkness. It's an easy decline from here. Just a few minutes to the road where Jordan parked his car. I remember the road leads up from Caney Fork and that we passed one or two homes set back into nooks in the mountains around us. I didn't bother to notice much more than that.

I feel the watching again. But my senses are fused and it's hard to separate bliss from fear. I try to pass it off as excess psychedelic energy but that trip has faded. I wonder if they are still at it or if they've reclined across each other and are smoking a joint in peace. I stop and look back to see if the watching I feel is just the trio coming up on us. There is nothing but darkness.

I hear the sonorous cries of hound dogs growing less distant. What at first sounded like one or two dogs barking in the night is now a symphony of yelping.

The trees form a stockade along the edge of the forest. We emerge from the tree line and into the road, leaving behind the tension of the hike. But up the road I see a dark figure moving toward us. The absence of light prevents me from discerning exactly what it is. We move closer to the car and I take Laurel's hand.

The dogs seem to be just over the crest of the road in a faint glow. We move around the front of the car to the passenger doors, relieved to find them unlocked. I try not to act delirious or frighten Laurel. But she catches the shock on my face as I hold the door.

"What's the matter, Scott? What are you looking at?"

"I .. uh ... I'm not sure," I say. "I ... I must be tripping out, you know, seeing things. Let's just get in the car. I think it must be hunting dogs coming."

I pause and look back up the road as Laurel slides across the seat. The figure is upright now, like a man, but its girth is incredible. Rounded shoulders backlit by the growing light coming over the crest. It stands seven or eight feet tall. If I was sober I'd swear it wore a crown of feathers but was part bear. It raises one arm and in the moonlight I can make out the claws.

As the vanguard of the dog pack comes over the hill followed by the floodlights of an International Scout, the figure darts into the woods just behind us. I'm in the car next to Laurel and pulling the door shut in an instant.

"Are you ok Scott? You are whiter than a sheet."

"I think they are hunting a bear. I just saw it before it went into the woods. I can't believe I don't have my camera. It was the biggest bear I have ever seen and it stood up and sort of like waved its claws at me."

Laurel pulls close to me and takes hold of my arm. The road is flooded with Plott Hounds of various sizes and as they pass there are a few men walking among them. One of them stops by the car and looks in. He's carrying a scoped rifle.

"You'uns all right in there?" he asks while pushing the brim of his Stetson back off his forehead. I lean over Laurel and crack the window as the Scout rumbles past.

"Yeah mister, we're fine. Been hiking up the Knob and we are waiting on a few friends to come down."

"Well not smart to be up there after dark this time of year. Bears are coming out of hibernation. Real hungry. We been tracking one all the way up from the creek."

"Yea, I think I saw it just ahead of your dogs. It moved into the woods."

"They're smart creatures for sure. But we got some dogs with a few years on 'em too. They'll sniff him out. You'uns take care now. We'll be seeing you."

I close the window back as the man walks off toward the Scout that's stopped about twenty feet up the road. The man gets in the truck and as it pulls off I see Jordan coming across the road. He's leading Kim by the hand. Will gets in the front passenger seat as Kim opens the door next to me.

"Can you make some room Scotty?" she says. I move over to the middle as Laurel scoots to the driver's side. Jordan starts the car and gets it turned around to head back down toward the main road. I think about telling them about the bear, or whatever it was that I saw, but no one is speaking and for once I think I should just keep quiet.

I can't see anything seated in the middle of the back seat and so my eyes fix on the gravel road caught in the whir of Jordan's headlights. Will stares immovable out of the passenger window and I notice Laurel doing the same next to me. I wonder what thoughts connect them at this moment. I wonder what desires separate them from their shared past.

We bottom out of the gravel road and Jordan pushes a cassette into the car stereo as he picks up speed on Caney Fork Road. At the end of a straight stretch we pass Johns Creek Church and shoot right with the creek as the road snakes. The music in the car grows from a clean arpeggiated mood to a frenzied, hypnotic rhythm. Layered distorted guitars with a man's high pitched voice dancing across the landscape:

Erotic Jesus lays with his Marys.
Loves his Marys.
Bits of puzzle,
Fitting each other.
Oh my Marys!
Never wonder...
Night is shelter
For nudity's shiver...
All now with wings!

Bluff

We take NC 209 off the highway in Waynesville and drive north for what feels like forever until I see a small sign for a place called Bluff. Brook told me to just roll with it until I see the sign. Now he starts looking for a gravel road just before a switch back to the right.

"Slow down, Scott," he tells me, handing the sheet with the directions on it to his girlfriend Darcie, who sits in the backseat. There's no traffic around us. We'd followed motorcycles after crossing into Madison County, but only passed cars going the other way for the last hour. We're just below Hot Springs, almost to Tennessee. The sparse humanity out this way is comforting, allowing us to enjoy in solitude (accompanied by Exile on Main Street blasting from the Boston Acoustic speakers in my car) the verdant splendor of the area. Not many flowers are out this early in spring, but dogwoods are in bloom set amidst thick rhododendrons and mountain laurel on the roadside.

We've passed a few clearings among this dense forest, although the valley back at Spring Creek was lush with neatly rowed fields and a crisp coat of white paint on the aged clapboards of the Methodist church. We've climbed back up along the spine of a ridge line toward Bluff. Brook spots the gravel drive before a sharp right curve twenty yards ahead.

"This must be it," he says. "We'll have to take it on faith." He's described our destination as a refurbished cabin at the end of a solitary road cut years ago into the forest. A logging road cut by day laborers toiling for merciless overlords in the heyday of the Depression of the 1930s, when aimless men were as expendable as the felled trees being made into boards shipped north to fuel America's endless consumptive thirst. Nothing but hardwood forest lines the gravel road that's barely wide enough to let two cars creep past each other on a straight stretch. Forget it if they meet at road speed in a curve.

The road rises to the right then falls before rising again for ten minutes more. Beyond the switchbacks we float up a last incline. An opening at the top appears and then the rear of three cars. As we approach the clearing, the land levels and I see the cabin. A rustic cedar porch lips out from a log cabin. Rich brown logs held together by slate mortar until a gabled roof topped by modern green aluminum. We pull to a stop behind an early 1980s Mercedes station wagon. Its brown paint faded in spots with rust eating the bottom of the left rear quarter panel. Beyond the clearing where the cars are parked is a newer stick built cabin, more like a barn or storage building, but obviously an expansion of the living quarters raised in recent years.

A Buick sits in front of the Benz wagon. An Isuzu Impulse covered in Widespread Panic and Grateful Dead stickers is parked to the side and I pull behind it.

A smiling man with Steve Perry hair and a pencil thin mustache emerges from the main cabin. He's holding a brown tabby cat and followed by an attractive woman, maybe in her mid-40s. Her hair is dirty blond and falls to her shoulder in an even arc, as if cut by a machine. It's feathered across the front and rests naturally, as opposed to the big hair so popular with the girls my age. "That's Sam, Noah's dad," Brook says.

We get out of the car and exchange greetings.

"Welcome!" Sam says. "Welcome to the house at the end of the road. Did you find it ok?" His kind smile is relaxing and in tune with the spot's natural beauty. High ridgelines dwarf us and I notice both cabins seem built into the very contour of the land itself.

"Yeah, no problem finding it, but it's definitely off the beaten trail," Brook says. "How far off the road are we?"

"Only about four miles," Sam says. "But it might as well be forty. There's nothing around us in any direction. Noah, Andrew and the girls went hiking after lunch. They should be back soon. I was just about to practice some new chords, so go ahead and take your stuff over to the new place. When you get settled, have a look around or feel free to come on in here and have a listen."

Sam turns to go back inside and the woman smiles at us. I take the fresh, pure air into my lungs as deep as I can. I pull in several meditative breaths and let it fill my senses. The forest exudes that thick, musky mix of sweet and pungent as the rot decaying under layers of duff and leaves mixes with the emergent life of spring. The soft rustle of squirrels and other small animals wafts into the breeze that gently moves branches and leaves across each other creating a buzzing friction beneath a breathless blue sky, visible in a dome over the clearing.

I pop the trunk and take Brook's bag in addition to my own so he can help Darcie and cart his six-string case at the same time. Darcie is ahead of us as we approach the newer cabin. Entrance is on the side and a nice plank deck extends out of sight around the back. A row of high vertical windows on the front reflects sun and tree and sky as we approach. Inside, the main floor is open with only a couple of chairs and a small card table near the sunlit windows. Across the far side is a large brick hearth and fireplace. A small kitchenette to the left compressed into the corner. Sliding glass doors beyond that give way to an extended patio with wooden Adirondack chairs.

Steps beyond the sliding glass begin next to the hearth and lead up to a loft. After placing the bags along the front of the hearth, I follow Brook and Darcie up. Sleeping bags and a cot are along the wall and another door leads to a redwood deck. The sun has heated the wood and as we lean along the rails at mid-tree level we finally take a moment to pause.

"What I wouldn't give to have a secluded place like this," I say.

"Yeah, nice, huh," Darcie observes. She's snuggled next to Brook who drapes his arm across her shoulder.

We dangle along the edges of the redwood deck, absorbing the sunlight like emergent flowers. The cornucopia of sound - small birds floating on the breeze, the occasional automobile far off in the distance, the slight movement of our foot or torso against the wood holding us up - encircles us and mixes with the forest's density.

In peace I watch the tiniest of insect march along the porch rail - miniscule wings up with translucent fibers perpendicular to the ribbed body with six legs behind a stinger topped head - until it hops onto my hand and I brush it off to fly out into the pulsating forest.

Serenity fills me. Devoid of anxiety I try to lose consciousness of the moment and enjoy the simplicity of "is". Darcie and Brook must feel it too because we linger silent in one of those fleeting moments you know will fill your memory in thirty or even forty years down the road. You will say to yourself "I was alive then" and you knew it was happening as it happened so you chose to let go and step back and watch it unfold from the future.

We perpetuate the moment in stillness - as if daring the first among us to break the spell - until I can't stand it anymore and I move across the deck to the far side just to check the view. I figure even the slightest movement will eradicate the serenity but at least I remain quiet. Over the edge I peer down twenty feet or more to the side of the cabin.

I hear movement along the gravel in front and a voice calling out for Brook. It's Noah, so we step back inside and meet on the main floor. Noah is a peaceful soul, all smiles and cheer despite the deformity of his left leg, a birth defect that requires him to walk with a limp and a cane, though you would never hear him complain about it. In tow is Noah's friend, Andrew Ergot. He's tall and thin, with a face of equal features, like a witch's face from a book of children's fables. A stark nose dominates his long jaw and chin, almost a caricature. Andrew has darkness about his eyes, but it's softened somewhat by the long brown hair that falls to his shoulders and a forced pleasantness. Noah wears jean shorts and a Phish tee-shirt. Andrew has on earth tone khaki shorts and a smoke gray tee declaring something about Panic. Behind them shuffle two bored looking young women who seem put out by our rustic surroundings.

On closer inspection, Andrew's shirt reads "Widespread Panic" and Brook seems to have heard of the band.

"Oh yeah we saw them open for the Allmans in Atlanta in the fall," he says after greetings are exchanged. "Real clean tone and solid groove. I think they met in Athens in the dorm or something."

Uneasy small talk hangs in the air as the group dynamic struggles. There is too much going on. Noah and Brook try to catch up on lost time as they chat across the room. The two young women seem to be attached to Andrew and he is occupied with entertaining them. Darcie and I are content to let Brook converse with Noah and we stare at each other from time to time in between glancing at Andrew and his two pussycats.

I watch the light grow with the moving sun until vast rays push through the tall windows and fill a quarter of the room with shine filtered by the drifting fabric hanging from rods atop the sill. Conversational din hums, staggered at first, until my mind has drifted with the dust particles rising in the sunbeam across the floor and the voices merge into midrange frequency.

By late afternoon the sun hangs across only the highest leaves, longing to slink behind the hills. We've hiked a short trail up into the woods, around a ridgeline behind the cabin with Noah. Andrew and his two friends elected to remain behind.

Noah says he met Andrew last summer in classes at UNC-Asheville, but that Andrew has since dropped out of school to follow jam bands around east of the Mississippi River.

"He follows the Dead, Phish and this new group Widespread Panic," Noah says. "He's built a nice collection of bootlegs. I've been trying to get copies but it's hard to get him when he has time."

"What's up with those two girls?" Darcie asks. "They don't seem real open to making new acquaintances."

Noah laughs as he leans on his cane and we pause to look down the forested slope toward the duplex. "Hard to say. Maybe just worn out from last night still," he says. "Andrew has a vial of some incredible liquid acid and we took some about eight o'clock last night."

He says one of the girls, Jill, the taller one with the longer auburn hair and sullen stare, freaked out in the middle of the trip and spent the night in the bathtub hiding from lizards.

"She locked herself in and we spent two hours begging her to open the door."

Andrew was peeved, Noah says, because he aimed to get laid and the other girl, Nellie, was in no mood after having to deal with her friend. "They're gonna leave about six if they feel up to driving back to Asheville."

"There seems to be a lot of strong acid floating around the hills these days," Brook says. "I think I'll be glad to get away for the summer. Seems to me as if a frenzy is hanging over the horizon."

Noah nods. "Andrew says that there's this old hippie chemist who relocated back from exile in Europe or something and settled here in the region," he says. "They think he chose this area because it's so close to big southern schools, Georgia, Tennessee, Clemson, even Virginia Tech. Not to mention the list of smaller schools like Western, App, UNC-A, the piedmont."

"Makes sense," Brook says. "And the tour scene comes right through here, Atlanta, Greenville, Charlotte. It's a good location to set up."

"Yeah, the Dead comes the middle of next month. Will you still be here?" Noah asks him. Darcie perks up, as if most of her immediate plans hinge on his answer.

"I'm not sure," Brook says. He glances off into the forest like he's looking for a sign or some place of comfort. "I'm going to Mexico in June. I might want to play it easy before then. Like I said, things are getting a bit crazy in certain circles." He's looking over at me. "I know my friend Jordan plans to go and hopes to hook up on some liquid. He says he plans to push the edges out this summer. Jordan can be careless sometimes. I'm not sure I want to be around for it."

"That Jordan, he's a nice one," Noah says. We all laugh. "He was up in Asheville about two weeks ago with this girl I had never seen. Isn't he still dating Kim?"

"Yeah they are still together," Brook says. "But they have both gotten into this poly relationship thing in the last few months. I guess it's cool you know. Whatever floats his boat."

Darcie clings tighter to Brook's arm as he talks about Jordan. "I'm not sure if he's keeping score or collecting mementos or what. Scott got a firsthand look at them in action this week."

"For the third time," I say. "They've gotten into it with some random girls twice this semester when I've been among the last at a house party at like three in the morning. I snuck off both times. The second time I was with the girl who rented the place. It was all I could do to keep her from throwing them out."

"Unintended consequences," Brook observes. "It's not like running a scale on the guitar or beating out a rhythm pattern. Those all resolve. Even dissonance resolves to a root. I worry about Jordan sometimes." He shakes his head. "Kim gets out of it what she wants - comfort, security, status ... but Jordan ... I don't know if he sees the boundaries anymore."

Crisp mountain air breezes between us and Noah suggests we should check in on his dad. "He's making progress on his songwriting, but he's still frustrated," he says. "So if he seems distant or becomes snappy all of a sudden don't take it personal."

We wander back down to the duplex. Along the way I see a dozen or more shots I could frame if I had my camera, a camera, any camera lucid enough to capture the vividness of this now for future reference. I linger behind to let Noah have space to move down the threadbare path. He and Brook are talking and Darcie falls behind.

I catch up to her as the path opens. Huge rhododendron arc over the clearing like a crown.

"Those two chicks give me the creeps," she says. "So does that Andrew. Something strange, almost usury, about him. He seems like a disaster waiting to happen."

"I felt something strange about them as well. Maybe they are just tense?"

"Tense is what you were when Jen showed up last night," she shoots me an elbow lovingly in the kidney. "What these people are is strung out. Doomed almost."

I'm rubbing my side as Darcie laughs at me. "Jen said you were phenomenal, Scott. She's hooked. If you break that girl's heart I will knee cap you." Darcie pokes her slim but forceful finger directly into my pectoral. She's loving and playful, protective and dangerous all at once. "So what are you thinking?"

"Nothing's changed for me, Darcie. I like Jen, a lot, but I'm not feeling a deep commitment or falling in love with her," I say. "You gotta understand, and so does she, that I mostly just want to be honest with her. I see so many people who lie about love to gain sex and I'm too honest for that. I enjoy her company but she lays it on too strong sometimes. And the one thing I have to be is honest with myself."

She is studying her fingernails as I talk and look out over the parked cars toward the newer cabin where Andrew and his playthings are coming out of the door. Brook waits in the grassy area in front of the cabin tuning his Gibson acoustic. As Darcie thinks for a moment she twirls one of the sandy brown locks of hair that's braided with colored thread in layers of red, gold, green and yellow.

"Well, we had a talk about that," Darcie says. "I think Jen understands. But I don't think that changes anything. I think she's in love with you Scott. So keep being honest. I think you are right about that."

We join the group near the parked cars. Andrew is draped over both girls, who seem more relaxed now. The taller one, Jill, seems alive at least, not achingly sullen as before.

I don't think any of the three have acknowledged me, or Darcie for that matter, since we've been here. They seem enraptured with each other, as if the acid has them still in a bubble. Acutely self-aware and still open to the source of consciousness, they are too wrapped up in themselves. As if the trip has them off on a cloud somewhere. I doubt much interaction with them is possible.

Darcie's written them off. She deposits herself right on Brook's hip and remains there for the next few hours. Brook is caught up with Noah and Sam and their conversations make good listening.

After coming in off the porch the main room opens to the left with a fireplace along the far wall. Sam has his guitar and a small amplification system set up next to the doorway leading to the back of the cabin. Heavy cushioned furniture and concert posters dominate the room, centered by a glass topped table fashioned from juniper. The rich amber streaks in the wood's fiber set off by lighter areas that constitute the balance. Hendrix and Joplin are frozen in frames announcing concerts in Monterrey or Atlanta in 1967 or 1970 in one corner. Doc and Merle invite you to come to Deep Gap in 1982 in the other. A gaunt Charlie Poole holds his banjo in a print frame next to an autographed photo of Earl Scruggs.

To the right of the entryway, where I am now, is the combined kitchen and dining area. Sam's friend, Ellen, has spread out a meal such as a group of stoned college kids could die for. Vegetable platters with tomatoes and carrots and hummus dip and pita bread in the center of a rustic six foot hardwood table flanked on the ends by chicken breast topped with garnish and oozing juice. Asparagus in stacks like corded wood next to potatoes whipped into a cream fury resting like the mountains outside. The lingering odor of the fresh bread she pulled from the stainless steel faced oven, still warm from the effort.

The room glimmers with Sam's laughter. He answers Brook's questions and Noah recalls the time when the nothing of something was the everything of then. Darcie nibbles asparagus and then bits of bread, her eyes yearning for Brook to pay her exclusive attention. He's oblivious for the moment.

It's an odd grouping, but the fun at the head of the table balances the silence at this end. I sit next to Darcie at the butt of the table and Andrew is just across from me. His playmates huddle together, rapt almost in proximate whisper, still in a cocoon. The food is so good I don't bother with conversation.

After dinner we gather in the living area so Sam can run through his new songs in front of a small audience. He has a Yamaha four track set up in a small nook behind a couch and an end table. Being the odd man out so to speak, I volunteer to run the device and capture the performance.

Before I dive into my cove beneath a skinny lamp with a burning bright bulb we pause as Sam gathers his pick and wipes down his Taylor acoustic. Andrew and Nellie recline on a rattan chair in the corner's darkness - the void seems to absorb them both. Jill is seated on the edge of the hearth. She's as close to them as she can get without being in the chair. Ellen sits on the thick cushioned couch across the room near the front windows and Darcie and Brook take up position beside her. Noah seems unsure if he should pair up with Jill or not and so he lingers, standing beside his dad as Sam gets settled in.

I've an abiding interest in music. Having lived with three musicians, I know how to run the four track. Sam has his vocal microphone in one, his straight guitar signal from the PA in two and a pair of nearfield condenser microphones in three and four.

"I've been recording for a few days so the levels ought to be good," Sam says to me. "If one starts to peak, just kick the clip knob down a bit at a time. Try to keep the meter in the green and into yellow, but avoid the red." He's running his finger up the path of LED bubble lights that march up the face of the four track. "Push here," he points to the large red button marked *record*. "And make sure the counter is running and then give me the thumbs up."

He settles on the stool, behind a vocal mic pointed at him from the end of a flexible ribbed stand, and strums a few open chords. Their suspended voice hangs in need above the tonic until he resolves in steps. I kneel behind the couch and move along the wall until

I'm next to the recorder, at the end of cables and wires on the floor beneath the lamps on a slatted end table. I can just see Sam's face and he mouths "ready" and I push the record nob and watch the lights bounce. The counter marches from zero and I give Sam the thumbs up. My back rests against the wall. I think about what a great angle this would make for photographs and what techniques I could play with. Radial blur to capture the movement of his hands on the strings as he strums or frets a chord. Adjusting the ISO or the aperture to play with the differential between light on his face and the room's surrounding darkness. Crisp, focused shots to process in black and white to accentuate his aged face's stark features, worn with experience but still emitting hope for more than moderate success.

I can see the years on his face as he begins to sing. His stage presence is forced, as if the repetition has dulled the excitement. I can see the worry playing like a churned sea storming behind the performer's facade. The thinning mustache and the mulleted black hair are at least a decade out of step with the times. Maybe he gets steady work in dive bars and beachside cantinas in the summer months, but I wonder how tired he is of the same circuit he's floated in for the last twenty-five years.

I close my eyes and my body hangs with the diminished and suspended chords. The music is pleasing. His finger technique is sharp and his clean sound pierces the room's increasing stillness. I wish I could move this couch or hover invisible near the ceiling and take in the effect Sam's rhythms have on the room's ambience. Does Andrew pull a hand tighter across Nellie's ample hip as Jill looks lustfully on? Did Noah saddle up next to Jill only to feel her move closer to the action in the rattan chair? How far into Brook's side is Darcie forcing herself? Is she chewing her stimulated thumbnail like valerian root or twisting a finger in the braid that falls from the back crown of her golden hair to the soft prominence of her shoulder? How many times has Ellen heard these songs in the week or so they have been here? Does she feign interest or retain a genuine appreciation for the music?

Sam moves through a couple of generic rhythm and blues numbers that fall somewhere between James Taylor and bluegrass. Hints of jazz appear along the way but tend to resolve directly to straight blues. After twenty minutes the chatter between songs has stopped. Is the crowd feeling weighted eyelids or the stiffness of boredom? After the next song, even the clapping of the seven people in the room disappears.

The professional that he is, Sam probably feels the need for variation. He's run through three songs about middle aged loss and four about appreciating nature or the milieu of the parent to child proximity.

"This is a song I just wrote this week," he says gently into the microphone. "I hope you'll like it."

He begins an upbeat and driving rhythm, nicely shaped pop movements with a quick turnaround from four to five and back to one. There's a gravel road off a snaking highway, trees and birds and clean air helping him leave the worry of the city behind with the tension of a commitment he can't quite fill. He's forgetting the heavy load because "he's at the house at the end of the road!"

It's the best song of the night by far and I'm ready to get up and boogie because the tune is catchy. I'm hemmed in by the wall and the couch and so flexing my hip and buttock muscles is all the dancing I can do. By the end of the second chorus I can tell he's giving it all he has because the levels are peaked, bouncing just between safe yellow and the danger zone where the signal plays into the edge of red like a child splashing at the seam of the ocean. I peek around the sofa and see Sam's face on fire. He's performing with all he has, a wide grin and perfectly shaped vocal delivery.

At once he stops and stomps his foot so hard the stool moves and his guitar bumps the microphone stand. The low frequency of boom waves between the walls for an instant before silence.

"You people are not even listening!" he growls. "I invite you up here, I feed you, I give you my beer and wine and you can't even listen to me?"

His just elated performance face is bunched up in anger as he snaps. "Come one, get into it," he shouts and dives right back into the song. "You're at the house at the end of the road ... one more time ... we're at the house at the end of the road!"

I'd give anything right now to see if a look of shock or feigned indifference hangs on Andrew and Nellie and Jill's faces because I know he was snapping at them. Darcie wanted to claw their eyes out earlier and I've been laughing at their hipster solipsism for several hours. I know he was dressing them down for being so dense. But I'm in shock. I want to become a mouse here behind the couch and sneak away in silence to a hole in the wall.

Sam brings the song to a close and says "well that's enough for tonight." He puts his guitar gently into the stand's hooked tip and walks around the corner to the back of the cabin. I see Ellen follow suit and in silence I wait for someone else to move. I wonder if I've been forgotten here in my sofa isolation? Then I remember I'm running the four track so I lean over and watch the levels respond as voices are picked up by the microphones.

I roll the master level softly to zero as the colors fade. Then I press stop.

We filter back to the other cabin. Andrew and the twins left directly without saying a word and are nowhere to be seen. Noah comes in the room after fifteen minutes.

"Make sure your dad knows I had a great time," I say. "I was really digging that last song. It had all the right elements."

Noah sits on a stool next to the hearth. "It's ok. He's under a lot of stress," Noah says. "Progress is slow and he's frustrated. But I think it's coming for him. He just wrote that last song this week."

Sam's really been struggling with mid-career reflection, feeling defeated, Noah says, about being in the same scene, at the same bars and clubs. The same worn circuit from Atlanta down the Florida coast and back up through Savannah and Charleston, the Raleigh-Greensboro-Asheville path along I-40. "A newspaper in Orlando called him pedantic last year. He took that really hard."

"It's a rough business," Brook says. "Hard to get into, hard to stay afloat, hard to give up. It gets into your blood, but it can eat you up."

It's not yet ten o'clock but there's no real spirit to revel in after Sam's outburst. Brook and Darcie make a pallet on the floor near the hearth from some quilts and blankets Noah pulls from a closet. I take a heavy blanket and head outside. The Adirondack chairs are cushioned and I stretch out in one.

Overhead the stars dance in holy reflection across the eons. I think about how little anything we do or say matters to the cosmos and wonder if it's liberation or punishment.

I sleep deep and restful out in the purity of air and darkness and wake up just as Brook is stepping onto the deck. He holds two coffee cups and hands me one with the steam hovering above the roasted liquid like memory bliss.

"There's fruit and cereal in there. Ellen brought it over," he says to me.

"You sleep all right?" I ask.

"I think we found some rest eventually," he offers with a near giggle. "Once the action settled down, you know."

"Don't come knocking?"

"You know it man," he says. He lifts the coffee to his smile and the elation moves to his eyes.

He tells me that Jill and Nellie left at first light. "Darcie's in the shower. If you wanna grab something to eat I think we plan to gather on the patio above for party favors."

We step inside and I fold the blankets and pile them where Brook has. He's taken up his Gibson and strums a few bright chords. "I never did get to play with Sam last night," he muses.

He could play any old song he wants to, and for a twenty year old he has a vast songbook in his head. I could name any song from the sixties and most rock from the seventies and he could lick it out in a heartbeat. But he writes songs as well. Mostly bluegrassy honkytonk that settles somewhere across genres in a little nook he's carving out for himself.

He maintains a peaceful stance on the stool, bent slightly at the waist, his slight legs crossed with his bare feet - one on the ground and the other dangling in the air, thigh holding the dreadnought in place for him to hug and caress sounds that pierce and fill and soothe in unison.

"Play 'Dirt Weed'," I implore him after swallowing a bit of cereal. His lips recede to reveal a slanted smile - half laugh, half meditative acknowledgment - and he nods in agreement and digs into the fast-paced rolling fingerstyle tune. His elbow swings out as he paints the turnaround, two finger arpeggios and double-stops palm-muted then hammered on and then back to the onset. His guide index and middle fingers slide from the headstock up a few frets into key providing that bluegrass swing. Half-step bends and string skipped pull-offs flavor the tune with baroque hints, just slight enough for you to think maybe it's a classical motif, but he slams right back into the finger roll at the crescendo and cries "And you'll never be smoking Jack's dirtweed again!"

A sprinkle of melodic lead notes like raindrops in a sun lit puddle ripple through the air and he drags his thumbnail backward from high to low, finding the tonic bass to end the tune.

"Jack's dirtweed, eh?" Noah says from the bottom of the stairs.

"Yeah, the best money can buy," Brooks smirks. He places the guitar in the black case against the wall and stretches his back. Darcie's out of the shower now, the darker streaks in her golden hair accented by the lingering dampness as she combs it out. Her head cocked to the side, she smiles at Brook.

"Why does everybody love that song?" she asks.

"Cause I got it like that I guess," he says.

"I think it's the vocal delivery at the end," I offer. "He hits it perfectly. Just barely into absurdity, the way he flexes his throat and offers it up, so sincere. It's hard to tell if it's a lament or a celebration."

"It's all we had at the time," Brook deadpans.

"You can't tell if Jack ran out of dirtweed, or if Jack left town, or if you left town and are missing Jack," I say. "It's the unknown quality of the refrain ..."

"Let's move this debate up to the patio," Noah offers.

Andrew is already on the patio slackly leaned against the redwood rail just outside the slant angled shadow of the cabin roof. His arms rest folded across his chest and his head is tilted at a downward angle as he regards some aspect of the wooden boards. He wears a white tee-shirt and maybe the same pair of shorts as yesterday. Forest brown Hi-Tec three-quarter hiking boots adorn his feet, crossed in thought one atop the other. His white tee shirt has a hideous stick figure head drawn with tufted flat-topped hair and a grievous emanation from its mouth spewing the words "Geezer Lake".

"It's a band I saw in Charlotte a month or so ago," he says. "They are from Greensboro. Crazy demented noise with a trumpet player on some songs."

Brook and Andrew discuss the emerging band scene and Andrew seems to at least be aware that other people exist in his immediate surroundings. We trade eye contact and I laugh at some of his descriptions of clubs or some of the bad bands he's seen open on a Thursday night in some average college town.

"Widespread Panic, though, watch out for them," Andrew says. "They are just about to peak and blow through the scene. Everything is coming together for them."

Someone lit a fatty and we're passing it among the five of us. I remember that I have a canister full of refer but there's been so much around I haven't even thought to pull it out.

"So who's going to see the Dead when they come through next month?" Andrew asks. Darcie says she'd really like to go but she will be starting an internship in mid-May over in Asheville and since Brook is leaving she will probably skip it.

"What about you, dude?" Andrew asks me.

I demure as I pull on the joint a few seconds and pass it over to Noah. "Me? Probably not. Not my scene. Their music is ok in the background but I'm not much for those crowds," I reply.

Andrew has positioned himself up on the rail that runs parallel to the patio floor. He's locked the tips of his boots between the vertical slats of the structure. For some reason the joint has been passed back to me and so I don't hesitate to suck it again.

I'm in the second puff and no one is speaking as we linger in harmony and the sun warms the patio. The angular shadow has moved slightly with the sun, and as I'm just about to pass the joint to Andrew, his body leans, slightly at first, to his right toward the wall of the cabin.

I'm not sure what I'm looking at, but when his head smacks the wall the sound tells me at once that he is out cold. His shoulders touch the wall for a moment as his head recoils back the other way. His upper body seems disconnected from the logical structure of joints and tendons that hold any of us upright. I'm ditching the joint and stepping toward him as his right foot comes off the vertical slat and his boot toe aims straight for the sky.

I step quickly right to avoid being kicked just as his buttock loses tether with the porch rail and his upper body begins what would be a twenty foot descent to the ground below. His torso twists like dough and the density of his head pulls the rest of him perfectly flat above the earth. It's in this frozen moment that I am able to get a hand under his ground facing chest and stop the momentum just enough to get my other hand onto the top of his thigh. His upper body dangles momentarily bent over the patio and my body weight hits the rail. For a second I think the structure will give way and I gasp what may be the last breath in my life before I take a dive on the rocks below.

But the rail holds and now Brook has me by the waist. I gain my balance and lift Andrew into a standing position. He's still out cold, and frozen in disbelief I forget what I'm doing. With no awareness to combat gravity's pull he crumples to the patio floor. I do maintain a grip on his upper body just below the armpits, and as his knees then hips hit the deck, I prop him up to prevent his head from slamming into the wood. The rest of him becomes motionless and I slowly let his shoulders and head follow suit until he is prone.

But in an instant his eyes open and he sits up as I step back in amazement. I'm speechless as he cracks a smile and uncoils to his feet like a cobra snake rising to the atonal vibration of a demented scale.

He's trying to play it off, but the shock on all our faces is inescapable.

"It's ok. I just did too many whippets last night," he says. He holds our gaze with an innocent countenance, as if the blackout has wiped his slate clean and he's just some fresh-faced school boy without a scheming bone in his body. His oblique grin hangs over his parted lips while his upturned eyes dare us to question his sincerity.

I'm floored. Speechless. Darcie finally closes her mouth and turns to go inside. The bell-tipped braid swings gently behind as she shakes her head in time with her steps.

Brook picks up the joint and lights it again. Noah and I pass it around but Andrew waves off from his seated position at the white plastic table and chair set next to us.

Drift

I stretched the mic cable into the darkness and began to recite Lincoln's Gettysburg Address so Dooley could check the levels back at the truck. We'd set the four-track on the lowered tailgate a few minutes earlier. Now, Anne and I were twenty feet out toward a series of ledges that led down to the banks of the Tuckasegee River.

"Four score and seven years ago," I whispered into the mic and looked back to Dooley. He gave me thumbs up, signaling the levels were good. Anne and I looked out across the land rippling down toward the river. We stood silent in the July darkness listening to the cicadas. A lone car whisked around the curve on the state road behind us before disappearing down the mountainside.

"What are we listening for," Anne asked.

"This," I said as I guided my hand out over the valley floor toward the hill that rose on the other side of the river. It made a borderline in the darkness separating earth from sky. I held the microphone out in front of

70

me and grabbed Anne by the waist, pulling her close to me again.

I let my hand drift down her hip, just below her skirt, and ran my fingers along the smooth surface of her thigh. Anne leaned her head on my shoulder and sighed.

We stood face to face in the darkness twenty minutes earlier in the middle of the short gravel drive that led to my basement apartment. She'd moved in upstairs a month before. I'd been living here a week longer. A friend had tipped me off to the duplex, a two minute walk from the edge of campus along Centennial Drive.

It was the second summer term and campus was dead. Traffic along the road just above my place was sparse. As Anne and I stood in the warm July night she leaned in to me. We'd begun to kiss and I moved my hand below the pleated hem of her short skirt. She hadn't flinched and soon I found my fingers running along the edge of her panty line to play softly with the damp, inviting flesh below.

She'd just moaned into my ear and wrapped her hand around the back of my neck when I saw the headlights veer off the road and angle down toward where we stood.

My acoustic Fender guitar hung from my shoulder, with the body of the guitar around the back, the strap across my chest. Anne and I pulled apart and I reached behind me to grab the tip of the neck, bringing the dreadnought body out front.

The truck came closer and I could see that it was Dooley. It wasn't yet 9:30, but since I was known to be single and always welcoming to a friend, it was nothing strange for people to stop by late if the lights were on.

I would soon learn to turn them off.

I couldn't be too upset with Dooley. He'd been a good friend for the three years I'd been at university and I knew he was lonely. His girlfriend of two years, Christy, had left him sometime after spring break. Dooley's normal countenance was dour but over the last few months he'd been especially morose.

I finger picked a bluesy D-7 chord and vamped to an A as I heard his emergency brake ratchet up and the headlights died. Anne leaned against the quarter panel of my Volkswagen and fidgeted with her nails.

"What's up, Dooley? Out late this evening," I said as he walked closer. I picked out a little run to end the tune.

"Yeah, man. How's it going over here? Working on a new song are you?"

"Oh you know it brother. All the time," I replied. "As a matter of fact Anne of Green Gables and I were just about to strike up a tune when you pulled up. What were we going to sing about GG?"

Anne rolled her eyes and laughed. "You have got to stop making up names for me Steven. I can't keep them all straight."

"Some habits die hard," I said. "Especially when you're a poet. Words just seem to flow from my tongue at times. Tends to get me in trouble."

We shared a laugh but Dooley wasn't fazed. I could tell he wanted something.

"Say man I tried to call Eric, and then Peyton, but none of them are around. You know where I can score a bag?"

This put me in a tight spot. If he hadn't been among my closest circle of friends, and the guy who played bass in my fledgling psychedelic rock band, I would have been pissed. Anne and I had only known each other about two weeks, since the time she heard me playing guitar on the stone steps along the side of the house.

I was playing a new chord scheme and humming, then scatting, some lyrical rhythms, when Anne appeared at the top of the steps.

I hadn't had cause to tell her all my secrets. I surely hadn't told her about the weed connection I'd developed that spring. In fact, I didn't like to deal out of the house at all. I preferred to roll out to a friend's house to deliver and catch a smoke. I wasn't dealing large quantities, just a handful of quarters and twenty dollar sacks for friends in order to make my smoke quota.

But I had a feeling Anne was ok. We'd smoked a few times together and giggled in her living room watching Beevis and Butthead. Tonight was the first time I'd kissed her, but I figured we might soon have little, if anything, between us. So I let Dooley's gaffe slide.

"Well now Dooley what kind of question is that to ask a guy standing in the middle of the driveway? Let's go inside. I need a cigarette."

I reached out for Anne's fingertips and she moved the rest of her hand into mine. I led her toward the muted yellow glow coming from behind the antique glaze of the single pane windows at my doorway and Dooley fell in behind us. I slid my arm around Anne's shoulders and let her go first up the steps to the porch and inside.

I moved my Gibson SG from the chair and put it in the worn black case leaning in the corner. I grabbed up my lyrics notebook and chord sheets from the coffee table and placed them next to the four-track. Anne took a seat and picked up the Electric Ladyland tab book sitting on the coffee table. Dooley sat on the couch, leaving me standing in the room still holding the acoustic. With no-where to put it down I thought it was a good opportunity to go in the back room and get a sack ready for Dooley.

"Let me put this guitar up in its case," I said and stepped into the narrow hallway and took a few steps around a corner to the bedroom. I didn't have a case for that guitar because I'd purchased it at a pawn shop earlier that summer. So I leaned it in the corner and opened the third drawer on my dresser. I still had four quarter bags, two twenty sacks and my personal stash from the last quarter pound Peyton had fronted me earlier in the week. It was heavy on shake with a few seeds and that had pissed me off good, but at the price he was letting it go for I could easily move it for $30 a quarter and smoke most of the shake.

I'd been enjoying the taste of joints that summer and so shake was ok with me. A few of my regulars had mentioned how the quality was less than stellar, but it was the middle of the summer and weed was hard to come by. I just wanted to get stoned on the cheap so I didn't really care what they thought. I stuffed one of the quarters in my shorts and grabbed my personal stash.

At the doorway to the living room I paused.

"Anyone want a beer? Anne, can I get you something?"

She nodded and Dooley got up to follow me into the kitchen. I pulled a few Becks from the refrigerator and set them on the slate gray countertop as Dooley came into the room. After I fumbled for the bottle opener I looked at him.

"Keep your voice down," I whispered. "I don't want her knowing I keep weed in the house to sell. I don't know her roommate that well. She's a local, kind of uppity toward me." I put the bag up on the counter. "Put this in your pocket. We'll smoke a joint in a minute but don't say anything about that bag."

"How much, man?"

"Thirty," I said and he handed me three wrinkled tens.

As I popped the bottle tops I called to Anne.

"You want a glass, GG?"

"No," came the reply with a hint of laughter. "Bottle's fine."

Back in the living room I sat on the couch next to Dooley. It was perpendicular to the chair, my chair, which Anne occupied. She still thumbed through the Hendrix tab book.

"Do you like that album," I asked. She said she wasn't familiar with it. "Oh my God. We will have to rectify that tonight. It's an amazing album. Has to be my favorite from beginning to end. Hendrix and Eddie Kramer did wonders with stereo pan and early attempts at delay with vocals and pitch modulation. It's fascinating."

I lit the finger-sized joint and after getting it going passed it over to Anne. I leaned back into the couch and exhaled the smoke. It cast a shroud in the dim light coming from the fixture in the ceiling.

"In fact, I've been experimenting with delay and pitch modulation this week. I got a friend's Microsynth and hooked it up to the digital delay pedal ... It's the blue double switched one next to the four track."

I pointed to the makeshift counter I'd put together. It consisted of a large black trunk covered with a tie-dyed sheet that I'd picked up somewhere along the way. The trunk rested atop four milk crates stacked in pairs so it was just high enough to be chest level when I was seated.

"I run the guitar signal into the Microsynth and then put that into the delay pedal. Then I send the out on the delay into whatever track is open on the four." The joint had come back to me and I pulled on the moist tip of white paper and let the sensation fill my lungs. Purple flowers. A wisp of the fragrance you'd catch on a mountain path early on a cool afternoon. The ember gave off a heavy stack of smoke and I leaned in to pull the remnants from the air with my nose. I held the substance in my expanded lungs and passed the half-smoked spliff over to Dooley.

I moved over to the stool in front of my workstation and exhaled once I sat down.

"I've been closing in on some Fripp and Eno type sounds today. Simple phrases which I can overdub with solo work."

"Can we hear it," Anne asked.

"I don't have any speakers but I can play it for you on the phones. Let me get it going."

She smiled as her soft brown eyes looked my way. I rewound the tape back to zero and thought of the afternoon's bliss as I developed the piece from a three note phrase, modulated by the filters and oscillators on the Microsynth. Once I was happy with it, I clicked the digital delay's infinite repeat button and spent an hour adjusting the controls, cutting the repetitions as I slowed the meter of the phrase itself, processing the original notes into something worlds apart.

Anne listened to the sketch I'd created that afternoon and we polished off the smoke. She bailed first, a wave of the hand signaling "enough." Dooley and I took a few more turns until he said "No man, I'm good" and I set the roach down in the ashtray to join the dozen already there.

It was only about 10 o'clock now and that particular interaction of fire, marijuana and white paper had fused the room with a pulsating energy. I can't say that my music had anything to do with it. Quite the contrary, it was a slow, spacey piece I'd tentatively titled "Cosmic Engine Failure" because toward the end I'd had the vision of a spaceship crashing on a desolate planet.

When Anne finished listening we all seemed to feel the need to get up and move. Maybe it was the weed. Maybe it was the tension in the room with one person too many being present.

I suggested we take the four track and a mic outside to capture atmospheric sounds so I could use them to augment the piece. No one hesitated and I felt that if we spent an hour or so outside Dooley would get the picture and take off. That would leave plenty of time for the evening's activity to run its course.

In the darkness you could not see the Mountain Laurel or the orange tipped Tiger Lilies lining the hillside separating my driveway from the road above. But in the cool stillness that surrounded us you could smell the bountiful fragrance.

I ran an extension cord from the living room to the bed of the truck and moved the four track there. I grabbed one mic and a cable and was back outside before Dooley had time to get his bearings.

"What are we doing exactly man," he said after taking a pull from the green beer bottle.

"Recording the life of this particular evening, Dooley. Just for a few minutes. I want to get some atmospherics on tape so I can experiment with them tomorrow. You got time to help me with that dontcha?"

"Sure man, anything for you Steve."

His blithe tone came close to hitting the raw nerve that triggers my aggression. Just as I was about to vent on him I remembered all he'd been through in recent months. The breakup with Christy, the extra strength sadness, how he'd tried to sabotage a relationship I had with a cute local girl a few weeks ago. But we'd been friends for too long for me to let that come between us. I'd been sad before. I'd known the weight of being alone. And so I'd let that slide too.

But our relationship was drifting. If I'd not needed him to round out the band I so desperately wanted to be in we would've seen less of each other. In fact, back in April he'd asked me why I hadn't been coming around and I told him straight up that it was all I could do not to hit him for the way he'd come between me and Marie right after Christy dumped him.

In early spring I'd moved out of the popular A-frame party spot where my band's drummer Dewey lived. The house was too active. Too many people coming and going. And too much distraction as I'd tried to salvage my relationship with Marie after a fit of jealousy led to rage on my part.

Dooley took my spot in the rotation and as I tried to make a new scene for myself I only popped by for band practice and to occasionally hang with Dewey. One day after classes and our obligatory afternoon buzz I was running scales on Dooley's small organ he'd moved into the A-frame. Dewey took off to run errands and I'd stayed behind to work out some melodies that'd been running in my head for a few days.

A short time later Dooley came back from campus and after exchanging the quietest of greetings we passed fifteen minutes without speaking. Music had always pulled us together and after he got a taste of the major seventh and ninth chords I was working out he came and sat on a stool next to me.

We made light small talk for a bit until he'd commented about it being nice to see me come around. I'd been holding in the bitterness toward him and let it out as I stood up and kicked the stool across the room and stomped out the door.

He tried to play like he didn't know what he was doing with his self-deprecation and constant passive aggressive posturing. We'd been close before and I knew he wasn't simple. So I figured manipulation, like a composer lulling you to that listening comfort before flipping it back around, was his game. And after Marie and I moved the intensity of our relationship back a few notches he was on her like a scale resolving to its root.

But Marie and I hadn't split up completely. We still spent time together in the afternoons and often made love in the evenings before I took her back to her mom's shotgun shack one block east of the paper mill that dominated the small town a few miles away from campus. She told me how she'd been at the A-frame with some mutual friends and how Dooley got her off in the dining room alone and tried to serenade her with the Pink Floyd song that'd been the foundation of our relationship. I knew what his game was.

Marie and I tried to work the kinks out of our affair and I went all in, shutting off everything but school, band and Marie. But she didn't go to school. She was a local, but wildly popular in our underground set. I didn't know at the time but in those last few weeks she was using me as a tool, trading the occasional physical act for access to a ride or a buzz or a meal to get her through the cyclical lull in her life before another serene summer rolled around.

And so it was about the middle of May that we stopped seeing each other much more than once a week. I knew in my heart she was seeing someone else and so I made the decision to let go. See, I'd been a 20-year old virgin prior to the night in my bedroom that past year when I flipped Marie back down onto the bed as she tried to break off our make out session. There was a full blown party downstairs and when she'd said "no they will hear us" I said "bullshit there's twenty people partying downstairs" and had my moment in the sun.

It had been very hard for me to come to grips with the disconnect between sex and love. But as Marie and I drifted apart I began to grow beyond my mother's working class Christianity that haunted a certain small region of my brain. And just as I did the floodgates opened.

Cara had been up first about a week after I moved into my current apartment. Dewey, Dooley and I had played the second slot of a huge house party. When we came off stage about 11:30 that night Cara was standing there and came right up to me. What she whispered in my ear still gives me a shiver after all this time and the things we did that first night and the three other nights we spent together in June are a wellspring of joy that I've only tried to describe to someone once. But words failed me.

I noticed that same glint in Anne's eyes the first few times we hung together in her living room watching MTV after her roommate went to work. When I found myself standing face to face with her in my driveway this evening I didn't hesitate to see what was what.

But Dooley.

I led Anne around the yard from the native rhododendrons at the driveway's edge to the base of the poplar tree at the house corner. I held the microphone out to get the crunch of our feet on the damp grass along the side of the gravel drive. I drifted my hand across the rhododendron leaves and let the mic capture the fiction's rustle. I pointed it to the sky as a tic hound barked somewhere across the river.

Anne and I began to whisper gibberish into the mic and she giggled as I moved it back and forth between her mouth and mine. After a few minutes I looked over to the truck and saw Dooley had finished with his beer. Anne and I made our way over to him and I carefully coiled up the slackened mic cable.

"Well that ought to be enough," I said. "Thanks Dooley."

"Hey no problem," he said flatly. "I appreciate you letting me hang out here for a bit, but I guess I'll head on home now. Thanks for the beer and all."

I caught the hint of his defeatism but wasn't biting.

"Don't go Dooley. Sure you don't want another beer? We could get a few more extension cords from inside or daisy chain the mic cables and see how close we can get down to the river."

Anne kicked me in the leg. She didn't know I was fucking with him.

"No man, I appreciate it but I guess I'll head on home and see about getting to bed."

I gathered up the four track and took it back inside as Dooley backed up the driveway before making a two point turn to get pointed in the right direction home.

I was just gathering the extension cord up when Anne spoke.

"He seems like such a sad person. What's the matter with him?"

"Dooley has always been dour GG. I don't know if it's the drugs or something from his family life. He's as smart as anyone and has been known to have a sense of wit, but he's morose more often than not."

"That's too bad for him."

"Yeah and it doesn't help that his girlfriend dumped his sour ass back in March. He's been insufferable since then."

"Who was she?"

"You've seen her here a few nights last week. Christy is her name. She's tall, a really white skinned girl. You'd like her. She's from up north just like you. She drives that maroon Chrysler van. A tall girl, not too thin. An oval face. She and Dooley lived together the last two years. I'm not sure what happened, if she got tired of him or what. I think she's moved out to her own place on the other side of campus, down Wayehutta Road."

Anne was leaning on my Volkswagen and looking out across the night.

"I'll put this cable up. You want another beer or anything? I could do with one."

She smiled. "That would be good, but I'm going to go upstairs first for a few minutes. I'll be right back. Can you wait for me?"

"Certainly," I said.

She bopped up the stone stairs into the darkness and I took the bottles and the extension cord inside. In the kitchen I was pulling out two more bottles and wondering if I was being naive or if I was moving toward the third act. I thought briefly about my parents, the finalized divorce, my mother's middle aged sadness and my father's timely advice about not getting married. Ever.

Back outside the clarity of the stars was brilliant as I looked between the trees to make out part of the Big Dipper. The handle stuck up high in the darkness as the dipper's edge sank behind a ridgeline.

Anne came back and we sipped the beers for a few minutes and I took her bottle and set it over on the porch. As I kissed her softly, tasting the husky remnants of cigarette and other smoke amidst her freshly brushed teeth, she ground into me and whispered "let's go inside."

I widened the disconnect between sex and love that week and it was as if I'd placed an ad or taken out a billboard that screamed "will fuck for fun". It was like I'd repented of all my slavish fears about my body and my mother's morality and what it would mean in the long run.

For about two weeks I alternated between Cara and Anne in what seemed like an infinite loop of lust. Anne made it clear that first night after we came inside that while she was with me then she might just want to be with one of my friends next. Cara would call me on the phone from her job at a group home for troubled teens and arrange a meeting place for after dark. She'd dated one of my casual friends for about a year and was working her way out of a living arrangement with him.

"I'm not looking for a relationship with you," she'd say on the phone. Our second night together I was supposed to pick her up in a gravel parking lot behind an area where road crews stored materials for patch repair. She didn't want anyone to see her car at my place just yet. We started into each other in the pitch black of midnight once we got back inside. By the time the sun came up and light filtered across her face, sweat bonded us together. In the shower an hour later we made love again and I understood that momentary bliss would never be exceeded.

More than fifteen years later my mother died suddenly from a stroke. Amidst the wreckage of her final years, in a small trailer where she'd isolated herself as she tried to hide from youthful shame she'd never truly shed, I found a set of pictures stuffed deep in a dented two-drawer filing cabinet.

Because of the suddenness of her death, and the paralysis of grief that gripped my sister and me, we made choices on the fly about what to keep and what to throw away. I wanted pictures and a few other mementos from my childhood - a ceramic Santa Claus she'd made, a framed needlepoint with the words "houses are made of bricks and stones, but homes are made love alone" - and I stuffed these items in the small cardboard box my uncle secured from the liquor store down the road.

Months later as I was sorting through the box after grief turned to guilt, and I needed to bathe in her memory, I was gripped by a set of photos. My mother out west with a half-brother she never knew existed. A dazed vacancy on her face as she looks at the camera. It's a year after my parent's divorce. She is forty-five years old.

One of the photos is of an overcast sky, a down quilt of clouds taken from her seat on an airplane. The grayness somewhat blurred by the motion and the mistimed shutter speed. A metaphor of the vagaries tormenting a life spent searching for clarity. I feel the grief that she endured in those days as the certainty of her lineage fell apart the same way her marriage had only recently as well.

I pondered over the gray stillness of the clouds - beautiful but tinged with sadness, as if there to hide the beauty of firmament from those put on this earth to suffer. I could see my mother taking the picture from her window seat on the cross-continental flight but I wondered did she capture the moment on the way to Seattle or as she left to return east?

I flipped the picture over as another tear traced the now double-circled wrinkles of my once youthful eye. On the back in computer print the words "July/August 1993". A hollow pain emptied my stomach as I thought about how alone she must have felt then. I sat down in my chair and stared at the words and then the picture again and remembered how Dooley had hung himself during that first week of August after Christy asked if she could spend the night with me.

I didn't even think twice about saying yes to her.

The Other Side of the Window

As the officer brought the customer through the heavy steel doors leading from the vehicle portico into the holding area, Sanders didn't really want to get up from his newspaper.

"Fucking incessant," he thought to himself. The officer led the heavy-set man across the shiny-waxed floor interspersed with eight cold benches and outlined with holding cells across the way from the glass windows separating Sanders from the prisoner holding area.

It had been a relatively normal Saturday at the booking office. A few walk-ins in the morning looking to charge somebody with a petty misdemeanor like harassing phone calls or trespassing. The clerk from the grocery chain brought her stack of summons for bad checks. A Forsyth County deputy brought a haggard mother in to finally get commitment papers for her out of control son who was too long on the crystal.

Now, just a little before lunch time, Stewart was the first police officer of the day to bring in a real customer. Sanders guessed DUI. Still hung from the previous night, the man probably made an erratic turn, or crossed the centerline, or weaved in and out of his lane of travel, thus catching the watchful gaze of senior patrol officer L.C. Stewart of the Winston-Salem Police Department, who was itching for a collar to get his day going in the right direction.

Stewart was a stalwart veteran of the city's east side. As square jawed and flat topped as they come, he had seen his share of the drugs and violence that infested that part of the city. Since the WSPD began tracking arrest stats a couple of years back, veteran patrolmen like Stewart fought like tomcats to get assigned to one of the 12 beats in the city's inner east or south side. That's where the action was, and if an SPO was ever going to make sergeant, he could get his numbers in that fertile field.

Sanders put the sports section down and got up from his chair to move into position. Stewart led the man into one of the four holding cells. The man was dressed sharp for an arrestee, wearing a button down shirt that hung over his belt line, a pair of dark, designer jeans and mandatory Lugz. A subtle leather jacket topped off the ensemble. But it was something about the man's countenance that caught Sanders' attention. The man looked down as he walked, a forlorn look on his wrinkled brow, resigned to something, and not at all like the aggressive, defiant types that officers from the busy part of town normally carried in tow.

Gathering his pen and notepad, Sanders moved to his window and waited for the officer. Stewart was a little taller than most officers, military trim, and no nonsense. He moved with confidence, posture erect and certain of his actions. After shutting the holding cell door, he turned to gather his clipboard from a bench, taking off his black leather gloves and adjusting his belt.

As he approached the window, he looked at Sanders. "Can you buzz me in for a minute?"

Since moving to the new glamor slammer from the dingy office in the basement of the courthouse, the senior magistrate had instituted several new rules. No smoking at your desk, no eating at your desk and no buzzing in every officer on the force into the nice new office. Sanders liked the cops and didn't really fall into the power play between the magistrates, who were really no more than glorified clerks, and the patrolmen. Sanders buzzed Stewart in without hesitating.

"Officer Stewart, how's it going?"

"Good. Listen," Stewart said as he hitched his thumb up over his shoulder aiming back to the holding area. "I came across this guy over in the circle holding a gun on another guy down on his knees. When he saw me he took off. He's going to give you some sob story, but he needs to get locked up."

"I hear you," Sanders said. Piedmont Circle was a public housing project off N. Liberty and East 29th streets, just below Smith Reynolds Airport.

As officer Stewart went back out the door into the holding area, Sanders looked back toward the man in the cell. He was still looking downward, listless as if in thought. Kind of an odd time for a robbery, Sanders thought. Kind of an odd perp for an armed robbery too. But after three years as a magistrate, Sanders wasn't really surprised by much anymore.

His first day on the job, 22 and fresh from dropping out of college again, his knees got a little wobbly when he said "bail is set at $50,000 secured" to the large black man on the other side of the thin Plexiglas in the old office. That guy was charged with rape and it was only the heinous thought of the violence of the act that gave Sanders the mettle to look the man in the eye and send him packing. After a few months, he had developed a reputation for firmness that most of the officers appreciated. As the scourge of crack and violence among otherwise hapless young men spread across the city, the police department had responded with a zero tolerance policy for petty crimes such as trespassing, loitering and littering along with a strategy of stacking charges where perps ended up with several charges for one instance of drug possession.

Sanders played along by being tough on the petty crimes, routinely locking up every thuglet that stood before him charged with trespassing with a $500 bail.

Stewart moved into position in front of Sanders' window, placing his left hand on the Bible and raising his right hand.

"Do you swear?" Sanders said coyly.

"I do," Stewart replied. "Your honor, this morning I was on routine patrol in Piedmont Circle and as I came past the 1300 block I observed a black male on his knees at the edge of the sidewalk with another black male standing over him holding a pistol to his head. When the man holding the gun saw my patrol vehicle, he turned and ran between a row of homes. I activated blue lights and siren and proceeded around the far side of the row and saw the man toss his gun onto the ground and run along the sidewalk. As my vehicle approached the suspect, he stopped and turned around and put his hands in the air. I exited my vehicle and drew my weapon and ordered the suspect onto the ground. He complied with my commands and I placed him under arrest for robbery with a dangerous weapon."

The story was familiar but the perp was out of place, Sanders thought as he took the officer's notes back to his desk to type up the arrest warrant. Pounding the letters on the typewriter into the preformatted fields on the warrant, Sanders' mind continued to mull over the details of the story. The man's demeanor just didn't fit with the normal circumstances.

More often than not if an officer brought in a perp whose actions outlined the circumstances Stewart just described, he would be bucked up and cocky, rapping a lyric from a gangsta rap song, staring coldly into his new surroundings as if all too familiar with what comes next.

Sanders ripped the finished warrant from the typewriter and made his way back to the window. He signed the warrant and separated the triplicate forms into their necessary segments: one for the officer to execute, one for the perp and one for the court file.

He was just finishing the personal information on the blue release form when Stewart brought the man to the other side of the window.

Sanders looked up.

This guy was soft and domestic, you could tell by his plump face and drooping eyes that he was no more streetwise than Theo Hucskstable.

"Mr. Gilmer," Sanders said, "You are being charged with armed robbery ..."

At those words the man collapsed his upper body on the counter across from Sanders, raising his cuffed hands to his round face in sorrow.

"Naw, sir, please, please, oh lord," the man cried. "I'm sorry, sir, please, I never done nothing like this ... oh lord, please ..."

Stewart jerked at the man's upper arm.

"Stand up there and listen to the judge," he said as he pointed to Sanders through the window.

The man raised his face to Sanders as tears filled the corners of both eyes. As Sanders continued, those tears fell in great drops along his cheeks.

"You are being charged with armed robbery," Sanders said. The man's lips quivered.

"Sir, I'm begging you sir. I just needed some money to get milk and diapers for my baby. I don't know what I was thinking. Sir, I'm sorry, sir," he said, raising the back of his wrist to wipe the tears from his right cheek.

For once Sanders believed. The facts all added up. He looked at the man. He looked at Stewart, who paused to look up from his half-completed arrest sheet to see that there was an uncertain look in Sanders' eyes.

Sanders fidgeted with his pen in his right hand. All he had to do was fill in the bubble with a bond amount and send the man to the jail. But other thoughts filled Sanders' head.

He thought about the hardened pricks that came before him with their scornful smirks and disinterested looks. He thought about the times he had been spit at in the other office, as the perps stooped down to put their mouths up to the small, waist-level hole and spit across the counter as Sanders moved to one side. He thought about the time the man said "fuck your gramma" to Sanders and how he almost lost it, coming around the counter and out the office door toward the man until a police officer put his hand on Sanders chest.

This man wasn't like that.

"Please sir, I never been in no trouble," the man continued.

Sanders looked at Stewart who was furiously scribbling something. Sanders looked down and saw that Stewart was writing on the back of the arrest sheet tablet.

Suddenly, Stewart slapped the back of the tablet up against the window.

"NO MERCY!!"

"DRUG DEALER"

Sanders knew what the officer wanted. He wanted a felony collar with a stiff bond so he could walk the man twenty feet over to the intake, where two black-clad jailers stood ready to take the man in.

Stewart wanted to dump the man off with the jailer, hand him the arrest sheet and get back in his vehicle and back to Piedmont Circle and East 29th Street so he could find another perp and get another arrest.

Sanders knew what the man wanted. Or rather what he didn't want. And Sanders didn't think the man deserved it either. In the bottom of his stomach Sanders felt a swell of empathy. But there was Stewart, still holding the tablet up to the window and staring a hole right through the glass.

The man collapsed again on the counter and Stewart had to use both hands to hold him up as Sanders said "Bail is set at $5,000" and ripped the top form from the perforated tab and handed it to the officer.

Stewart nodded to Sanders as he propped the man up and began to lead him across the holding area.

"Oh lord. My baby," the man continued to cry as he walked away.

Sanders placed the second copy of the release form into the white file and placed it in the basket for the clerk to pick up Monday morning. It would be just one of hundreds from that weekend.

Stewart was diligently straightening his arrest sheets as Sanders turned away from the clerk's basket. Their eyes briefly met and Stewart nodded before taking the arrestee by the arm and leading him across the holding area floor toward the heavy doors that led into the Forsyth County Detention Center.

The man shuffled as Stewart guided him toward the gatekeeper, who was already putting on his Latex gloves and instructing the operator in the control room to pop the lock. The man continued to wipe his cheek on his shoulder as if drying those tears would somehow make a difference in what lay ahead.

By the time Sanders straightened his area near the window and readied it for the next customer, the gatekeeper was probing the man's mouth with his Latex covered fingers, checking his ears, patting him down and emptying his pockets probably for the fifth time that day. After the gatekeeper was convinced the well dressed perp wasn't hiding anything, SPO Stewart handed the man, and some papers, off like a baton in a relay. SPO Stewart headed back out across the holding area toward the sally port. Eagerly he threw a hand up to Sanders and said "Be back soon!"

Sanders watched as Stewart entered the vestibule between the holding area and the main exit to the sally port. Stewart unlocked his gun from the box in the wall, holstered the pistol and replaced the key. Ready to resume his patrol, he asked master control for permission to exit. Safe in the assurance of the video camera on the wall, control opened the lock and Stewart disappeared into the midday sun.

Sanders wanted to return to his newspaper, but arriving back at his desk he took one look at the stack of worthless check summons he needed to process and resigned himself to his fate. Though the state dutifully provided forms with neat boxes to be filled in, other boxes to be checked and yet more boxes to be signed and dated, the interaction of Sanders' fingers and the typewriter keys, the process of positioning the paperwork, removing the finished product, signing it in triplicate, tearing this perforation here, folding along this line there, placing the copies in order neatly in the specially designed white sleeves and stamping the envelope across the single black line at the top, added much misery to Sanders' day. Neatness was not his forte. As a child he did not like to color within the lines and ever since that time he searched for still more lines to cross.

Crossing lines was to Sanders as natural as the rich blue sky that cast an amber glow across the tops of the city skyscrapers that September morning when he made his way to the booking office. Strange it was (two years ago then) that Sanders, just a few weeks past his 23rd birthday, had found himself in a white-carpeted office across from a diminutively frail woman who sat behind an incredible oak desk and interviewed him for a job at the Forsyth County Clerk of Court's Office. A few hours earlier he had been at the employment office at his father's urging, taking the typing test, searching the computer system, entering codes for the career field he might have interest in. At least it wasn't the Army, Sanders thought at the time, and when he found an entry for "deputy clerk of court" he thought that might be an interesting way to spend 40 hours a week in return for monetary consideration.

After a phone call from the job placement counselor, and a return home for a shirt and tie, Sanders found himself sitting across from Mrs. Francis, the elected clerk of court for the county, as she looked at his test results and pre-formatted application.

"My, but things are happening fast for you today young man," she said as she offered him a job working in the basement of the courthouse processing paperwork, as she put it. After a few months of training Sanders was placed on the second shift, 4 to midnight, and spent two years listening to every type of neighborhood complaint, domestic dispute and otherwise general disagreement imaginable among men (and women!) when he was not otherwise processing mounds of paperwork or signing arrest sheets for the officers.

To be sure the collars, as the cops called it, were the most interesting part of the job and Sanders never ceased delighting to hear their stories. Not all of them were as dramatic as Stewart's well-dressed robber but many of them were nearly as entertaining.

The great majority of them were mundane rehashes of the same testimony, well coached by the brass at the police department in conjunction with the district attorney, with a goal of minimizing appealable error by the officer in the performance of his duty.

"Your honor, on this date I was on routine patrol in the blah blah blah block of yadda yadda yadda street when I observed (fill in the blank here with unimaginable nonsense on the part of other humans beings) ... and proceeded to exercise my lawfully sworn duty to serve and protect ..." was the basic mantra repeated over and over. At times the fill in the blank may be interesting along the lines of "saw a man with flesh hanging from his arm approaching my patrol vehicle in the 700 block of East 19th St. Upon exiting my patrol unit the victim advised he had been slashed at with a butcher knife by his girlfriend Towanda Hairston (that's her in the curlers and housecoat, he says, with a thumb over the shoulder) because he spent the $8 dollars she gave him for milk and bread and a pack of hot dogs on a six pack of beer, one pack of Kools and a bag of pork rinds."

Or something uglier still such as "responded to a call in the 1400 block of Sherwood Drive to the home of Mr. and Mrs. Van Story and their daughter Melanie. While there I was advised that Melanie is being harassed by a young man, Trey Weaver (yes *that* Trey Weaver's son) by means of telephonic communication. Mr. Van Story, tired of the phone calls and his daughter's tears, decided to record the last phone call from the younger Weaver. Yes I do have it here on tape, your honor, and I would like to play this for you as evidence."

The tape crackles as the voice reminds Sanders of the many times he endured similar taunting at the hands of the youth of that well to do section of the city. "Yeah, uh, Melanie, I don't know why you won't go out with me. I tell you what. You think you are so great. You're ready. Yeah, you know you want it, I got a dick as big as a Louisville slugger for you. You know you want it. I'll talk to you after second period."

Sanders took the fair and impartial aspect of his job seriously. Probably a little too seriously at times, but you can rest assured that he much enjoyed looking at the younger Weaver, with his ruddy cheeks and nice Polo shirt tucked in to neatly ironed khaki pants, as he stood beside his family lawyer on the other side of the window and said "Bond is set at $15,000" to which the lawyer recoiled "Your honor, this young man is from one of the finest families in the city. His parents are right outside. Surely you can release him to their custody."

"Then they should have no problem raising the money or hiring a bail bondsman for a fee of 15 percent," Sanders shot back. Powerless, the attorney angrily gathered his papers and placed his ink pen back in the inside pocket of his dark blue suit coat as the police officer smiled at Sanders and led the young Weaver across the floor to the gatekeeper.

That was as much punishment as the young man would likely endure for such a vulgar display toward the Van Story girl, Sanders thought, and he was going to make sure Young Goodman Weaver spent at least a half hour in the jail processing area while the bail paperwork was being arranged and cash paid, or the bond quickly appealed, in the courthouse across the street.

Sanders knew he could expect a complaint to be filed by the lawyer with Mrs. Francis, they always did when they did not get their way, but so too did the police commanders.

These thoughts toiled around in Sanders head as he drifted through the rest of the afternoon. In the back of his mind, though, somewhere deep in the recess of gray matter, neurons and chemical interactions, Sanders kept wondering if he served justice when he put Stewart's well dressed robber in jail that morning. When Stewart slapped the back of the writing pad up against the other side of the window and Sanders read the words "NO MERCY" he knew a visit from the patrol captain would take place later the next week if he did not accede to Stewart's demand.

But something about that case bothered Sanders. And it grew inside of him as the day progressed. When it was his turn to be relieved at the end of his shift, Sanders was still thinking about the man, and his choice, as he retraced his steps back down Third Street from the new ten story jail, passed the local and federal court houses on the right, across Church Street, passed the glass bank tower on the left with its nauseating seawater green reflective windows and up the hill toward the corner gravel lot where he paid $35 a month to park his small Honda.

The Boy's a Time Bomb

In a delirious fury Samuel dances in the dark with the soft red lights of the graphic eq smiling at him like a demon from a spot in the wall. But not even a demon would scare him now. He could stare down the gnarliest monster to come his way if anything interrupted this frenzy. Farrell is screaming from the two speakers set to a volume just above ambient, piercing the stillness of the third hour now with the words "happiness ... it's a cloud! And hope is just another form of prayer! It's a cloud!" Samuel gyrates like a pagan in the darkness, sweat gleaming across his naked body in the low lights coming from the stereo like coals in their last moments before fading.

He's normally ashamed of his body, hiding its girth under two layers of shirts or the bagginess of a loose fitting jacket. But in this ecstasy he's shed his clothes into a rumpled pile by the bed and in the darkness finds a center of delirium and slithers to the waves pulsating in the room. He taps a primal instinct, one he's seen other guys exude at parties or on stage amidst vivid bass grooves, he forms his hands into position on the frets and above the bridge to strike across the strings and send a swell of energy into the disturbed air which collapses in file at the sonic torture.

In this anaerobic state the endorphins flow and he now sees the languid blues and soft yellows of concert lights glowing on the faces of the opalescent crowd. Their roars rush into him and amplify his inexorable madness. His feet pound in rapid fire succession on the cold wood of the sparse floor. His hips this way while his shoulders the other. His hands now reaching for points hidden in the darkness and then pulling at the hair on his head or moving the gathering moisture from his forehead or smoothing it into the skin above his racing heart.

Farrell is glorious now - singing "All the guys that really have the money!" - and Samuel is putting six, sometimes eight, inches between his feet and the floor, that poor wooden floor that is thankful at this point for the concrete beneath and the firmness of the earth below that pushes back against his mad leaps. The music transitions to deep, monstrous octave riffs. His feet plant and his knees bend as he leans, holding the oneiric guitar against his dripping body. He thrusts the agreement of the two notes separated by eight tones out into the darkness and then jumps onto the bed as if it were a speaker cabinet. With the lubricant between his back and the wall he pulses as the music fades and he collapses in relief alone on top of the sheets.

There begins a soft song now and as the cool air fills his lungs a bead of sweat rolls over his eyebrow before following the track of his nose to the tip and then glistening in the darkness for an instant before dropping to the white sheet. "Children are innocent a teenager's fucked up in the head ..." and he comes slowly down from that crest and back into the stillness of the black darkness. "... adults are even more fucked up ..." and he rises now to pause sitting naked and sweating on the edge of his California style bed before standing to put his shorts back on.

It's been about four hours since he dropped Foxx off at the bar and made his way home, stopping at the package store for a pack of Camels and a few bottles of beer for the long night ahead. He started slowly at first with a small rail of the somnambulant powder spaced out by two smokes and a beer. But he was always ready for more and as long as the pile was visible he would do more until the pile reached that point where it became finite. And like a man who fights the boredom of middle age as the final crest comes into distant view he begins to savor and bargain and make plans to stretch the pile out as far as it will go.

He's made a deal with himself to not crack the bread tie twisted around the second baggie and as he pulls the chain on the reading lamp he sees that the first gram is near the end of its lifespan. He turned the music on half an hour ago after pulling a line as big as his pinkie finger and finishing a cigarette tipped with what little bit of coke would stick to the edge of a well-packed smoke moistened by the tip of his tongue.

Outside the dry air of late winter in North Carolina hangs in silence as faint stars gleam ancient waves of light across the void. Each star shimmers and fades in its own way as the wavelengths bend with each pulse to move across the space between first and last. Underneath the endless rooftops across the city people sleep with purpose amidst the dreams and responsibilities that constitute life.

But as the fifth hour moves to its halfway point there is one being awake and sending small pieces of light back across the emptiness. He sits now in the nook of the rear of his house just outside of the back door that leads to his kitchen in the downstairs apartment of a duplex on the corner of Sussex and Lockland. Five or six candles are spread around him as he sits with his back to the frigid brick, his sock feet shivering in the February air but with no signal of cold making it past the chemical barrier in his brain that separates his current state from the reality of his surroundings. A small knit skullcap covers his head. In the pale light can be seen the faint threads of red, green, yellow and black. He's polished off five or six cigarettes in the time he has been sitting and staring at the candles and every so often changing their position.

He smokes a bowl each time he moves the candles and blows the acrid smoke across the flames to leave a mist in the increasingly damp air of impending dawn. He knows he should go in soon because the earliest risers will be waking any moment now to greet the sun's path across the horizon.

Leaning forward he blows out the first candle – the red one – and blesses it for its gift, thankful for the companionship of light it shared with him so briefly. He holds a séance over the remaining candles – each blessed according to its color (green for the people, white for the sky, blue for the possibility of memory) – and peels away from the layer of frosted sweat binding his upper back to the wall that's held him up for the last ever so long.

He reenters the lamp lit room but it's not the same place he knew in the third hour. That center is gone now and in his confused mind he feels the vacancy. He's done and wants to escape the fantasy and come back home – to this room, to that low lying mattress and box spring in the corner, to those real dreams he has in the few hours in between consciousness. But he's fractured the stillness of that space, and gravity has yet to pull the pieces back anywhere near a semblance of order. For a moment though, he sees the complete picture of the room – the six empty bottles on the floor by the table with the lamp, the overflowing ashtray on top of the table, the empty baggie lying beside the ashtray with a milky residue obscuring its translucence.

He thinks he might be sick, so he gets a small glass of water from the sink and sips it slowly, the moisture slides down his esophagus and hits his stomach like a bomb. He puts the glass down. His left hand wanders across his midsection like they wish the hand of God would wash stillness over the war torn blocks of ancient cities by the sea. For another instant he thinks of more and the second bag hidden above the upper rim of the bookshelf in the corner opposite his bed. But there is one ounce of sanity left somewhere amidst his strafed psyche, and in his remembered concept of time he thinks of starting over and he's afraid, really, of being that guy you read about in the papers who OD'd.

He's able to lock that notion away, but doing so leaves him still in the vacant confusion. He lights another ciga-rette and flips the matchbook onto the table, he watches as it slides a few inches more and pulls deep on the filter before raising his arms up and resting his hands on his head so his lungs open fully. He takes a deep breath and exhales the smoke as he stares vacantly through the wall and back into the warmth of Gatsby's Pub. He's sitting at the bar now nursing his Long Island. Derrick is playing pool, Britt and Jenna are laughing and then she comes in with her friend Laura. He sees her glow even in the low light of the bar. Her name is Kristin, she probably just turned 21 because he's only begun to see her in the last few weeks and he's stared at her like every other guy in the place because she has a magnetism that very few can wield.

He's pondered countless times what it must be like to have a kinetic seductiveness that's like a scimitar cutting down the weight of loneliness. Kristin is surrounded at all times but he's made eye contact with her on more than one occasion and she's held his gaze and offered a slight upward curve of her richly colored lips. He's noticed her pearl skin is as flawless as her shoulder length, lightly feathered hair, the color fascinates him.

Maybe it's a base brown or strawberry even, but it has a royal touch – a slight shade of violet in certain light mixed with a hint of burgundy that matches her full lips. He wants to ask her what the color is because he can't escape the taste he imagines it smells like.

He's spoken to her but she is guarded, like she knows how both sexes are seducing her repeatedly as she tries to just pass a few minutes with her friends after working her shift at the upscale bistro. He's gone there twice in the last month hoping she would be his waitress, but it's as if they can read his mind and he gets stuck with a Will or Steve.

It's a tight knit circle here; she doesn't have to worry about people constantly hitting on her like she would at a club or one of those college bars up the street. So he knows he has to play it cool, or risk being on the outs with the hipster clique that wields the real power in this room. He tried to speak to her gently once as she walked past him, she paused and said softly "I'll be back by" and kept going.

And it was that hint of chance that elated him then, as it does now. When he's finished, he pulls his shorts back up, wipes his hand on the edge of the sheets and rolls over, trying to find the darkness.

But dawn has again conquered the constancy of night and black gives way to a dull gray as his eyes remain open with his heartbeat elevated while his body fidgets from one side to the next until he gives up.

He moves to the bath, runs some cold water in the basin, rubs his hands together and then onto the roughness of his unshaven face before looking at himself in the mirror. He's still soft on the edges, but the darkness under his eyes has grown; he hears those voices from across the years, quickly looks away and turns off the light. He moves aimlessly between the three rooms in his apartment and decides since dawn has broken and the traffic of labor now vibrates every so often past his window that he should go outside.

His hands shake lacing his sneakers and his breathing labors, but he hopes the fresh air will calm him. His therapist, Jeanette, is always telling him he should walk more to alleviate his depression. All this gels in his current frame, and in a few minutes he's moved a few blocks down Sussex toward the park at the bottom of the hill. The light air is crisp and he moves with overdone steps along the brittle sidewalk path beneath the now barren limbs of the mature trees lining the streets of the original section of Ardmore.

Samuel is talking to himself in a low mutter as he moves toward the entrance to the park. He's passed a few older women walking small, flannel covered dogs on short leashes. A younger woman jogging with a fleece headband keeping her auburn hair from her face as the ponytail sways with her staccato stride. A trim man in his 30s with a steaming coffee and a dull briefcase held him at length while picking up his newspaper before getting into his Volkswagen. He continues the hard look as he drives past Samuel on his way up to Miller Street.

Perhaps they could hear his thoughts as he walked along and his mutter increased to an audible cadence – "I'm so fucked up. I need to get out." – was the pulsation currently at work. By the time he reached the end of the block, the traffic was heavy on Miller Street as thousands made their way to the hospital down the hill to begin the day shift as an equal number were leaving to go home as the night shift ended. Thousands more followed Miller Street down to First Street to either go right toward downtown or left toward the Stratford district's banks, retail shops and commercial notions.

There were two or three women and a few men waiting at the crossing to go over to the park on the other side of the road. It was a stern woman with graying black hair who spoke to him first. She wore blue scrubs and white floor shoes beneath a padded down jacket.

"Are you ok sir? Are you cold or having some kind or reaction?" she asks him.

He's been languishing deep inside his knot of isolation and when he realizes she is speaking to him, he pulls his darting eyes from the traffic flowing past and looks to her upturned face. A few others have stepped to the side or backed up from the apex of the curve where he stands inches from the path of the cars.

"No," he says. "I'm fine." He pauses. "Well physically I'm fine. But are you a Christian?"

Her brow contracts and she seems perturbed, but she steadies and says "Yes, yes I am a Christian."

"Then pray for me." He looks to the handful of faces within ear shot whose heads perked up at the exchange. "If any of you are Christians just pray for me. I'm lost and have no idea what to do."

Before any of them can respond the light has changed and the traffic stops, he sees the white stick figure across the street in the crossing signal and he steps lively into the road, the first one across the street then down the granite steps and into the park toward the footpath.

The nurse pauses for an instant only when she reaches this side of the road and then turns and heads on to the hospital. He forgets her but he's ripped another chasm in the fragile silk of fabric that holds peace together. As opposed to calming him, the cold and the effort have sped more agent through his agitated blood stream.

He passes an older man walking on the path.

"Are you a Christian sir?"

The man walks another step and stops as they both twist to face each other. Frustrated, the man replies "What? Yes, yes. I am a Christian."

"Then pray for me."

"What's the matter with you son?"

"I'm lost and I've got to get out."

He's turned and walking swiftly again before the man can respond. The man raises a brow and begins to shake his head as he turns and continues on his way.

He forgets the man and is almost to the bend where the footpath goes down into the woods but he decides to veer off the path and cross a small field to another set of smaller steps that lead back up to Miller Street about 200 yards closer to the hospital from where he began.

Maybe he feels a buzzing numbness in his fingers or a damp chill in his lower extremities, wet as they are from crossing the grass moments ago, or maybe he doesn't. Maybe he quivers from the toxins his liver is struggling to filter or perhaps his body shakes as it begins to work the knot from the inside out. A tall man in green scrubs pulls on a winter coat he's carried in his arms since he left the hospital a block away. An ambulance wails as it pulls away from the intersection in front of the medical park, which he can see now about 100 yards in the distance.

The shrillness of the siren pulls a trigger in him and he realizes the commotion in that direction offends his nerves and as he spins to go in the opposite direction he bumps into an attractive woman hustling behind him.

He touches her elbow to brace her and prevent her from falling.

"I'm, uh, sorry. Excuse me."

"It's ok. I'm fine." she replies as she adjusts her shoulder bag and moves to step around him.

He wants to say something to her, but is happy just to have not bowled her over. She notices the anxiety in his expression.

"I'm fine, really. No harm done."

She turns to continue on her way and he calls out to her.

"Miss ... are you a Christian?"

She's stopped and turned her head to him for an instant, but with a quizzical look turns away and moves on. He watches her for a few seconds, her shoulder length hair bouncing steadily as she walks. She seems to greet a few people she passes and then he sees two security guards and a policeman come around a corner up the block. They stop to talk to the woman and he turns and begins steadily walking back toward the entrance of the park.

"You, stop!" he hears but pays no heed to the call. "Hey you by the stairs stop." He can hear pounding footsteps now and he glances over his shoulder to see the policeman jogging up the sidewalk about 20 feet from him.

He's one step down from the sidewalk and in half-step to the next, but stops and faces the officer and pulls his hands from his pockets. He steps back up to the sidewalk as the officer, walking now, comes up to him.

"You got some id? Several people have reported to the security guards that you are impeding pedestrians and acting in a suspicious manner."

"Me, well, uh, no sir I just live over off Sussex and am out for a walk. I bumped into that lady by accident when I turned around. I apologized to her."

"Yea we saw that, but several others before that said you seemed agitated. Sit down on that wall for a minute."

He comes to face down with his nose shoved deep into the crevice where the seatbelt mechanism extends from the molded plastic of the police cruiser's back seat. He feels stiffness in his left shoulder and a searing pain stings the back of his head. It's when he tries to move his right leg to roll over and sit up that he realizes his legs are held together by straps and his hands are clasped together behind his back.

"Move again and I'll crack your skull," the gruff voice standing in the door says to him, so he lies real still and hears the door slam. The armrest on the closing door pushes his feet up and the force of his knees hitting the back of the seat almost causes his body to fall into the gap between the front and rear of the cruiser.

When the car takes off, the momentum forces his torso back in the other direction. His face slides across the blood that's oozed from his head onto the seat. His head feels like a thunderstorm, he tries to raise his head but realizes the space in the rear of the vehicle is moving in two different circular directions, so he decides it's best not to try.

"10-4, we're en route to the ER bay, notify intake he's got a large gash on the back of his head. Possible separated shoulder. We're pulling off Miller now."

He tries to think back to the last memory he can recall. He remembers the officer calling to him. He remembers sitting on the wall. He remembers heat, a body wrenching surge and a lunge but after that nothing. The car makes a sharp turn and he slides in the seat until his feet hit the car door. He notices a pain in his ankle when he pushes back against the motion.

The car suddenly halts and he's thrown forward again, his heel and backside coming against the rear of the front section of the car with his hands shoved between the two. The steel of the handcuffs makes a clacking sound as it strikes the plastic and pushes the metal into the tender meat on the underside of his wrist.

Before he can push off against the back of the seat with his toes and fingers the door is opened.

"Sit up motherfucker. Put your fucking feet down and sit up."

He tries to move but can't. The officer grabs his shin with one hand and forces it down off the seat while gripping his upper arm and pulling him toward the opening of the car door.

"Don't even think about resisting again or I'll finish you."

He's in a daze and barely able to hold his head up but softer hands now are touching him and applying pressure to the back of his head. The cop has him by the rear of his left arm and is pulling him to a standing position before handling him into a wheelchair where a large black orderly is waiting. He notices several other officers have arrived in cars behind the one he was in and the place is loaded with security guards and police.

There seems to be a lot of attention being given to one officer with a bandage pressed to the side of his head and he recognizes him as the officer who asked him for his ID in his last moment of clarity.

A muscular, flat topped older cop, clean shaven and wearing a white shirt with a gold bar on his collar gets out of an unmarked black SUV and gestures for the wounded officer to move inside. With a commanding air of authority, the officer clears out several cops standing around eyeballing the guy in the wheelchair having large black zip ties readjusted on his ankles and his now un-cuffed hands strapped to the armrest of the wheelchair.

"Take him to bay three," a female nurse with a clip-board tells the orderly and the officer in the white shirt follows behind.

"If you struck the suspect then I'll need a report," the lieutenant says to the cops standing around as he's wheeled toward the ER doors. "If you saw the altercation I will need a report. If you just came on scene then you can clear and move out."

He's wheeled into the ER bay and laid face down on the table after his wrist restraints are removed. Firm hands hold his head in place as others jab stitches into the wound on the backside of his skull. Softer hands take his limp left hand and hold it gently, stroking his thumb joint and outer wrist softly while he transfers some of the pain by squeezing tightly.

Live for that Look

I'm dancing on the chair *again*.

My pants are on this time. The groove has my feet moving and my spine tingling. I know Troy just called and asked me to come across town to Carmen's house but I need *this* right now.

The transition from *Blowing It* into *I Live for That Look* lifts me and if I could I would float in the air, across the room with the ugly puke orange, green, yellow and brown carpet that still covers the floor of my parent's basement. My dad's gone and my mom's at work. I quit my job last month and just got home from Butner but I still have $4,000 of my state retirement fund in the bank. I've got nothing really pressing to do so I think Troy and Carmen can wait a few minutes while I dance on this chair.

I don't know if it's J Mascis's deft touch on the frets or his melodic walk up and down the neck in the solo bits that gets me in that spot where existence pulses. There's something bitter sweet when he cries "I don't know a thing to say to you" just before he reaches down low, too low it seems for a normal guitar, and pulls a note and pushes it skyward. He holds it and holds it until he releases the tension and moans "Hey I live for that look!" and I'm jumping off the chair and up and down on the floor screaming "I know why! I know why!" Murph is absolutely killing a straight four-four back beat and just because the song can't stay perfect for more than a few bars they have to end it.

I move over to the Sony stereo my dad gave me just before he disappeared. I turn the large black knob down from eight toward three and push the stop button on the cd player. I'm not sure if my sister is home or if her friend who rents my brother's old room is here and to be honest I don't care. They know I have my moments and that the only cure is frenetic grunge turned as loud as it will go.

I've turned the music off but it still rolls along the stereo in my head. I take a Camel Light from the box and open the brown door and step into the nascent spring. Late March's cool air amplifies the chill bumps already on my arm and up my spine. The thin tee shirt provides little comfort now, despite being the perfect attire for my brief rock and roll frenzy. I smoke the Camel in four drags and flick it into the bucket by the door and step inside to find my black Adidas and a jacket. I grab my keys and head back out the door to the driveway and get in the Prelude.

Soon I'm rolling across once open farm land that's now formless housing developments that morph into one stream of bourgeois depravity across this part of the county. Down Robinhood Road and into the outskirts of town. Past the shopping centers of my youth where I spent days upon days with my mother and my brother and my sister going to the grocery store or the drug store or shopping for discount clothes or begging her to stop at Wendy's for a Frosty. I've driven down this road so many times I don't really notice it any more. But I did exist in that parking lot on several occasions and I've been over there in the back of another car reading a book I just picked up at the library as my mom drives us home. Or over there getting slapped across the face with my dad's huge right hand as he keeps his left on the steering wheel and since he's six fucking foot seven yeah he can reach me all the way in the back seat after I said something smart or whatever. I've driven this road at three in the morning coming home from the bar at 90 miles an hour just daring a cop to be anywhere near the vicinity and almost killing myself more than once. Especially the time I rounded the curve and there was a car stopped to turn left and I barely had time to stomp the brake and decelerate to about 40 before the car turned off and I avoided death just like that somehow.

But for now I am just cruising on a Tuesday afternoon across town to Carmen's mom's to see Troy and probably go shoot pool. I'm cruising Silas Creek to the south side. Floating in and out of traffic listening to Rollins

Band. Trying to keep the Prelude under 60 miles an hour because that is the speed I drive. I just don't slow down for much anymore. Life is moving on and I am moving with it and Henry Rollins is asking "Do you really wanna fuck with me, huh, me, yeah, me, no I really don't think so!" I suggest you move your car over to the right lane like you are supposed to when I come rolling up on your bumper. I mean rules are there for a reason.

I make it to South Main Street and into some older neighborhoods where Carmen is living with her mother. I see Troy's white Honda down the street and I look for a place to park the 'lude, wondering again what the parking rules are in these overpopulated working class areas. I remember the time we were hanging with the sophomore girl behind Jefferson Middle School while her mom was at work and I parked in front of a neighbor's house and when I went to get my sack of weed from the glove box the man was standing over me as I tried to get up saying "Son get your car out of my yard!" But there are no unlined street fronts here. Each house has a drive and a mailbox and, glory to heaven, a curb to park alongside.

I'm out of the car and up the concrete drive to the side door. Through the kitchen lit by the now warming March afternoon sun and through the small area where the kitchen, the hall and the living room come together. Here sits Troy and Carmen on the couch that's covered by a rich red tapestry draped across the cushions.

Carmen's light blue eyes light up as she greets me and I feel welcomed as always to be around her. If she wasn't my best friend's off and on I would seriously have to consider how I could get to know her biblically.

"Hey Thomas," she says as she gets up and gives me a hug before plopping back down on the sofa beside Troy. "What took you so long?"

I think for a moment if I should really tell them the truth? That I had to have a manic moment because it's spring and the energy is pulsating in me and my skin is alive and I can feel life moving all around me in whatever I do or say. I demure and make up something about running an errand to the bank or whatever. Carmen looks me over and smiles again as she repositions herself on the couch. I smack hands with Troy and say *whattup nigga* and move to a deep brown upholstered chair next to the sofa.

"Your hair is growing back nicely, Thomas. Why *did* you cut it off in the first place?"

She doesn't know the whole story and I don't really have the heart to tell her that it was another manic moment. That when the barber came into the ward at Butner on the fourth day I was there I had been reading The Gulag Archipelago. I decided to exhort two or three other patients to shave their heads as well (*it makes for quicker showers!* I had told one of them) even despite the caution of the staff that the doctors might find it strange and extend our stay. So I run my fingers through the growing stubble and just say "Thanks, C! I wanted a fresh start for spring."

"Well fresh is what you got, that is for sure. Did you get any writing done today?"

"I did, actually, thanks for asking. I worked on outlines for two chapters and made some notes for the last third of the plot," I say. "I think it's coming together nicely, if I can just stay focused this time."

"And stay the fuck away from Brent," Troy says, referring to the orderly from Baptist hospital who has set up shop at the bar up on Burke Street pushing a rich strain of wonderful coke. Two footmen work the bathroom and the back pool table sliding matchbooks back and forth in exchange for twenties and fifties and Benjis.

"Ain't that the truth," I say and shift uncomfortably in the chair hoping we can change the subject. But Troy is my conscience, as he has been for two years now, a perfect complement of reason and logic to my swash-buckling mentality.

"I know you're bored and drifting bro, but if you want adventure and excitement you need to find it in something lasting, not in putting that shit up your nose like everybody else in Winston who doesn't have anything better to do," Troy says.

He's lectured me several times this year and I know he means well. We're as close as brothers but he's got a wholeness, a sense of being that I'm searching for, a contentment in his family and his existence that escapes me.

"You're right Troy, I know it. I'm gonna turn a new leaf and try to stay on the straight and narrow now," I've said this a dozen times in four months – to my friends, my doctors, to myself- but everyone knows I can't be contained.

"We all care about you, Thomas," Carmen says. "It's just that you've got so much to offer. We don't want to see you go down like so many other people have in the last few years."

She smiles at me again, her blue eyes glistening in the room's sunlight. Her burgundy lips set against the crispness of her powder white skin. I can't see why they are not a couple. I wonder again about what angst is driving her, what demons she struggles with when she is not smiling and trying to make the rest of us believe that she has her shit together.

"Let's talk about something else guys and stop lecturing Thomas," Carmen says. "I know, let's listen to this compilation disc I got from my friend's record label in Spartanburg."

Carmen gets up and crosses the room and puts the cd in. As the first few reverb heavy bars of another R.E.M. knock off group from South Carolina begin, she hands me the disc case. It's got intertwined circles and swirls on the front and some sort of animalistic figure subtly embedded across the back of the case in a thirty percent mask underneath the list of artists. As the tracks play on we smoke and I try to feign interest in the music but it's the same shit people have been putting out in this part of the country for 15 years now: jam band mush or twangy ballads about "she did this" or "she said that", half rock, half pop with too many hints of country for my tastes.

I know I'm a purist for Hendrix and the Dan and King Crimson and if your tunes are a knockoff of REM or half-baked white funk then I'd just as well listen to that rock station from Charlotte we can pick up on FM in town now.

About midway through the disc there is a decent song with a frenetic bass line that grabs my attention away from looking at the shrubs in front of the house across the street. My head starts to nod and then my fingers begin to play the bass notes on my upper thigh. Before I know it I feel like dancing again but I gotta keep it under wraps and so I shift in my chair and stretch out my legs and put my arms up and rest my hands on my head.

Troy and Carmen are talking about some more of their friends I have never met and who works where and who dates who and what so and so said about such and such yesterday after thus and so did something. I'm still focused on this bass line and as the song fades I feel a sense of longing. But that's soon replaced by ecstasy as the next track begins.

This one is the total package in my book. It's got that four-four beat, a moving chord progression in two parts – 1-2-3-4, 5 and 6-3-4, 7 and 8-3-4, all beneath a descending flurry of crisp Mixolydian tones that stone me to my soul. The verses drop into a standard two chord movement so the lyrics become the focal point but the shift back to the chorus unleashes the muse again. I can't even begin to care about the lyrics of the song with music this good. I'll even give the song a pass for being about "she" doing something or other. There's a few references to colors and pottery and a jeweler's stone, but it's still basically a "boy meets girl, loses girl and writes song" song that goes nowhere lyrically, but that's ok this time because the arrangement is tight.

I'll have to ask Carmen to borrow the disc.

Right after Troy says it's time to bolt and head up South Main Street to town Carmen makes me promise on all that is holy that I will bring her the disc back in a couple of days. I swear that I will bounce it to tape tonight and keep the disc in the car so I can give it to her next time I see her.

"Bring it to me tomorrow, if you can Thomas. I don't want you to disappear for two weeks again without giving me the disc back." She smiles and laughs as she says this, but I know she's motivated by a serious concern that it might just happen that way.

"You can bring it to West End after lunch tomorrow. How about that?"

"Definitely," I say as she takes the disc out of the stereo and places it in the case and hands it over.

"And most of all, Thomas, be good to yourself," she says as she hugs me and I move to head back out through the kitchen and the side door and down the driveway to the street where the 'lude is parked.

"I'll meet you at the piercing shop bro," Troy calls out as he gets into his Honda. I throw up a wave in acknowledgement and climb into my car.

As I put the car in gear I wish I had a cd player so I could listen to this disc again, but that will have to wait. I whip a three point turn and soon I am heading down Konnoak and turn over to South Main Street to go uptown. As I make my way north I pass Sprague and Waughtown and I think about my grandparents and my dad and how he grew up east of here off Waughtown in a neighborhood whose streets were named after battles in World War I – Argonne, Marne, Verdun, Bretton and Bellauwood, which was my dad's street.

The tiny mill worker homes packed up against each other along narrow streets barely big enough for the 1975 Plymouth my grandfather drove in his last days to pass between the equally large cars parked along the side of the street – like a tank driver maneuvering the field between battlements and trenches. The School of the Arts floats by on my right and I move down the large hill toward where Waughtown meets South Main and head up to the stoplight in front of Old Salem. The centuries are filling me now with a sense of connectivity and purpose despite the hollowness of my current paradigm.

I pull into the small lot in front of the piercing shop run by Troy's friend, Chris. We're at the very bottom of Liberty Street now heading into a row of small buildings with brick fronts, a set of four small shops at the south edge of downtown. The shop's called Mystic Eye Piercing or some shit like that. I quit paying attention to the neo-hippie underground set after I had a bad experience with some people I thought I knew as good souls who went all gangsta' a few years back when The Chronic came out. They all of a sudden went from Grateful Dead, patchouli smelling freaks to scowling wannabes walking around with a g-lean talking about "*hell yeah*" in that deep pitch Dre does so well.

But I'll feign interest in their beanie kick sacks and their twirling sticks, their elongated earlobe jewelry and nipple rings, even their pierced tongue studs – so long as they speak clearly when they ask me a question. Troy is already in the shop and standing at the counter talking to Chris when I walk in.

I've been around Chris a few times but I don't think he's ever said more than *whattup* to me so I look at him and nod and he does the same. He and Troy continue talking about some flier they are looking at. Chris is the total package for the early 20s underground set. He's medium height and fit. Rich skin, approaching olive, which gives him an exotic look despite his name being Jones. Stark, narrow facial features set beneath the obligatory lion's mane dreadlocks that all the rave set sport these days. His girlfriend Sharon is a clear eyed blonde, full in all the right places, curled up on a couch in the corner looking at a magazine.

"So yea bro if you can just pass some of these around the crew that would help me out a lot," Chris is saying as I make my way across the room.

"Let me check one," I say to him and he hands me a copy — runestone letters on purplish blue paper cry out *"Rave, Rave with DJ Judah!"* and I remember Chris, in addition to being all things possible in underground suave, is a fucking rave DJ as well. It's then that I recall his mom died and left him some money that he spent on this building, piercing equipment and proper turntables and a PA. I haven't been to a rave since late 93 when I ran into Mary and Mack at the club after we watched a black hard core band called Egypt that was made up of some of the dudes from 24-7 Spyz and we ran into the singer after the show and he said he wanted to check the town and we heard there was a rave across the street at the coliseum so we walked across Deacon Boulevard to check it out.

The rave scene had some appeal to me when it seemed alien and strange and contained a sense of other-worldness that was fresh and curious. Now with every kid under 24 adopting the dim stylings of the scene it comes across as just another lumpen cliché. And I am the anti-cliché, wed to the dogma of freshness with a violent Jacobin reaction against anything stale. But now was not the time to make a stand. It would be uncool given that we're standing in dude's own shop. So I hand him the flier back and say "cool."

Two teenage girls come through the shop door and begin to ask Chris about getting their lips pierced, or their tongue, and again I'm shaking my head on the in-side and laughing but then I remember that they are probably looking for the same escape from the staleness of mid-90s white America that I am except that as an introvert I prefer to get twisted on the inside. Troy is talking to Chris' girlfriend on the couch and I'm jealous again because he knows all of these females and can bounce from house to house in one endless stream of friendship. I wonder what that's like – to have more than one or two people who actually know you and enjoy your company – not having to wait around for the phone to ring or someone to show up at your door to break the monotony. I wonder how it is not to feel like you are forcing yourself on the crowd or to feel the need to prove yourself by talking constantly. Soon I'll learn to ask more questions and actually listen to people's answers instead of pouring my thoughts out of my mouth in a vain effort to fit in. But for now I haven't gotten that far and I'm still stuck bouncing between silence and sibilant nervousness.

I chose the silent route now because Sharon is so attractive I couldn't talk around her if I wanted to. I content myself by standing across the room flipping through a stack of CDs by the bookshelf stereo next to a display of piercing studs. I position myself so I can look over at Sharon as she talks to Troy. She has the freshest glowing skin tight across her dimples, angular chin and high cheekbones and clear blue eyes. She can't hide her figure under that loose tee shirt, probably her boyfriends, and I wonder how firm her breasts are and what they would feel like in my hands. I stare one second too long and she catches my eyes before she looks back to Troy and I back to the underground collection of local music that Chris has collected on the counter.

After a moment, I look back and my eyes linger across her waist and down the leg of her jeans that are curled up under her as she sits on the couch and across her exposed ankles and bare feet with one or two toes covered by silver rings. Her thin sandals lie on the floor. I glance down briefly at the cd and then back to her face that is full of laughter as she smiles at Troy and he is smiling about something and then says to me "You ready to roll dog?"

I pretend I was not paying them any attention and look up and nod. Sharon stands up with Troy and gives him a hug and he wraps his arm around her waist for a moment. I'm about to head to the door but she comes across the room with Troy and sticks out her hand.

"I'm Sharon," she says.

I stick out my hand and wish I knew her enough to get my arms around her, but I just say "Hey, I'm Thomas."

"It's nice to meet you Thomas. Troy has a lot of good things to say about you. Do you think you will make it to the rave?"

"It looks like it will be a blast. I'll get some people to check it out."

"Chris would like that. Hope to see you there," and with that she moves to hug me and I am a bit stunned. I lean into her and feel the fullness of her breasts against my body and briefly grip her waist. She raises her palm to my chest and applies just a small bit of pressure to let me know it's too much and so I let her go.

Though it was only a second at the most it makes me want to dance again.

With Intent to Sell and Smoke

It was a Tuesday, my birthday actually, when they came and got me and took me to the sally port and put me on the bus handcuffed to Number 4.

Since it was my birthday it was the first week of October. What I could see of the air seemed typical of Winston-Salem, a rich blue sky and a still warm breeze and the first hint of gold in the poplar trees downtown. I couldn't see much on the ride to the courthouse, just a thin strip of sky between the building tops, much like the slice of sky I could see from the narrow horizontal window in my cell. I'd been in solitary confinement since May so I'd grown accustomed to not seeing the sky.

But it was my birthday and I knew the weather would be glorious. This made me sad. Thoughts of my childhood and crisp days with my grandparents soothed me for a moment until I remembered I was handcuffed to Number 4.

We had to wait while the other bus unloaded at the dock to the basement of the courthouse. I sat in silence and looked up the sidewalk that passed by the office I used to work in as a minor court official processing mountains of criminal papers each day. I remembered the pretty reporter from Bristol, Tennessee that I'd leaked information to about the murder arrest of a trucker from her town about a year earlier. I thought about the dark thing that consumed me later that year and the anger of failure that drove me to bleaker levels of despair. I thought about how I'd cracked in March and did the ugly thing and went on the run until I sobered up enough to turn myself in.

Today I was pleading guilty on my birthday and hoping to begin reclaiming my life. But right now I was handcuffed to Number 4.

He hadn't been there long, just about six weeks. He'd come into the cell block quietly about mid-morning but was on the 12 o'clock news. His peace was short-lived. I passed the days as usual, reading and sleeping and occasionally talking on the phone to my mom or my friend Doug. They took my phone calls when they eventually let me out of the cell at 3 a.m. for my hour on the floor. I didn't think much about Number 4 or what he'd done. I made friends with a trustee and a crazy black man who'd been there for two years and would come by my cell door to tell me about the cartoon fantasies he created in his frequent psychotic states. The late summer passed quickly after I told my lawyer I was ready to plead guilty for the ugly thing and move on.

Unmemorable things happened each day until this brick of a man appeared at my cell door one afternoon. I'd seen him the night before when I was looking out the cell door window at the inmates shuffling about.

"White boy gimme a cigarette," he barked at me. His large black face was covered in a thick black beard. His chest muscles evidenced years working out in prison.

I was known as the quiet man they never let out of his cell except every other night and only then chained at the wrists and ankles with a thick leather restraint belt limiting the movement of both. I figured the trustee told him I was good for a square.

"Yeah I got one for you. What's your name?"

"Donald," he said.

"I'll give you a cigarette, Donald, but you have to answer me a question."

"Bet? What is it, bruh?"

"Well, see, I never been in trouble before. I never been to jail."

He laughed. "I can tell that's true."

"So, I wanted to know, if I have to go to prison, is prison rape real? Should I expect it will happen to me?"

A wide, soft grin spread across Donald's face.

"Nah, my dude," he said. "There is so much free ass in prison it's not a problem. You'll be alright. But that guy, Number 4 .." He looked down the row. "They got a

TOUCH YOUR DEFENSES ~ 137

special place for him. They'll take him in a closet with a broomstick and make him bleed."

I gulped and rolled two cigarettes under the crack of the door.

"Here, have another," I said.

He bent down to pick them up.

"What are you in for," I asked him.

"Murder, my man," he said. "I'm here so they might reduce my sentence." He walked off and put one square behind his ear.

I thought about this as I stood handcuffed to Number 4 at the entrance to the courthouse holding cell. We waited two by two as a deputy took the cuffs off and we stepped in.

I'd been in solitary for 139 days and only once had I been around other inmates. The week after July 4th the cell door popped open suddenly in the afternoon. I was sitting on the bed reading about Fagin in the condemned cell. I put the book down and went to the door. It was open so I pushed out. Every inmate in the block was loose. Some jumping about but most rushing to start a smoke on the lighter embedded in the wall.

I knew I should not be out. I was on the highest level of administrative segregation possible and Jenkins and Saunders made it clear each time they came in to shackle me that they'd love for me to flex just once so they could crack my head open.

I sat down at one of the metal tables anchored to the floor. The trustee, Henry, resided in number 8 next to me and he came out and sat down. We made small talk about the chaos for a minute until Parsons, a white jailer who was often decent to us, came stomping across the block right at me.

"Ashton, get in that cell right now," he exclaimed pointing toward my door. I got up and went in and Parsons came and slammed it shut. I looked out the glass and saw SRT coming in hot to deal with the rest.

The courthouse holding cell was jam packed already with about 25 inmates. So far I had not run across anyone who remembered me from the office days. Most guys milled about. Some stretched out on the floor. I saw space on the bench near the corner of the cell and made a move in that direction. I was freed from Number 4 but instinctively he followed me. I took a seat a few feet from the corner and Number 4 sat down right next to me. I still pretended he was not there.

I adjusted my glasses and gathered my thoughts and tried not to look around or look at Number 4. I was staring a hole in the cement floor when I saw sock feet and jailhouse flip flops. I looked up and a young black man with jangly dreadlocks was looking right at me.

"Ain't you the dude from the booking office? What are you doing in here?"

"I fucked up," I said.

"He's in for arson," another voice said. "It was all over the news." I looked over to see a white dude built like a stump stretched out on the floor. He wore a white trustee jumper. Dreadlocks wore gen-pop blue that complimented the bright orange Number 4 and myself sported from solitary.

I remembered them both. The white dude was Daniel Redmon. I went to high school with his older sister and had booked him at least twice and committed him to psych ward when his mother came to the office with the papers.

Dreadlocks looked me up and down. I had booked him a half-dozen times in three years.

"Yeah, I remember you," he said. I cringed. After a pause he continued. "You was always polite, respectful even. That's what I remember."

"Same," Daniel said and I hoped he didn't know I was the one who committed him, "I remember the first time you was real courteous explaining the details of the charge and what I could expect."

"Why you in segregation," Dreadlocks asked.

"I dunno man, punishment I guess."

"They afraid he'll get his ass kicked," Daniel said. "They don't even let him out the cell every day. Only every other day and sometimes they make him go three or four days. They even make him walk naked and chained up to the shower."

"Man that's fucked up," Dreadlocks said.

The jailers came and took a few guys off to their court appearance and Daniel went with them. Dreadlocks walked off and sat down next to a guy that couldn't have been a day over 19.

"What you in for cuz?"

"Possession with intent to sell and smoke," the kid said indignant. He was riffing on the court language of the most frequently charged felony drug crime. "Mother-fuckers came up on me out of nowhere. I had just got a half pound of mexicali and was rolling a blunt when they got me."

"Man, that's cold," Dreadlocks said. After a pause he looked down the row toward me, whispered something to the kid and got up.

There seemed to be increased chatter among some of the younger black guys and I could feel them eyeballing me. The hair stood up on the back of my neck and I prepared for what I thought would be an attack from someone I had not been so courteous to at the office.

Dreadlocks came and stood in front of me. He seemed to be welling up spit in his mouth. A few guys made a battle line next to him.

"Hold up," he said. I widened my eyes to take it all in, to be prepared for the flank attack but Dreadlocks looked at me and made a "get out of the way" motion with his right hand. That's when I realized they had come for Number 4.

I got up just as the loogies began to rain down on him. He shuddered and another inmate took his cock out and began to shower him with yellow urine. I noticed two in-mates standing in front of the glass window at the door looking back at us. A couple of guys struck him and one made a karate kick to his head. It bounced off the wall and Number 4 fell into the floor and took a beating. He got up and moaned his way to the toilet in the corner.

"That's nothing like what you gonna get in the pen motherfucker," Dreadlocks said to him.

Number 4 dropped his jumper and sprayed shit all over the toilet and the floor before he hit the metal seat. He wiped the murk from his face and stood up and pulled his jumper over his shoulders.

"That molester motherfucker didn't even wipe his ass," one of them said.

Number 4 took a few shots to the head as he walked back to the only place left for him. He curled in the corner and buried his face in his knees with his arms over his head. He took gulps of air, his body heaving, as he tried not to cry.

I'd barely the time to take it all in when the guys at the door scattered. A jailer opened the lock and shouted for me. I went before the judge and pleaded guilty to the ugly thing on my birthday. I was ready to begin living again but I still had to ride back to the jail handcuffed to Number 4.

Mariah

I met Mariah through an old friend of mine, Carmen. Actually, Carmen was my last friend as I had succeeded in pissing off all my other conformist friends. But not Carmen. She respected me as no other, and though she was beautiful, we were able to maintain a pure friendship, one that could withstand my habit of fouling myself with that which was wrong for me.

I ran into Carmen at a bar downtown just after New Years. She walked through the door in a long black coat covering her party dress. Her radiant smile set against pale skin and dark hair, impossible not to notice. I walked over to say hello.

"Matthew! So good to see you. How have you been," as she kissed my cheek and we embraced.

"Fine."

"Where have you been for so long? I haven't heard from you," she asked as we stood face to face and hand in hand.

"I've been away, haven't you heard?"

"No! What happened?"

"I landed myself in trouble again."

"Matthew, no! Did you get busted like Troy?"

"No, it wasn't for drugs. It was worse. But I'm over it now. I paid my debt."

"You don't want to talk about it?"

"Not here, later I will tell you. How have you been? Let's have a drink."

As I ordered myself another beer and Carmen a vodka and cranberry, she told me of her life during the past eight months while I was away.

"I still work at the bistro, still hate school and still love to party. I mean, Matthew, I am only 22 and life can be so dreary and long. I figure I will put it off as long as I can," she said with a furtive glance at her drink and a sip on the straw. "Or until Mr. Right comes along."

"Good point," I said.

"I just moved in with an old friend from Charleston, she just moved here from Greenville."

"South or North," I asked her.

"South Carolina. She graduated from Furman and is looking to go to grad school here. She's a few years older than me and a little more disciplined, you know, with school and all. You'd like her. Her name is Mariah, she might be here later."

"I'd like to meet her."

"She's out with her latest thing, you know, she runs through them like they won't make any more tomorrow."

I felt I knew what she meant.

A week later I found myself at Carmen's apartment on the south side of Winston in the mid-afternoon. It was a Thursday, I believe, and Mariah was out.

"Well show me the tour," I said after a brief greeting.

Carmen led me through the apartment, three rooms downstairs with a kitchen and three bedrooms upstairs.

"We use the middle room for storage and Mariah's study. This is her room," she said as we walked down the hall.

The room was centered by a large wooden bed, sturdy dressers and chests and pictures everywhere. Without asking I walked through the room and gazed at the daintiness of a girl's things. It seemed so foreign to me with all the frills and lace and floral impressions. Especially compared to my recent surroundings before I came back to town. I picked up a picture, one of a wedding party, six maids all in a row.

"Which one is Mariah?" I asked and handed Carmen the frame.

"This one," she said, pointing to an attractive blond of medium build with an aura of happiness. I wondered if it was the appearance or the constitution. Gazing around at various pictures I noticed lots of different young men posed with her.

"She is not in demand is she?" I asked, looking at one picture of her surrounded by a cadre of private school chums.

"She keeps herself in demand," Carmen said with a wave of the hand. Hearing something she turned and walked down the hall. I set the picture down and just as I exited the room I heard footsteps coming up and Carmen said "Well here she is now!"

I looked to see a vibrant young woman trudging up the stairs with a loaded laundry basket, a heavy bag slung over her shoulder and a pocketbook. Sunglasses perched on the top of her head. Mariah looked exhausted and so I took her laundry.

"Thanks," she said. Carmen set about introducing us as I carted the laundry back into the room. Mariah knew I was snooping just prior to her arrival, but she didn't seem to mind.

Carmen and I went downstairs and sat in the living room. She put on a Bob Marley cd and offered me a beer.

"I'd love a beer. Dr. Ellis wouldn't like it, but he's not here is he?" I said and followed her into the kitchen.

"I'm so glad to have a day off. Two days, actually. That place gets me sometimes," Carmen said referring to the small upscale restaurant where she worked. As she closed the refrigerator door I noticed it was covered in more pictures of Mariah and her minions.

"She loves pictures, huh?" I asked as Carmen handed me a bottle.

"It looks that way, doesn't it? I'm not that vain," she said and I noticed the sarcasm. We went back to the living room and sat and Mariah came down and we all talked and laughed and I remembered how good it was to be free and young and chasing a buzz. We smoked some pot and listened to reggae music and they talked about recent male conquests as if it were a game. I knew Carmen to be a flirt, but not a hussy, she was too full of self-respect and happiness for that, but as Mariah talked I sensed she was different.

I fell back into my place over the next few months. A petty job to pay the bills. A seat on the train to the garden in the darkness. The spot in life where those of us with memory attempt to hide, juggling work and play in the mirror and reflecting balance to the world. A screen between what we want and what we need. It was hard for me to find a good job, what with my recent history hovering.

I would see Carmen and Mariah out and about. I would go over on the weekends and grill out and drink and eat and talk and go home as their nights were beginning. Carmen was still after Prince Mr. Charming Right, but over time I began to notice a pattern in Mariah. She did run through them like they were not going to make anymore tomorrow. Other mutual friends I had with Carmen would come by their house and sure as sugar Mariah would hunt them, conquer them, and send them away. I would listen to Mariah complain of loneliness and a desire for stability, but the only man stable in her life was Jack from Tennessee. He was an old friend of hers. Jack Daniels, Old No. 7 Tennessee sour mash. Slowly, I began to meet some of Mariah's friends and they all told the same story.

One night I met Mariah's friend Faith. Faith took to me and we ended up on the floor in the spare bedroom in the darkness, passionate for two hours. Afterward as we lay in the moonlight that fell across the floor, Faith told me she was worried about Mariah.

"Have you noticed anything strange about her?" she asked.

"Well I have only known her for about five months."

"Have you noticed anything?"

"Other than the obvious, no."

Perching up and propping her head on her hand she asked me what the obvious was.

"I think that for such a lovely girl, she drinks way too much of that shit," I said.

"I know and she is putting on weight too, she used to be so thin, but that's when she was partying a lot."

"Yeah," I said as I reached for a cigarette, which I lit, and then handed one to Faith.

As we lay smoking in the darkness she told me the sordid details of Mariah's life since college. I learned she was the only daughter of a wealthy South Carolina family and was the toast of Greenville during her years at Furman. She had met her Prince Mr. Charming Right during her last year and was supposed to marry. But he cheated on her one night at a frat party with a younger student. Mariah took to Jack on a permanent basis as a result of a binge and a one-night stand after her breakup. Faith began to make sense of the pattern I'd noticed in Mariah's life: short–lived flame outs, falling in love today and fucking somebody else in a drunken stupor tomorrow. I felt sorry for her.

Faith and I sparked for a few weeks and all seemed to be going well. I too have a propensity to fall in love easily, and as such I think I am more in love with being in love than with the woman I fall in love with. I never said these words to Faith. I never got the chance. Two weeks after I met Faith I was at Carmen's place hanging out. She was not in a good mood and was upset with Mariah.

"She brought some complete stranger home from a club last night, and left him here when she went to work," Carmen said with fury. "I got up this morning and found a note under my door saying he was asleep and she would pick him up at lunch, but dammit Matthew, I was scared as hell to leave my own room. In my own house! I don't know this person."

I could tell she was upset. We were preparing a meal. Both of us liked to cook, and she was good at it. I tried to change the subject but she kept on about Mariah and her different man every week.

"It's getting old, and I am tired of it. I don't know what to do."

"The best thing is to tell her, I guess."

"What, tell my best friend that she is a slut?"

"If the shoe fits ..."

"Oh it definitely fits," Carmen said, cutting me off.

We changed the subject and went on to eat and then we went out drinking. The next night I had a date with Faith, but when it came time for me to call her she was not at home. I called her cell phone and she answered.

"Hello," she sounded drunk.

"Faith, where are you? I thought we had plans?"

"We did but not anymore."

I was stunned. "What happened?"

"I can't go out with a crackhead," Faith said. "Goodbye Matthew."

I knew what that was about. Weeks earlier while I was out with Carmen and Mariah and Mariah's flavor of the moment that notion crossed my mind and before I knew it I was in a stall in the men's room with a straw in my nose and power running through my body. Carmen knew what was up and asked could I get her some, which I did. We partied well into the morning and I drove home like an idiot at about 5:30. For a couple of weeks we fell into a pattern of me, Carmen and Mariah getting blitzed before we went out. I have a propensity to be in love with bliss; not the bliss you find in Webster's, but a twisted happiness that is born of despair. Carmen told me later that Mariah, in a spiteful tone, told Faith I was a crackhead, which Carmen couldn't believe since we had all done blow together many times.

"She seemed to be purposefully undermining you," Carmen said.

I was very angry and did not come around for a while.

Over the next few weeks I found myself reeling from the bitterness imposed on me by Mariah's animosity. Shedding skin like a reptile, cold blooded and always moving into an uncertain future, I slithered from group to group looking for a place to unwind. I'd been working a steady job, even promoted to a management position, until the owner of the company asked me to lie to a coworker about a job order. When I refused he fired me. Fuck him.

Registered with unemployment, I was guaranteed a few hundred dollars a month, enough to have a good time and not worry about things. Some new friends of mine, specifically an athletic brunette named Dana, began frequenting a Mexican restaurant on Mondays to take advantage of their beer specials. Mexican draft for 99 cents and Newcastle, the king of all beers, for an unbelievable buck seventy five. A week after my affair with Faith ended, nine of us were hanging, laughing and generally getting drunk at Ernesto's when an old friend, Lucas, showed up. I'd known Lucas in college but had not seen him for a few years. He was an aspiring jazz trumpeter, lost in the wavering world of Miles and Dizzy, and he was pretty good.

"Lucas, hermano, *qué pasa!*" I said.

"*Senor!* It is good to see you, no?" he replied with a laugh, and as we shook hands he sat down. There were eleven of us now and we began to raise a ruckus. The wait staff was ever so friendly, especially Frankie, a slender man from Acapulco. He was about my age and of the most pleasant temperament. The other waiter, Ignacio, somewhat smaller and more round (not fat but healthy) was friendly but quiet. Whereas Frankie would joke back with us and answer questions (will you take us to Acapulco next time you go?), Ignacio would just smile and walk away and return time after time with pitchers of beer and frozen mugs, until we had dried their keg and drank their stock or run them clean out of mugs. They loved us to death. As the rest of the group merrily interacted, Lucas and I began to catch up.

"Man, I have not seen you in what, four years," I said.

"At least that," Lucas said. "I think since that house party on the south side right after I graduated and came back here. And here I am once again stuck in this town."

A common complaint of those who grew up here, went away to school or travel and returned, was how boring our town was compared to larger cities. I understood this complaint, but to me it was inherent to the nature of the thing in itself to be a small, industrial, quasi-religious southern mill town, forget the fake southern gentility crap, that was all b.s. to me. It was about small people in a small town living small lives.

"What have you been doing," I asked him before he could ask me.

"I just came back from Europe three weeks ago. I spent nine months with a quartet led by Bill Rhodes, the piano player."

I had heard of the guy. He was no Red Garland, but who was?

Lucas continued. "I've been to Denmark, England, France, Germany and Austria."

That blew me away because the most interesting place I had ever been, besides New York City, was prison, unless you count the state hospital I visited for five days right before that. I could see why he was unhappy to be back here. This place compared to Copenhagen in the late 20th century must really suck, but compared to Yanceyville, Salisbury or Butner, I was quite content. He had heard of my troubles. Being less than discreet, he tried to get me to talk about it, but luckily Dana came to my rescue.

"Are we drinking another pitcher of beer guys?" she asked with a slyness inherent to a 21 year old.

"I'm game," I said.

"We know this much," Dana said. "You always game. You so game you broke the frame."

"True dat, true," I said and anyone listening would have thought we were crazy, which Lucas did.

"What are you talking about?" he asked, perplexed.

Dana jumped in first. "Ebonics, man, it is all the rage. Matthew is making a dictionary and even spreading it to I.E."

Still confused Lucas said, "Dare I ask what I.E. is?"

"Initialized Ebonics," I said. "But let's not go there right now. Are you still drinking with us Lucas, mi amigo?"

"Si senor! These pretzels are making me *thirsty*," he replied and we laughed and drank until closing time, our group thinning slightly to five when Frankie brought our tab.

"Thank you," Frankie said. "We see you next Monday, ok?"

"Yes, definitely," it was Dana, always flirtatious. "We'll bring more next week."

"Ok, Ok," Frankie laughed. "Perfecto. Hasta luego amigos."

As we walked out Lucas and I exchanged digits and he went on.

"Man you have to come to In The Sky, this little bistro off South Main Street. On Thursday, they have jazz open mic and a bunch of us jam from seven till eleven. Matt Kendrick is the host and leader. It's smoking."

I told him I might come, and he was without doubt elated. We retired to the parking lot and said our good-byes and me, Dana and J.C., one of her other friends, headed downtown to raise more hell. I still had my pager from work and it was about this time that it went off. Instinctively all three of us checked our pagers.

"It's me," I said as Dana rummaged through her pock-etbook. "You could lose an army in there. You can stop searching, D."

"Thank god. I don't think I'd ever have found mine anyway."

I looked at the number on the display. Not recognizing it, I called it with Dana's car phone. A man's voice yelled into the receiver amidst loud noise in the background.

"This is Matthew, somebody from there paged me."

The voice yelled, "Anyone page a Matthew" and I heard a familiar voice say "Yo, it was me!"

In a few seconds I was talking to Moody.

"M-dog, what's up?" he asked.

"No muy mucho," I said, beer buzzed and still in Mex-ican mode. "Where you at, Mood?"

"The Bear, waiting on your drunk ass to get here. Y'all still at Ernesto's?"

"We're just leaving to come down there. You got what I want?"

"True dat," he said.

"True dat, true. We'll be there in twenty," I told him.

"What, then?" he said.

"What, then hell. I was waiting on you. Peace!"

"Peace out," he replied in our new found language of the street.

Downtown from Ernesto's on the northside was a 10 minute drive through the city, which is just enough time to get cheesed. I only hit the bowl twice, which was enough since J.C. had a small piece of some of that funky stuff. It was proper.

"Man, where on Earth did you get this shit," I asked him.

"I could tell you but then I would have to kill you."

"I don't want that for sure though," I said, passing him the pipe as I choked my brain out of my eyes and my lungs out of my throat.

Dana laughed at me. "Getting old M, you are becoming a lightweight."

"No sweat," I said. "Nothing Barry White can't fix."

"Oh, so you talking to Barry tonight?" she asked me with a raised eyebrow in the driver's mirror.

"Yeah, I might speak later at the Bear. Why, you wanna talk to him?"

"You know this man," she said and drove us through town as J.C. puffed the pipe.

The car stank by the time we passed the university and the police department and the library on Fifth Street and soon we were on the two block area of downtown where the city fathers in their benevolence allowed us a small red light district. We parked in a gravel lot behind an antique shop and crossed Burke Street to the Black Bear. The door man Chris opened up as he saw us coming and soon we were in the netherworld of pitchers, smoke, trips to the head and all the young twentysomethings who's goal in life was to get fucked up and roll with the flow. Gotta love being twenty something sometimes.

I had been in and out of the scene a few times, and nearing thirty was somewhat of an expert on who was who and who was new. Still young enough to pass for twenty three and old enough to talk with the thirties who were lost on bar stools, as always I first had to oscillate between my different cadres. I often hated having to select between this group and that, but since we all just can't get along, for they haven't imagined all the people yet, I was forced to cut short a visit here to make an appearance there.

Finally I found Moody.

"What up dawg," he extended his hand to mine.

"Jus chillin like Bob Dylan cause I ain't robbing or stealin," I replied as we did our handshake and he looked at me funny.

"Man, you just ain't right," he said.

"I know, dog, I know."

Dana came around with our pitcher of Newcastle. She handed me the glasses and I poured a round. I had known her for a year or so and we had become very close since I came back home. We were both Libras and had a lot in common except that she was a blooming flower and I was a fading light, or so I had convinced myself. We raised our glasses for a toast and I said to her "Libra twin powers activate ... form of beer ... shape of pitcher." We clinked glasses and drank, she almost blowing beer out of her nose due to the incessant laughter. I was good at making people think I was 'twacked out.

"You are not right, dude," she said and she searched again in her pocketbook for a smoke.

"I know. I know all too well since you are like the third person to tell me that in the last hour." I handed her a cigarette and lit it for her. She smiled and said, "But you know we love you anyway."

"True dat, true," I said as I lit my own smoke and puffed away at the fire stick of death as the American Heart Association calls it for the sake of the children. Halfway through the smoke, Moody tugged on the back of my shirt and with a nod of the head I knew it was my turn to transact.

The men's room at the Black Bear was small, a sink across from the doorway, three urinals across on the far wall to the right and one stall with a door, good for taking a dump or a bump. It was in this stall that a good deal of the street level transactions took place, were processed and stuck in a matchbook for distribution, or the product was put to use. Mood did all three at the same time, with feeling. As we closed the stall door I caught a strange glance from an older biker type who smirked and said "Y'all don't piss on each other in there." He knew the deal and I said "We never cross streams" as I pulled the door to and held it shut since there was no latch.

"Watcha want a g?" Moody asked me as he pulled out a golf ball in a sandwich baggie, with other smaller cousins secured with bread ties.

"Make it two, dog," I said. "I better be prepared for what lies ahead."

"What lies ahead?" he asked me as he used a matchbook corner to scoop the flavescent contents of the baggie into a smaller one.

"Who knows, but I know I'll feel good about it."

"That's for damn sure, because this here is the butter. Acetone based."

"It looks like the butter," I said.

"Yellow mellow, baby, so gimme your money, uh!, if the butter is what you want," he sang with a boogie and a transaction and a blast to get us started.

"Damn, Mood, that is the shit," I said and I tried to clear my nose and power began to make me feel like Freud in Vienna circa 1890.

"I told you," he said in song. "It's the buh-tear .."

"What, then?" I said.

"What then, hell, mothafucka I am waiting on you," and with that we went out one at a time, me lingering to actually use the bathroom for its intended purpose, although getting high seemed like a perfectly normal bodily function to me.

When I went out to the bar the crowd had grown in size and I was feeling fine, eight miles high as Roger once said, or was that David, I can't remember. Looking for Dana was not hard because she was taller than most men and when I found her lo and behold there was Carmen and her friend Tracy talking to Miss Dana. I had not seen Carmen in a few weeks, had talked to her on the telephone, and the first thing she said to me was "Mariah's over there with her new flavor and Faith is with her."

"I don't give a fuck," I said. "I really don't, because me and Barry are like that." I demonstrated by wrapping my middle finger around my index and holding them up.

Dana laughed and said, "I can tell by the funk on your nose."

"Oh shit, I forgot to get nostril clearance before takeoff."

They all laughed and Dana said it was not really noticeable unless you were looking for other signs, of which she was, so I handed Barry to her and the three of them put a big dent in him before they came out of the ladies room full of its four private stalls and a shelf in each one, supposedly for a purse or something but ultimately convenient for having a small conversation with Mr. Barry White.

Apparently while so engaged in the ladies room Carmen took the opportunity to tell Dana about my incident with Mariah. Further she went on to tell her how Mariah was jealous of my friendship with Dana and had told Faith that Dana and I were crackheads.

This all came to my attention when Dana returned. She handed me the matchbook, smiled and said "I'll be *right* back." I watched as she sashayed over to where Mariah, Faith and Mariah's new flavor were and you could clearly hear Dana over the entire bar yelling about a goddamned fat ass drunk slut bitch you better never call me a crackhead or I'll bust your fat ass bitch slut face in and I don't care who your fucking daddy is and let me tell you something else ... until Andy the barkeep, who was our friend, went over and told Dana to pipe down, which she did after telling them all to kiss her beautiful round ass, in so many words, and sauntered back over to us for a round of high fives from all but Carmen who was disgusted because she would have to deal with it all later.

We didn't care for now and we had a swell time for a Monday in a quaint, sleepy, quasi-religious mill town, never mind all that southern gentility crap.

We were alive!

Death Wish
on Acid

He found a risk inherent in certain forms, be it family, security or love. The specificity of risk excited Kyle. He could see the shockwaves pushing out from the epicenter of decision. The anticipation of reaction was his motivation. Imagine the problems this could cause!

He hadn't set out on this night to imbibe frenzy, but in less than two hours after he'd downed the Death Wish on Acid he found himself neck deep in rivers of chaos.

The drive to Asheville had been tame, which was lucky on a Friday evening. His shift at the warehouse passed quickly given the amount of anticipation he had for the weekend at hand. His friend Norah had invited him to drive to see her brother. Kyle knew her brother, but was more interested in what might occur on the drive there and back. He had a sweet spot for Norah, one that longed to be assuaged.

He was able to score two grams of coke within ninety minutes of clocking out and was in Norah's driveway by a quarter past seven. The drive from Greensboro was mellow until they hit Morganton and the anticipation grew and they began to pull lines every ten minutes during the last hour of the trip.

Somewhere in McDowell County he pulled the Celica off the interstate hoping to buy a tallboy. The clerk gave him a funny look while mouthing the words "dry county" and Kyle had to content himself with Sprite.

The dry sweetness did little for his thirst, pushing him to drive carelessly up the serpentine concrete until they crested Black Mountain and floated along toward the I-240 exit that led downtown. Norah's brother, Troy, and his roommate, Kevin, gave them shit in a round-about way for being fucked up but they didn't push the issue. Troy had moved up into the mountains to grow hydroponic pot, after all, and to escape the powder scene that dominated the mid-section of North Carolina at that time.

"Man, you guys are wired," Kevin said after they'd exchanged greetings and had the time to find a seat.

"Nah, bruh, just tweaked from the drive," Kyle said. "I tried to get us here as fast as possible."

Troy wasn't saying anything, just glaring at them because he'd specifically banned anyone from bringing blow into his house. Kyle tried not to look at him.

"So what's up with you two bitches anyway?" Norah said. "Are we going to hit the town or sit here and stare at each other?"

"Well we've been waiting on you, but now that you've arrived in style we can get the evening started," Troy said. "I guess you'll be wanting to smoke a bit so you can come down from 'the drive.'" He made quotation marks in the air before pulling a wooden tray from behind the apron around the bottom of the couch. A gray green glass pipe rested on its side surrounded by clumps of pot the size of grape clusters loosened from the bunch. Norah's eyes lit up and she licked her lips. "Yummy," she said and rubbed her hands together.

Troy pinched off a bit and stuffed the glass as Kevin got up and walked to his room just off the main living area. He opened and shut the door quickly, but not before Kyle saw the orange glow from the grow lights. "How's all that coming?" Kyle said, nodding his head toward the back.

"If by 'all that' you mean the grow room, then you know we don't talk about it," Troy said dryly. "But I can tell you that you'll enjoy this right here." He handed Kyle the glass and put the tray back under the couch.

Kyle's head still pulsed fifteen minutes later when Troy pulled his Civic under the I-240 bridge at Lexington Street. It was a good spot, just down the hill from Walnut Street. The lights from the storefronts and the rush of the crowd on either side gave him that electric Asheville vibe right off the bat. Straight-laced clean cuts in button down madras with badly dyed blondes in Eddie Bauer passed along amid dirty jeaned burnouts with unwashed dreads and ear lobes as hollow as their gaunt stare. Underfed women in formless cotton dresses tie-dyed the color of New Mexican sunrise tagged along behind hallucinating heroes tripping on the mellifluous din of a city open to possibility.

They crossed the street near Stella Blue and Kyle was almost knocked to the pavement by a gregarious high-class beauty dragging her high-heeled friend in a short skirt in the wake of her own flowing hair. Their toned forms backlit in the bluish streetlight as they ran toward the door. He thought to call out to them, and he would have in any other city, but he was trying to tap into that mellow Asheville soul.

He didn't want his reputation to follow him. Not here. Not when he and Norah had talked during the drive about moving up and joining the highland party. Not when he had the chance to leave his reputation for drunken brutality in the past and maybe find a way to tap into the good times vibe. If he could find a way to chill and leave the worries of the past in the past and not fret over them and chase the stoned just trying to mute the noise for a while.

"Where are we going, Troy?" he asked.

Troy had set a mighty pace and Kyle had fallen a few steps behind after he'd paused to watch the two dark-haired beauties rush into Stella Blue. He'd thought about running after them for a minute, but that's what got him into the trouble he was clawing his way out of eighteen months later. So he rushed to catch up to where Kevin and Norah walked arm in arm next to Troy.

"We're going to Magnolia's, behind that shop where you bought the ring last month," Troy said. "I met this cutie who tends bar there."

Kyle walked a few paces behind the group. He clenched his jaw and opened and closed his fists rapidly trying to pass the pulse of envy he felt at the sight of Norah's arm fed through Kevin's, the way her hip and long torso brushed against his portly frame. Nothing he could do about it, he reminded himself. She'd made it clear to Kyle that they wouldn't become lovers anytime soon. He'd cried on the phone a while back and said "I'll wait then" to which she replied "Don't" and he said "But that's all I have right now" to which she suggested that they not hang out for a few days so he could get himself sorted out.

He'd fallen in love with her quickly after Troy left town and suggested Kyle hang out with Norah in his absence. He'd only been out of prison for six weeks when Troy told him he was moving to Asheville to get a new perspective.

Kyle didn't talk to her for a week after he'd finally said the words, but she'd called on Monday and asked if he wanted to drive back up and see Troy for the weekend.

Magnolia's was a spacious bar with floor seating and dart boards on the wall and an opening that led to more restaurant seating and a billiard area next to bay windows. They shared a few drinks and caught up on small talk and Troy was able to make plans with his cutie. Norah walked off with Kevin to play pool and Troy finally turned his way.

"She's cute, huh," he said with a toothy grin as he turned to Kyle, who nursed perhaps his third Long Island.

"Very," he said. "But you always seem to make a good impression with them. I wish I knew how to do it."

"It just comes natural, bro, you just got to be yourself. I been telling you that for years now," Troy said. He smiled again with those easy eyes and then leaned back on his bar stool. "They're everywhere up here, man. You really should think about moving up," he continued. "And for real, you need to stay away from that shit in your nose. You're about to piss me off bringing that shit up here. And with my sister?"

"She's the one, homes," Kyle said quickly. "She's the one who calls me on the phone 'hey watcha doing? wanna split a gram?' You know I'm struggling, and all alone, so what am I gonna say when a 21-year old asks me do I want to go out and get wasted?"

Troy looked at his beer. "I know. Look, you should know that my parents are suspicious. Asking me all kinds of questions about who she hangs out with and is she hooked on drugs, so try to get her to chill."

"I try man but ever since she started tending bar at Stilskins shit is crazy."

"Yeah, my mom is about to come down on that, too."

"So, it's like half the time I am trying to protect her and half the time I am trying to do my thing. Did she tell you I almost got in a fight with a guy who wanted to hit on her about two weeks ago?"

"Yeah, I heard."

"I mean shit Troy I can't be violating my probation. I got thirty-six months hanging over my head. It's one thing to do dope, but if I get arrested, I'm fucked."

They passed a few minutes in silence and Kyle turned around and leaned his elbows on the bar. He watched Norah from across the room. He'd fallen in love with her because she was Troy's sister and he missed Troy with all his heart. He knew this much. He knew what his feelings for Norah amounted to. And that's what kept him from running off the rails like he'd done so many times before.

"I miss you brother," Troy finally said to him. "I hope you can get this way. It would be good for you."

"I'd really like that," Kyle said. "Maybe things will line up and I can make it happen. Make a few good decisions for once." The comment lingered between them, hovering in the possible space before being pushed away by the sound of Norah's voice from the other end of the bar.

"Kyle, get down here," she called, leaning her breasts upon the bar so that he could see her smile beyond the row of people between them. She was with Kevin and had picked up a couple more admirers, an athletic black man in a gray shirt stretched across his thick chest, and a tall blond school boy in khakis and a red and black polo shirt. Kevin knew them and they formed a tight circle around Norah. One had his hand on her hip near the space where her shirt rose up from her belt line to expose her taut midriff.

Norah was like her brother in that they both were wholly without malice and often the center of the party. But unlike Troy she was still very naive. "Not this shit again," Kyle thought when he saw the dark-skinned hand resting on her hip. He approached gingerly, as if afraid of being drawn into another conflict over who earned her attention.

"Dude, you have to try this," Norah said. She handed him a tumbler, with colored liquors stacked in layers.

"What is it?" he said and raised the glass to his nostril.

"Death Wish on Acid," she said. "It is so good."

Kyle didn't think it sounded like a good trip. He sniffed the liquor, picking up hints of rum, whiskey and mint.

"Don't be a fucking pussy," Norah snapped. He downed the shot, surprised at how effortlessly the concoction went down.

"Let's do another," she said. Kevin and the two suitors nodded.

"Why not," Kyle said.

Norah stepped up onto the foot rail and leaned in to get the bartender's attention. The school boy elbowed his dark skinned friend and they eyeballed her ass and the school boy made a groping motion with his fingers. They both looked up to Kyle, the school boy offering a lecherous smile as he pulled on his cigarette and looked away through the rising smoke.

She handed around the drinks and they downed them without a word. Norah turned and accepted the touch of her suitor. Kyle looked back down the bar to where Troy laughed with a new group of friends. Kevin and the school boy chatted about a mutual friend from the restaurant where Kevin worked.

Kyle lit a cigarette and contemplated the visible. The energy like atoms in constant vibration, giving, receiving, moving without reason. He realized he'd reached the point of inebriation that he called "liquefied" where the infusion of more alcohol leads only to nausea. He stood sipping a glass of water when Troy said he was ready to bolt.

Kyle rode in the backseat becoming increasingly disoriented. But he snapped to when Troy took a clover leaf curve too fast and came within four inches of the concrete barrier that separated them from the French Broad River flowing silently below in the darkness.

"It's all good!" Troy yelled as he worked the wheel, his hands crisscrossed as the tires screamed before he righted the small white car and they all laughed.

"Holy shit," Norah said. "I need a cigarette." She smoked for a minute and then asked Troy if he would stop at the grocery store.

"Will you run in for us, Kyle?" she said. Still buzzed from the hairpin curve he thought it would be a good decision to get out of the car for a minute. Troy handed him ten dollars and said to get a couple of cheap pizzas and a Coke and maybe a pastry for in the morning.

The store was incredibly bright and Kyle felt a strange rush of drunken energy, a manic, confused excitement, as if he was just getting his alcoholic's second wind. He did grab two pizzas and a Coke and some Pop Tarts and headed to the front. It dawned on him as he waited at the register that he hadn't seen anyone else in the store. Not a clerk. Not a customer. Not a cashier. He thought about laying the ten spot on the counter, but he looked around again, and seeing no one, he walked out the door.

The excitement bit into him. The electric tingle of fear as he waited to hear a voice calling him to stop, footsteps rushing in syncopated loss prevention.

He exited the foyer and went through the large sliding door. Down the concrete sidewalk and across the black-top to the white car. He could see Troy laughing in conversation. He glanced back into the store and still saw no one at the checkout. It was like an apparition of a grocery store, a third moment between what normally is.

Two Days at the Office

ONE

He hung the phone up knowing life had forever changed. A few minutes earlier Samuel Ashton was finishing the chicken salad and potato chips with the rest of the staff out in the open area of the warehouse where the night folks put the paper together and readied it for the carriers. It was a good luncheon. He made small talk with a couple of his reporters in a casual way that wasn't possible in the course of everyday editorial responsibility.

Samuel leaned back in the chair – the plush leather office chair that served as his command center from which he managed the 15 employees who worked to publish two newspapers a day and three on Tuesday and Friday – took a few deep breaths and let the memories and the visions wash over him. The smiles at the baby shower a few weeks ago. The elation when Shane received word that he won the fellowship to the D.C. bureau. The congratulations when he received his five year award and things were all smiles for once at the department head meeting.

Flash ahead. The eight month old mortgage. The four month old baby. The wife who just last month turned down a full time job at the university in order to focus on the baby. The baby. Healthy now and looking much more resilient than the week spent in Brenner in April with the large needle stuck into his skull as he lingered somewhere between death and permanent disability.

He opened his eyes and looked out the office door to the newsroom where the staff was now trickling back into the air conditioning from the warehouse. The bay doors had been opened to a late July afternoon in order to make use of the docks for the grill. He'd chosen the chicken salad over hamburgers or hot dogs because the real work lay ahead and a light lunch was less likely to induce sleep. So he was first to come back into the newsroom to get a head start on the afternoon – an editorial to be written, two pages of layout to complete – in order to clear the deck for reading stories as they began to flow in hopefully before 5 o'clock.

He didn't think much when saw the red blinking light on the phone.

Samuel had been back from vacation for three days when Shane and Michael approached him outside the newsroom looking intensely as he came down the hall.

His first thought was that the two eager cubs uncovered the story of a lifetime. Not like the time David approached him about the gay marriage one of the candidates for city council was rumored to have cemented in some far away New England state. No, whereas David was a drama queen who couldn't keep his ego from getting in the way of his instincts, Shane was a true newshound. And with Michael in tow that surely meant the story involved some deep hidden conspiracy among the local elite.

He had a lot of faith in Shane. In fact, he'd placed all his eggs in Shane's basket – reorganizing the entire coverage matrix to play to Shane's storytelling strengths – and let the chips fall where they may. Sure two reporters quit – good riddance actually in one case – but that allowed him to bring in Michael who didn't seem to mind playing second fiddle to Shane. Michael gladly took the breaking news assignment that he'd paired with covering the smaller of the two cities in the area. This allowed Shane to focus on county issues in order to dig and turn out stories of a higher quality than had ever come out of this newsroom.

The two had been together for six months and made Samuel's life infinitely easier, not the least of which was in terms of editing their daily copy. God he'd come a long way since those first days two years ago. He had to re-write about half of what his reporters turned in each day, working his way through a minefield of dangling participles, misplaced commas, incorrect word usage and basic crap that wouldn't pass as acceptable in a high school news writing class let alone a five day a week community paper with a lingering circulation of 5,000 copies.

So it must be a big story. He just knew it. It was written all over the eager faces of the two young men who would help Samuel Ashton establish a legacy here before he moved on to a bigger shop.

He took a sip of coffee and felt the excitement fill his limbs as he approached them – confident that the best of days lie just ahead.

Which is saying a lot. Because nine years earlier he'd pretty much given up on himself. The pot was fine for a few years after he dropped out of college the second time but soon the numbness returned and he took to the bar and a fistful of Long Islands. As the months wore on he tired of the alcohol. It wasn't a Fitzgerald novel after all, chap. In fact it was 1996 and the Millennium was just ahead and someone had even opened a local club called Millennium Center but it was staffed by the same group that ran the other popular club in town and so he didn't go there much. Since they beat down his cousin and robbed his friend Mack a few years earlier it was all he could do to suppress his lust for retribution.

That office job he scored paid him just enough each month to cover the bills. If he drank slowly, it afforded him at least one weekend of soused fun. He could fill the others with something, he told himself, as he calculated what was left and ordered that third or fourth drink but inevitably the clock struck two and then two thirty came and he had to leave alone. The shrinks told him that the sugar in the damned alcohol was going to keep him awake but he usually had a joint waiting at home. If he smoked it by three he was asleep by three thirty and that gave him four hours of sleep in order to make it to the office by eight.

And how much sleep did a 24 year old need in order to go to the office and process paperwork and apply the appropriate four digit code to a stack of 1,200 forms that crossed his desk each day? The answer was unclear but he intended to find out.

And so it was in the midst of this mind numbing repetition of processing – forms, alcohol and unrealized potential – that he made the decision to abandon the certainty of functionality for the hopelessness of chaos. This primarily took the form of buying as much cocaine as he could afford the week after pay day and spending the rest of the month trying to keep up with the jones.

TWO

After punching in his message code a female voice he vaguely recognized spoke.

"Mr. Ashton, this is Sheila with the Big City Daily News and I'm calling to get a comment from you about a story we are doing about the made up quotes from Shane and Michael. We've spoken to a few of the people involved who appeared in the man on the street feature and we are running a story in tomorrow's paper. So if you can call me back ..."

The rest trailed off – audible but not processed – because he was already calculating the damage. He waited a few minutes and tried to think about the work on his desk that needed to be completed. Trying to let the lunch he just enjoyed settle in his now rumbling stomach. Waiting to gather the strength in his legs and catch his breath before going into the publisher's office to confess.

The voice on the message was Sheila Vallejo, a veteran of the BCDN newsroom. She worked as a features writer when he first came to the small city in the northernmost part of the BCDN coverage area and so he'd not read much of her work, being himself a straight news and op-ed type. But some turnover in that paper's local bureau brought Sheila to the county where Samuel worked. His younger rookie reporters churned out hard news and features in recent months at a volume that was catching the attention of most readers. Even some of the paper's biggest critics had mentioned the improvement in the daily report since the current team formed at the beginning of the year. It seemed his strategy of bringing in fresh college graduates and letting them loose on the community was paying off. "Don't hold the reins so tightly," the publisher told him. "Learn to trust your staff, give them room to grow and you can focus on the managerial aspects and your op-ed writing."

This was music to his ears at the time. Attempting to manage in a vacuum of leadership and continuity had seemed impossible to him in the first 18 months on the job. It was his first management job after three years of successful experience as a reporter for dailies in North Carolina and Virginia. But his determination and force of will had opened a gap in the wall of mediocrity he'd faced when he arrived here at the Small City Review for his first day on the job. Dedication to professional standards drove off two dinosaurs in the first year and a refusal to accept mismanagement by his supervisor decapitated the monster at the source six months later.

The void of leadership remained but in the space below he was able to attract talented young reporters who wanted to work – reporters who reminded him of himself – eager, hungry, looking for advancement. He made a point in each interview to recall his experience as a rookie a few years earlier when he latched on to a pair of stories that caught the attention of the community and editors at larger papers within the company. Before he even settled into a groove in Morganton he'd been promoted to Fredericksville and whisked across state lines to explore Virginia and work a county beat before moving up to city hall. Within a year he won first place awards in state level competition. He equally won the ire of his older coworkers for his ability to turn out two and three bylines a day. He reveled in the sight of his name across the top of page one and again on the front of the local section. It's what he was made for.

But a love affair and a desire for a stable personal life drove him to consider marriage and somewhere during the second year of what was sure to be a long career in journalism he married the sardonic girl with the dry, playful smile, the powder white complexion and honey brown hair. He brought her seven hours from the small town she was raised in. Seven hours from her heritage, her beautiful home on the plateau where seven generations of her family roots connected her to the earth. She was not at peace across the state line where he was devastating his coworkers' daily comfort and blazing a trail of reportage second to none.

The honeymoon and the first two weeks of wedded bliss passed in languid sweetness. But as he prepared for work one early September morning in the third week of matrimony she came to the bathroom door and said the Pentagon was on fire. He replied that she must be mistaken because the Pentagon could not possibly be on fire. It was the foundation of a power that knew no equal. But she replied that the Pentagon was in fact on fire on the television and that in addition someone had flown a plane into the World Trade Center. The second fact amplified the first and as he thought about the implication of the Pentagon being on fire he grabbed a towel, put on his shorts and made it into the living room in time to see a moving image of a giant jet plane crashing into the second of the towers and he said "holy fucking shit" along with the rest of America.

Later that morning he felt himself pulled to his knees on the floor as he approached the screen—falling with the first of the towers as the Pentagon continued to burn. As with many that day a lot of things changed. But for him personally it seemed the unease he felt coming from his young wife grew and grew. The homesickness never really faded and so a few months later she was begging him to move back across the state line to Big City where she could pursue a master's degree at the same university her mother attended a generation ago.

But he'd left so much behind when he crossed that state line. Though it was a matter of less than 100 miles he felt a world away from the chaos of his personal life and the weight of a fractured family history that all but dragged him to the grave less than a decade before. Even though the line was a mere cartographical mirage he felt some real sense of separation. And it felt good. And it made him feel free of the weight, like a rock he'd set aside and refused to carry into his new commonwealth.

But love has its ways. The more she implied that she wanted to make the move back across that line, back closer to the past he'd fought to escape, the more he began to think that maybe it would be different now. Maybe a college degree and three years of experience on the job were enough to balance 28 years of personal failure and a family legacy that had kept so many weighted down with the impossibility of generational guilt.

And so applications went out. Cover letters with copies of clips in brown manila envelopes. Back across that line to the newspaper in Big City. The Big City Daily News. Another to a medium sized daily within driving distance of the university in Big City that the girl with the sardonic smile, the powder white complexion and the honey brown hair had her heart's desire set upon.

Weeks passed and he advanced a couple of levels in the interview process with the BCDN but then the trail went cold. No more writing tests. No more hoops to jump through and so it looked like the nice Ralph Lauren shirt and the nice Ralph Lauren tie would not be worn to this triumphant interview at the BCDN where they were sure to be impressed with his clip file, his work ethic and his nose for news.

After this reality set in he moved to plan B, which was a front line editor position at a very small daily owned by the same company he worked for at present. A small paper in a small town that had a bad reputation for violence and poverty and had seen its local economy decimated in the last decade as manufacturing in textiles and furniture and tobacco had moved across a real geographic feature that once separated nations and economies but due to the evolution of the container shipping industry had been traversed with ease.

The newsroom was small and the man he interviewed with was obviously a fascist, which probably explained why the newsroom—which had 12 desks and seemed to be staffed—was empty and desolate at 1pm on a Monday. He thought this was very, very strange for a newsroom and if he followed his instincts he would have handed the man who seemed to have fascist, overbearing dictatorial personality traits his writing test about the court case, the car wreck and the injured reporter back and said "I don't think this is the place for me."

But the girl with the sardonic smile, the powder white complexion and the honey brown hair—the girl he loved in a way he never understood before, who he wanted to please in order to keep her happy so she would stay with him and ease the loneliness and fill the void that had driven him to so many dark places in the past—that girl who was now his wife was sitting outside in the car thumbing through rental guides and her application to the university in Big City. So he sat down and completed the writing test with ease and of course was offered the job a week later.

Against his gut instinct, those instincts that had led him to news stories day after day in his three years as a reporter, those instincts that were screaming inside—this is not a good thing for you to be doing—those instincts that made it clear to him that a small town in the midst of a transformational economic decline was not the place for him, those instincts that told him maybe this is too close to the lingering smoke of the charred remains of your past, against all those instincts he accepted the job as front line editor for the Small City Review and agreed to report to work in three weeks.

And now about twenty-eight months later his instincts—though he tried to outrun them, out work them, unlearn all that had previously held him down—proved to be on target as always.

As he approached Shane and Michael that day standing outside the entrance to the newsroom he noticed they both held white envelopes. Shane spoke first, looking him in the eye briefly before looking down.

"Samuel, we need to talk with you," Shane said.

He thought surely they aren't quitting. If they were quitting they would just come into his office and hand him the two week notice and try to avoid a long conversation. He asked to see Shane's envelope.

"We'd rather talk in the conference room," Shane said.

He told Shane that he understood that. He didn't tell Shane that he knew enough after two and a half years as a manager in an impossibly unprofessional work environment that he wasn't going into a conference room with two employees holding white envelopes without knowing what he was walking into. Shane had moved toward the conference room. He knew Michael to be meeker than Shane, less certain of himself – after all he'd brought not one but both parents to the job interview – and so he held out his hand to Michael and demanded that if they wanted to meet in the conference room that he must first know what was in the envelope.

Michael handed his envelope over and the three of them made their way toward the conference room door. He entered the conference room and sat the cup of coffee down and then stepped back into the hall and opened the envelope.

The paragraphs there took him a few minutes to skim over but the implication was clear. He had a full blown ethical crisis on his hands and was about to have to fire both of his best reporters. The publisher was not in the office today. She never came to this office the day after the department head meeting. Those had been hot recently, especially since the office girl from the weekly across the county had been given a shot at ad sales and began selling ads to family members outside the coverage area and even had the incredible idea that she would sell an ad in a neighboring county. It was outside the coverage area but closer to her home than the main office over in Small City. And so she announced the day before at the department head meeting that news should begin to cover the other county so she could sell more ads there.

He almost spit coffee out of his nose at this and reminded the gathered brain trust that ad sales did not dictate news coverage and that there was a real but invisible wall between editorial and sales. Since he was not from around here and had more newspaper success in his three year career than those gathered around the large wooden table had in three decades, it should be no surprise that the other department heads looked for ways to make his life miserable. This presented itself in the form of off the wall ideas for him to implement in the editorial department – the department he attempted to manage toward the goal of producing two independent and unique newspapers each day with a staff barely adequate for one, with the added pleasure of producing a third newspaper on Tuesday and Friday. A secondary manifestation of this took the form of regular last minute changes to the available news hole, ads thrown in or removed hours past the agreed upon deadline, special section projects dumped on his desk with inadequate preparation time, canceled special projects his staff had spent hours to complete only to see a failed sales campaign eradicate the financial rationale for the section's existence; and now suggestions of expanding coverage beyond the already geographically challenging area.

The chorus of condemnation was as loud as it had been to date in the department head meeting that took place the previous day in the very conference room where his two best reporters were now sitting and waiting for him to decide if an ethical lapse meant the end of their brief careers. The advertising manager scoffed first with a slam of her pen while decrying the idea of this wall he mentioned that supposedly separated editorial from sales. Next came the classified manager with a recital of all his shortcomings in recent months, reminding everyone present that he had not been open to her ideas for news coverage or even willing to allow her department to avail itself of the news photographer for her revenue generating ideas. He sat in silence making a list of things to do that evening – journalismjobs.com, polishing his resume, recalling editorials he could include in his application package.

Yes he'd had enough of this nonsense. When the publisher said that if Jessica could sell an ad to the auto body shop in the neighboring county that surely Shane could go over there and report a story once in a while he resigned himself, figuratively, to the fact that his effort here was done.

As he again read the words on the page that was in the envelope he just opened he walked into the news-room and asked Carla the news editor - who was a whiz at layout and whom he was grooming to move up into management despite her lack of a college degree and previous management experience – if she could come into the conference room with him. As they walked back toward the hallway he handed her Michael's letter.

"Shane's got one of these as well but I haven't read it," he said.

Carla entered the conference room and sat down as he closed the door. Michael's letter said that he had been back in Chapel Hill for the July 4th holiday and that in the back seat of his car were several copies of the Small City Review. One of his friends noticed the paper and wanted to see some of Michael's work but instead noticed a picture of a mutual friend from the Carolina journalism program featured on the front page in an advertorial called "Two Cents Worth".

This was among the banes of Samuel's existence during his time at the Small City Review. Sponsored by a local financial planner, this was one of the irregular revenue generating ideas that sales had concocted that blurred the line between advertising and editorial. The idea was simple. Give a small business a prominent spot on the front page but include some eye-catching feature —it could have been a monster truck or a naked woman for all that mattered—just something to get the reader to look at that spot on the page and thus see the ad for the financial planner. Why they didn't just charge the financial planner for an ad and place it there—marking it up for the prominent location—escaped him. He'd asked for a year or more to have that content changed, but the animosity coming his way from the other department heads prevented any progress.

The news staff balked time and again at the idea of having to fill the spot every day with a man on the street quote in reply to some asinine question. And despite the fact that the staff of 14 was already charged with producing two unique newspapers every day—and three on Tuesday and Friday—the other departments insisted that this advertorial content was critical to the future of the newspaper.

In the spirit of "loosening the reins" and "trusting the staff" he had set an annual calendar that had each reporter responsible for a week's worth of content each month. There were five reporters, a sports reporter and a photographer – for a rotation among the two papers that gave each staff member one slot to fill each month.

On the hierarchy of need related to his responsibility to get these newspapers out each day in a way that enhanced his career as a journalist, the production of the man on the street quote ranked just below getting the date right.

And some days even that proved hard to achieve.

THREE

Survival was his first instinct. What did his training tell him? Obviously he needed to get up and go into the publisher's office once she came back in from the luncheon and tell her about the phone message. But he had time to think now. He looked across his desk at the pictures of his son – four months old now and growing healthier every day – a far cry from those first few fragile weeks when death hung over the newborn as he refused his mother's milk and was caught between the push and pull of forces beyond his control. What was eclampsia anyway? An insidious sounding word that elevated his young wife's blood pressure to dangerous levels, poisoning her breast milk in those first days as nurses and others stood over her all but demanding that she breast-feed the screaming newborn who spit the milk out with each attempt.

He would retreat to the far side of the house, not wanting to be an added stressor on her as she tried so hard to do what everyone expected of her. He would listen to the baby cry and cringe at the thought of how she must feel. Thoughts in his head wondered if he should step in and demand that they switch to formula. Would that be overbearing? Where was the line between giving her space and following his instinct?

He snapped back to the present crisis as he heard Theresa coming down the front hallway talking to the business manager about some reports that were due to the corporate office by tomorrow afternoon. She passed by the second of his two office doors and entered her own office that occupied the front corner of the building. Give her a few minutes, he thought. Focus on something. But the panic was building in him because he knew he was in deep trouble.

Major plagiarism scandals had rocked the journalism world in the last five years. Publications in New York and Washington had been caught with their pants down as prominent reporters were discovered to have made up entire stories – fabricating sources, presenting fictional interviews as field work and embarrassing hallowed institutions in the process. In his own company – in fact in his own career – two smaller versions of the same story had played out the previous year.

A former editor was found to have altered published stories prior to submitting them to the state press association's award contest. A dozen or more journalists who worked for Ronald Thompson—associate managing editor of the newspaper in Fredericksville—saw awards taken away as part of the scandal. Thompson resigned in tears and disgrace. A pitiful ending for a guy who was loathed and admired for his determination to get the most out of his reporters.

In fact, he recalled, Thompson drove him to excel. He owed a lot of his success to Thompson. Left to his own devices he might not have turned in half of the stories he had during the two years he worked there. Thompson's daily demands squeezed the most possible production out of him. And for that he was thankful.

But he'd also been stripped of two first place awards and an award from the state bar association for a three part series he completed on street gangs infiltrating the city and working their way into the neighborhoods and schools to find new blood to fly their colors.

Thompson had been the first person he turned to when his own boss here at Small City Review—the fascist asshole whose overbearing eccentricities bore little fruit in the way of a productive staff—took it upon himself to alter a nationally syndicated political cartoon and put his own name on it.

It was the opportunity Samuel had been waiting for and he took full advantage of it. An anonymous email address was created at yahoo and he sent the cartoonist an email advising him to get a copy of the July 21st edition of the Small City Review and look at page A12 at the political cartoon. It was less than 72 hours before the regional publisher called Samuel at his desk and asked him if he would be able to guide the paper by himself for a few weeks.

At first he thought the regional publisher was referring to Carla, his page designer, who'd been exceedingly difficult recently and only escaped his ire because without her he could not get the papers published each day. And so he hesitated a moment before telling the regional publisher that yes, in fact, he could get the papers out each day by himself. Even if he had to stay at the office 18 hours a day to do layout and edit stories it seemed worth it to have a chance to build a staff from scratch and mold it to his liking.

He ended his shift that weekend expecting a difficult road ahead of him. So he was delighted when the local publisher called him on his Monday off and said he needed to come in because "Harlan Stevens no longer works here."

He was never before so happy to be called in on his day off.

That was eighteen months ago. Back when the paper was still a laughing stock and seemed incapable of serious effort. But he knew that if he ever wanted to escape the mediocrity he found himself in and land that job writing op-eds for a metro somewhere in the southeast then he needed to have success here.

Samuel set out to transform the newsroom through force of will. When the local publisher left to move to Georgia he gained a free hand to guide the news staff in the direction he wanted it to go. The first thing he did was bring in a new page designer to help Carla. He sat down with Carla and the new designer and the sports editor and went over the publication schedule. Meet the deadlines. No typographical errors. Proofread your pages and get them to the pressman on time. I will provide

190 - JEFF SYKES

you with the best content possible if you will take care
of the back end. The three agreed to this and he challenged them to excel and they had more than met the
challenge.

This freed him up to focus on his strength: reporting.
He would sit at home at night and draw out designs for
how to divide the coverage responsibilities between his
five available reporters. And then at long last it came to
him. He split the geographic and topical requirements
down the middle. The entire staff seemed to be excited
to be out from under the fascist regime of the eccentric
former managing editor and everyone set about handling
their business.

There were very few bumps in the road over the last
year. There were two or three staffers who had come and
gone but the continuity seemed to remain within the
plan itself. When Andrea—a young prima donna of a reporter who thought she was too cool to break a sweat—
balked at his ideas he held firm and she left within a
month. When David pitched a fit over a basic editing
suggestion and had a complete meltdown in the face of
managerial firmness, Samuel followed the discipline pro-
cedures he'd learned at a first year manager's conference
and David was gone within 48 hours.

But each challenge brought new opportunities to
bring in fresh talent and sell them on the idea of in-
dependence and achievement.

And now that he had Shane and Michael as his hard
news anchors little else mattered. Those two excelled at

turning out news stories and the newsroom was a fun place to be as journalism was perpetrated on the local community.

But now it was falling apart. Against all the power of desire and denial he could muster he knew there was little else to do but go into Theresa's office and lay it at her feet.

When he re-entered the conference room where Shane and Michael sat he had every intention of firing Michael on the spot. Carla was right behind him and as they sat down beside each other and across from the pair of reporters who had less than a year each on the job he asked her for Michael's letter back.

He went right at Michael with the Socratic method he'd learned while being abused by it at the hands of Ronald Thompson up in Fredericksville each afternoon for two years.

"What is the foundation of a reporter's credibility, Michael?"

The 21 year old looked down at the conference table where his hands were clasped – the tension evidenced by the increasing whiteness of his knuckles.

"Hard work and integrity? Accuracy?" he floundered about looking at his hands.

"And do you think for one second that using your friends to do a man on the street quote exemplifies hard work and integrity?" Samuel asked.

He knew the answer. He'd been through this to a lesser degree with each staff member who had a slot on the man on the street schedule. They all hated doing it. But he thought back to his two years at the college paper. He enjoyed doing the man on the street. Hell it was an excuse if nothing else to approach the best looking girls on campus and talk to them. And who knew what might come of such randomness. But the staffers here said the town was too small. People were standoffish. Go to the community college, he had recommended. But there are only so many of them there, was the excuse. Or it's too far of a drive, was another.

And each time he raged on the inside, damning the unbelievable laziness of the person standing in front of him and cursing the day he ever decided to take a job in a small town. But he swallowed the rage, smiled, and in his best managerial voice went over the schedule with the person standing before him, advised them of their deadline and noted that this should be considered a verbal warning and that failure to adhere to the deadline again would result in a written warning.

He was through his second cycle of performance evaluations and had just completed his first cycle with control of the staff budget. He found the performance based pay carrot was a great pair with the stick of written warning. This would be his methodology to deal with petty issues of lack of effort. Feed the chickens and starve the turkeys he heard the president of the publishing division say and that was what he intended to do. Besides, ten minutes spent going over the same performance issue with the same employee time and again was ten minutes he could not spend writing an op-ed and advancing one step closer to his career goal.

He had wanted to be a columnist since the days he discovered Grizzard and Kaul and Raspberry and Ivins and Safire on the back pages of the city paper where he grew up.

And then after the baby was born he had such a traumatic first few weeks and then Samuel fretted over the newborn through all those sleepless nights in May and June and was barely able to function at the office during the day due to lack of sleep.

"Loosen the reins. Trust your staff. Give them room to grow ...." Theresa had said to him when he worried aloud that he was not on top of things at present given the totality of what he was going through. "Just make sure Carla and the designers get the pages out on time. You've got a proofreader. The new designer is doing a great job. Trust them."

And he had. And things seemed to be going well. And he didn't worry about the production issues. The new page designer, Charles, was doing a great job. Samuel enjoyed seeing the paper each morning. The crisp layouts. The well balanced packages, finally making the most use of the talented staff photographer.

But one day he noticed a grainy picture, dark and lacking sharpness, used in the man on the street feature and so he asked Charles in passing where they were getting the photos. He recalled then that he had noticed similar pictures, small head shots that looked as if they had been processed one too many times, a week or so earlier. He hadn't thought much of it then because he was "trusting the staff" as Theresa advised him. Charles replied that he only took the photos that were in the folder and put them on the page and didn't think much of it. Which was acceptable from his perspective because the Man on the Street, as the entire staff knew, was advertorial busy work, and so it was most efficient to get it done in the most direct way possible. He took the answer at face value and moved on without giving it a second thought. Maybe he would ask the photographer when he came in that afternoon.

He knew that the sports guys often used pictures from the high school yearbook or the sports guide or file photos they had taken at a game as man on the street photo and then followed up with the person to get their answer to that week's question. There had been a case where the high school intern was accused of using a picture and not actually talking to the person in question. The student's mom had come to the office and said her daughter was shocked to hear she was in the paper that morning and upset when she saw the feature because she had not been asked the question. The question that week was "what is your favorite ACC team" and the girl's answer was "Wake Forest" and this upset her very much because she was a Duke fan.

He'd spoken with the publisher then and quietly called the high school intern in and asked her to resign. It was late spring and the intern was about to graduate, having completed her requirements. She'd done such a good job of covering routine sports games that they kept her on and gave her more responsibility, such as being put on the man on the street calendar. The rest of the staff liked this because it moved their frequency back to once a month from every other week.

Internally he was upset again that the staff had shown such laziness that it influenced the high school intern but this was only the man on the street advertorial feature and so he went over the requirements and the deadlines with the staff yet again and felt surely that would take care of the problem.

But then just before the baby was born in April and just after Shane had been awarded the fellowship to go to the company's D.C. bureau for a month that summer Samuel noticed a repeated mug shot in the man on the street feature and so he asked Charles who took the photo. When told it was Shane's week he became livid because he'd been over this with Shane Vallow twice already and it was not believable to him that such a talented young reporter who graduated from the journalism program at the University of North Carolina at Chapel Hill just a year before and had already won a prestigious fellowship to go to the company's D.C. bureau for a month that summer could be so lazy as to not be capable of turning in five basic photos for a man on the street advertorial item that he had a schedule made out for a full one year in advance. It was beyond believable and so he called Shane into his office and looked him dead in the eye and told him in no uncertain terms that he was making it harder than it needed to be and that if he once more failed to adhere to the deadline for the man on the street advertorial item that he would receive a written warning.

"Shane," he said, "you are way too talented to let this get the best of you. In fact I have already fielded two inquiries from larger papers in our company about you. You will be out of here by the end of summer and on your way to a paper 10 times larger than this one. When you get there you will have feature calendars, business items, special sections, each with floating deadlines. It will be your job to meet the deadline and they won't give you a second chance to make the deadline. I want to be able to tell them that you are fully capable of this so please don't make this man on the street thing harder than it has to be."

He felt sure this was crystal clear to anyone who could graduate from the School of Journalism at the University of North Carolina at Chapel Hill and who could win a prestigious company-wide fellowship and so he thought nothing more of it.

But now he sat here in the conference room with Michael and Shane and faced a confessional letter from Michael stating that he'd fabricated the advertorial assignment and been called out on it by a friend from journalism school who demanded accountability in the form of a confession. Samuel was intent on making an example of him.

He could replace Michael. He would hate to replace him because he was a good news reporter who was dutiful and turned in clean copy. Michael followed reporting basics and got the story nine times out of ten so far on the first day and the paper was humming along because of it. He knew he would lose Shane in a month or two to promotion and he would have to start over again with two new reporters but he had the system down pat by now.

"Michael, you know this is totally unacceptable. The industry is in turmoil and has no tolerance for these types of fabrications," he found himself saying as he began to walk Michael down the road to inevitability.

Shane sat grim faced and silent next to Michael and it was then he recalled that Shane had one of these envelopes as well. Before he went too far Samuel thought he'd better see what Shane had to say for his friend. Michael's letter included an appeal to remain employed that basically said he was sorry and ashamed and if given a second chance would do his utmost to make up for his failure.

He was certain Shane's letter was an appeal to keep Michael on and so he wanted to take that into account.

"Shane, you have something to say about this?" he asked and Shane silently passed his envelope across the table.

FOUR

Theresa's office door was just outside of his and a few feet to the right. He'd worn a path along the short distance between the two over the last year – constantly seeking her advice or to reinforce decisions he'd made. Some days he feared that maybe he bothered her too much with routine management errata. But as a first year executive his policy was to err on the side of caution.

It was the height of irony that in this case he was coming to her after choosing not to seek her advice a few weeks earlier. He'd made the unilateral decision to admonish Shane and Michael and to not fire them. He'd made the decision that their error was one of immaturity and not something for them to be publicly crucified for. How on earth the Big City Daily News got wind of the story – or better yet why it mattered to them – were mysteries to him.

But he was clear on the chain of events that was about to unfold once Sheila Vallejo's byline appeared in tomorrow's paper.

"You got a minute boss?" he asked as he stood at the threshold of her large bookshelf lined office. She looked up from her laptop – docked as it was to a device that sent the laptop signal to a large monitor, mouse and keyboard. She seemed engaged in her own duties but looked at him as always with a friendly yet business like demeanor. "Sure, what you got?"

He moved to close the door. "Oh, it must be serious then," she continued. "Well come and sit down."

He moved to one of the two cushioned chairs that were arranged in front of her large executive wooden desk. He took in the photos of her family as he always did and looked across the smiling faces posing at the beach, at a ball game, at a family cookout, and thought about his own young wife at home nursing their four month old son across infancy from newborn days filled with the panic of fragility.

He was sitting now, but not yet speaking. Still looking across the room—at the random stuff on shelves and spread on flat surfaces that gave the brick and drywall space a feminine feel—he was searching inside for a place to begin.

"Well, Samuel?" she said after a few seconds. "You're whiter than a ghost. What's the matter?"

And finally he began. He spoke half in fear and half in frustration at the thought of having to begin again. As he recounted the revelation, the tension and the decision he took in those brief minutes less than three weeks earlier she seemed to exude a confidence that made him think perhaps the worst could be avoided.

"And so what did Ms. Vallejo's message say?" she asked when he'd finished retelling the chain of events that led to the present moment.

"She said that they were running a story tomorrow about the man on the street fabrications and that she wanted a quote from me."

"Have you spoken to Michael or Shane?"

"No. Michael is covering a city budget meeting and Shane was just at the cookout and I imagine is on his way back to the other office where he is covering while Amy is on vacation."

He continued.

"I really think we should call Carl or Arthur at the regional office and let them know about the situation and get some advice. Or maybe I should call Donna at corporate," Samuel said.

She turned grim and leaned back in her rich leather chair, a shade of coffee with just a hint of creamer for color. "If anyone is to call Carl it will be me. But I think we can handle this ourselves. We don't need to worry Carl with everything."

Samuel thought for a moment. He disagreed with her. He wished he'd turned to someone the afternoon Shane and Michael came to him. Get outside of yourself. Seek wise counsel. Lean on your mentor. Things he'd learned in his crash course in management and leadership over the last few years as he tried to grow into his new role.

"My instinct tells me that Big City will make a big deal out of this. This won't be some news brief on the inside of the local section. I suspect they will make a news feature out of it ... put some funky angle on it to make us look as bad as possible. Our folks have really been handing it to them in terms of breaking news and coverage. I think they will use this to damage us."

"I'm not so sure," was her reply. "Either way it's not that big of a deal and whatever ramifications come our way, I will handle them."

He felt reassured briefly at her expression of support. Perhaps the worst could be avoided. Perhaps Shane and Michael could be retained and the entire operation would grow tighter from the ordeal.

"Well what do you think we should do about Ms. Vallejo's phone message?" she asked him.

"I'm not sure myself," Samuel said. "On the one hand if we ignore her it will make us look like we have something to hide and we don't. This was a simple instance of immaturity which we handled as a personnel matter in the way corporate has trained us – to learn from the mistake and grow from it. But if I call her she will likely engage in a line of questions to try and make me say something dumb. So I'm just not sure right now."

The only thing he was really sure of was that he wished it would all just go away. He wished he were far away—back in Fredericksville churning out daily stories to the chagrin of his coworkers, filling the paper with his byline by chasing leads and working sources and developing information in a steady stream of effort that garnered him respect and admiration. In the last few years he had become a faceless android who bore all the responsibility of failure while receiving very little in the way of replenished energy from the daily delight of accomplishment.

That was the need he'd filled during his years as a reporter. Seeing the daily fruit of his effort in the form of a bylined story kept him moving forward and allowed him to gauge his progress and effort in real time. And for once he'd been part of a strong team—one piece of a complicated machine that he could get lost in. He was content to be judged by the quality of his work. There was no focus on his persona, no death by a thousand cuts to suffer the way it was once he stepped up on to the management scaffold and became something to be examined from below, like chattel on the auction block of judgment.

His thoughts were still with Shane and Michael and wondering if their young careers could be salvaged. He felt loyalty to them because they worked hard and treated him with respect. After the run of three or four staffers who caused him several pounds of pain in the form of backbiting, back talk and back stabbing he returned their negative energy by channeling them out the door as fast as possible. With Shane and Michael it was different. They sought his advice. They listened to his feedback. They seemed to want to earn approval. He returned their effort with deserved praise, a leeway of trust and his best effort to make their copy sing.

He wanted them to succeed and for the rising tide to lift the newsroom out of mediocrity and to build success where fair to middling had always been the norm. Then he could move on to something bigger and better, knowing he'd succeeded and not just cut and run because the task seemed insurmountable.

"Maybe I could call her editor and see what kind of angle they are taking on the story," Samuel heard himself saying, almost without realizing it. He was a problem solver. He had a way with people. Perhaps he could squeeze an insight out of the BCDN's editor in the bureau Vallejo worked from.

Theresa was thinking. Her index fingers pressed against her pursed lips as her two hands were clasped just beyond her chin. After a moment, "Ok. Let's do that. Then call Shane and Michael and make sure to tell them they are to have no comment if Vallejo calls them."

"Do you want to listen in as I call Bill Robinson?"

"I think you can handle it, Samuel."

But he wasn't so sure. He wasn't sure about any of it anymore. He thought for certain that they should call Carl or Arthur or Donna and get some outside advice, some perspective on the events. But she had flatly dismissed his idea and he really didn't have the energy to argue with her or feel he was in any position to push the issue. If he could survive the day he felt it might be ok. That he could keep his nose above the waterline. Theresa was a rising star in the executive side of the company. She mingled with the vice- presidents and directors not only in the publishing division but across the entire corporate structure. She was due for a corporate meeting in Concord the next day. She told him directly not to call outside her chain of command. Chain of command was emphasized across all managerial training and so he felt that responsibility was taken from him and he was to follow her lead.

But he still felt they should seek outside help.

"I'd appreciate it if you would listen in," he reiterated to her.

She exhaled as she rose—a bit frustrated perhaps at the distraction. "Well if I must," was her reply. And he felt as though she might not truly grasp the scope of the situation and the potential for extreme damage.

Back in his office, Theresa took a spot in one of the small fabric covered desk chairs shoved up against the confines of the white drywall that he'd covered with a few large prints in $100 frames. There was a Dali print of dry yellow butterflies in front of a crisp Sonoran land-scape of burnt orange and rich browns set off against the richness of a magical blue sky that took up about one third of the print. It was the deep blue's allure that attracted him to the work. The escape into the infinite azure complimented the larger photo print of a New York skyline from the late 1950s. Black and white, the dullness of the city scene was anchored by the Empire State Building with the city's energy pulsating within the length and breadth of the city blocks stretching to the shot's edge.

He called this his "window" since the office was likely a former storage closet converted when the two local pa-pers he now guided had merged management structures about a decade earlier.

It was an impossible task, really, to manage and publish two newspapers a day from one staff under the demand that each be unique. It was the overwhelming oddity of the enterprise and this duplicity of effort was the thing in itself that caused his many management headaches. How could he hold the staff to higher standards when each day he found himself bailing out the waters of confusion with a tiny bucket, struggling just to keep the boat from sinking?

He was struggling now with what to actually do. He wanted to just disappear or to turn the clock back three years to the day he accepted his first job here and undo the decision that brought him to the present. He wasn't a manager. But he was a chameleon, able to absorb the aura around him and fit within. Transformation was beyond his ability. Perhaps he could just cut to the chase and resign now and spare himself the effort of bailing out on this day. But he had a newborn at home and a vivacious wife who was in her own way striving to regain her energy after the last two months. He couldn't quit. He had no savings. He had no job prospects because he had yet to take steps to move on. And moving on had been a settled issue since they bought the small house late last December when hope still colored the horizon with the glow of possibility.

"I guess I will try to talk to him off the record .... See what they know .. Why they are doing the story," he said.

Theresa nodded. "Don't answer any questions. If it gets to that point, tell him you will call back with a prepared statement."

He looked up the number in the small county phone book. It was more like a car trader or thrift publication you can pick up on a small wire rack at any corner store or fried fish restaurant or grocery store, not at all like the thick tome of the city phonebook he grew up with. He found the number of the BCDN local bureau. He took a deep breath as he dialed the number and punched in the extension for their news room.

Robinson answered. Samuel introduced himself. "Bill, I have this message here from Sheila and I'm kind of curious you know why you guys are poking around my newsroom grasping at straws?"

He was a bit aggressive in tone, trying to set the stage and feel Robinson out. He didn't know much about him. His cheesy jovial mug shot in their paper each week when the bureau published a local section for the BCDN gave the impression that he was a happy go lucky guy. If Samuel had known how many years Robinson worked in the business or that he was a veteran of every section at the BCDN or that he was the managing editor's closest chum then perhaps he would have taken a quieter track or just resigned on the spot. But he was still pitching water with his bucket. It may have been a small bucket not quite strengthened by experience or traded in for a more skilled pump but in the absence of a lifeline from above he was going to pitch the water with all he had.

After a few moments of silence during which he could hear typing in the background Robinson replied.

"Sorry for the delay. I'm trying to get Sheila on IM. She is down at the main Big City office today. But I can ask you a few questions if that is ok?"

"Right now I'm not going to answer any questions. I may later, but right now I wanted to see if we could talk off the record. I am trying to get an understanding of what the story is, why Sheila is asking these questions. I mean, I've got a lot to do today in trying to get these two papers out."

"I see. So, yeah, we can talk off the record for a minute. So where we are is that we got a few calls from people who said that your man on the street feature wasn't using original photos and we dug around a bit and then found where a few of the ones featured last month included people who don't even live in the area. And we've got an intern here from Carolina and she recognized one of the photos after we reviewed all the ones from a few weeks ago. We keep the copies here in our office. So she said she recognized one of the people as a classmate from Carolina who is interning in Rochester. We contacted that person and faxed her a copy of the photo. Turns out she said she was with Shane Vallow on staff at the Carolina student paper but has not spoken to him for about a year. She thinks that he took the photo from her Facebook profile. You've heard of Facebook right?"

He thought for a minute. He had heard some of his new staffers in the last year or so talk about this online yearbook of photos called Facebook. It was restricted to college students with a university email address and since he was several years out of school he'd not thought more than two seconds about it prior to this moment, other than to think that technology was moving faster than he could keep up with.

But then he had another thought and he remembered back to the day a few weeks ago when he noticed the grainy, dark photos of smiling twenty somethings that ran for a few days in the man on the street feature. He asked the page designer Charles about it for two reasons. First the photos were dark and obviously not taken with one of the new digital cameras he all but begged corporate to issue him in the last budget. Second, the people in the photos were beautiful and young and smiling and in this county the young people fled in droves and it was a huge community issue that the college graduates never came back home to live and work in the county and the brain drain was another drag on the local economy, which had been suffering in the last decade of layoffs and factory closings. And so he asked Charles and Charles said he didn't ask where the photos came from, that he just put them on the page from the folder in the computer server and that it had been Shane's week.

And an outline of a frame for him to understand the picture he was looking at emerged.

"They are going to make us look as stupid as possible," he thought to himself. But that was ok because the company that owned BCDN and the company that owned

Small City Review were locked in a dogfight for readers across Virginia and North Carolina and this type of thing happened every now and then where one paper would go behind a competitor and say their reporting was shoddy or that one of their staffers had been charged with a DUI. In his mind he knew the blow would be hard. The industry had seen several major plagiarism scandals and this was close enough to a journalistic ethics breach that they could use it to make his company look bad. It was probably a proxy war over the price of each company's stock on Wall Street and so yes he would be embarrassed. But Theresa seemed supportive and if they could weather the storm together then Shane and Michael could get back to kicking out bylines and he could increase the stack of op-ed pieces in his clip file.

"Facebook you say? Yes I've heard of it. Don't know much about it," he said to Robinson over the phone line. He was stalling as his mind churned over what he envisioned their story would say. He remembered back to the fall when he met Sheila Vallejo standing in the small entryway of the office of the secondary paper he managed about 12 miles from Small City. A deer of all things had run from across the street and crashed straight through the double glass doors and into the foyer and after slamming into the counter took a right turn into the 15 by 20 foot space that served as the newsroom and pranced a path of destruction that left three computers smashed and two walls and a long glass window on the street front covered with blood before one of the staffers had the opportunity to rush and hold the door open for the deer to Bambi right on out again.

As the shocked receptionist continued to try and answer the business phone, one of the staffers—a vivacious if manic woman named Amy who covered the police and courts beat—decided to call down to the police department and tell them what happened. They dispatched an officer to the scene and Vallejo had heard the call go out over the scanner and arrived at the office just as Samuel arrived from Small City. He'd taken a phone call from the other staffer, Brian, who was looking for instruction on how to continue to complete his work for the day in light of the damages.

Theresa had elected for him to go over and ascertain the damage to the office and as he stood looking at the overturned computer monitors, scattered papers and chairs and the rich red animalistic blood smeared across the window, walls, carpet and desks it was then he noticed the short, obese woman with the high and tight haircut standing just to his right writing in a three-subject notebook with a ballpoint pen that was as short and fat as he was.

Amy was standing near to the door recounting the events in her manic fashion of disbelief and while he thought again that if she only could channel some of that energy to enterprise and trend stories that she could win awards on a regular basis it was then that he realized the small obese woman in the military crew cut was perhaps Sheila Vallejo because he had seen her boyish grin and haircut in her profile shot on the inside of the local section that the BCDN bureau produced each week.

"I'm sorry but who are you?" Samuel asked.

"I'm Sheila Vallejo from the BCDN," she said. "We heard the call on the scanner and I thought I would come down and see what was going on."

"Well, Sheila, I appreciate you coming but the office is closed right now and we've got to deal with this damage and we have blood borne pathogens afoot so I'm going to have to ask you to leave," he said a bit firm not only because he truly couldn't believe that he was standing in the office having to deal with the aftermath of a deer running through the room but that he really didn't like her or her newspaper. He had wanted to work for BCDN and cover police or courts or work in one of the three bureaus the paper staffed in surrounding counties and turn out stories of substance and grow as a reporter and hone his craft in the biggest of shops where he could meet veteran journalists and learn from them and absorb their knowledge but instead he'd become the manager of a local yokel small daily where he had to deal with such amusing events as deer running through an office and trashing the newsroom.

Vallejo left readily as he escorted her to the still bloody door where Amy was standing and as Vallejo exited he thanked her for understanding and then turned to the receptionist and asked her to call Theresa and have a carpet cleaner come to get the blood up. He found some gloves and towels and told Amy and Brian they could go to the main office in Small City or go home and write their stories and that they should call him in the morning to find out if the office was back in working order.

He told them first to get their own papers and books and put them in a chair to be saved because he was about to throw away whatever was on the floor and begin to clean out the damaged machinery and move the furniture so the carpet cleaners could get the blood from the carpet and the walls and the window and so he spent the next hour cleaning blood from old wooden desks and chairs that had needed replacing long before the deer took its trip across the street.

It wasn't until the next day when he got the first phone call from a radio station morning show host asking him about the deer that he remembered Vallejo had been there and that she might just have done a story on the white tailed visitor and by the time he found a copy of the BCDN he had taken two more calls from radio show hosts in Charlotte and Richmond who thought it was funny.

"It's just a goofy story we'd like to talk about," one of them said to him when he asked in exasperation why they were calling him and what he would be expected to talk about. Just a goofy story. That's what his career had become, he thought then. No hustle. No worn shoe leather and filled notebooks with details of that big story all the good reporters are constantly chasing. Just a goofy story for Billy Bob morning show radio hosts to make fun of with that constant nauseating forced laughter that was one of the main reasons he bought a car with a CD player so he would never have to listen to the radio again.

That was what Vallejo and Robinson and the BCDN would do with this man on the street photo story, he thought. They will make fun of us. Make us look like buffoons again.

"So you are definitely running this story then Bill?" he asked the editor of the BCDN local bureau who was still on the other end of the phone line.

"Yes. As I said we've talked to a few of the people pictured and they say they never had their photo taken and so we wanted to get a comment from you all. I think Sheila has tried calling Shane and maybe another reporter there," Robinson said.

At that his ears perked up. His dander rose because he remembered Vallejo scribbling as Amy prattled about the deer and how she had dressed Amy's words in the most facetious fashion possible and how corporate was angered that he had not better trained his staff not to talk to competing media. But he had gone over that with staff in the days after the deer incident. He blew it off as another one of the endless concepts he would have to school these recent college graduates. Samuel wondered at the time just what other life skills and standards of professional conduct he would be responsible for instilling in these graduates from the University of North Carolina at Chapel Hill.

He thought about telling Robinson that he didn't appreciate them going behind his back to talk to his staffers and that out of professional courtesy they ought to run this thing through him but he knew enough about competition and metro journalism to not bother. Get the story was all that mattered. And with that he actually agreed.

"Well Bill, we are a small property within the company and you know I will have to talk to my superiors about this but if they agree then I will call you back and make a comment," Samuel said.

As they hung up he was in fighting mode now. No longer pitching water he was lacing up the gloves and ready to go toe to toe.

"Those people," he said looking at Theresa. "It's bad enough that we are kicking their ass every day with breaking stories and increased coverage and that Charles and Carla are designing first class pages and that our team is performing like no other. But they have to stoop to this level to make us look bad. I can't understand why they don't just leave us alone and try to report their own stories. I mean if they are going to have a bureau then they might as well produce some news instead of this constant fluff ... "

His voice trailed as Theresa interrupted him before his motor got going full.

"Samuel, Samuel. I've told you over and over not to get worked up about the small stuff. This is small potatoes. They obviously know that we've got new blood here at the local papers and that we are moving forward and so you should take this as a compliment that they feel the need to take you back down a notch."

"We will get through this. Keep the staff focused on their work. Tell them that we've learned from the situation. That is all we can ask is that we learn from our mistakes."

"So do you want to respond to them with a comment or no?" she concluded.

He thought for a second. She still didn't see this from the journalistic ethics perspective. He did not share her confidence about this being "small potatoes". But he also from the deer experience felt BCDN might still put the ludicrous spin on the story and so what could he really do. He damn sure could not stop their story. He could ignore it and let them take a broadside at his cubs. But he was fighting it now. The memories of the deer experience and the "goofy story" quip from the radio jock tripped the trigger in him and he had moved from the detached rationality of survivor mode to the jab and step aggression of the sweet science. They want to punch us in the nose? Well I can at least stand up for my people.

"I think maybe we should make a comment that implies how we are focused on improving this paper and somehow slide in something about how we are getting the best of them and poke them back," Samuel said.

She nodded in agreement and so the two of them spent the next ten minutes putting together a few lines.

In the meantime he had called Shane back at the other office.

"Shane, I got this call here from Sheila Vallejo about the man on the street," he said.

"Yeah," Shane said. "She's called me like five times today."

"And you didn't bother to tell me?" he asked "I just saw you at the cookout. We stood and talked together for half an hour."

"I didn't know what to say. I was hoping it would just go away."

"Well, have you talked to her?"

"No. I told her the first three times that I couldn't make a comment. That it was a personnel matter and that we had been told not to comment on the situation."

"Good. Well keep it at that. How are your stories coming today?" Samuel asked, trying to refocus them both on important matters like daily bylines and not spending any more energy on this man on the street nonsense. He'd already spent too much energy dealing with it over the last several months as he tried to get the staff to handle such routine responsibilities with ease while meeting the necessary deadlines.

But with Shane he was almost fed up. He could tell that Shane had talent and it showed every day in his copy but there was also something dark, mystical even, about the young man whose floppy hair, dark, discrete eyes and sour countenance emoted both sympathy and frustration from him as Shane's boss.

On the one hand he could tell Shane was talented and could go as far as his work ethic could take him. At the same time Shane's inability to handle such a routine deadline belied an aspect of weakness about his commitment.

Previous cub reporters had also shown periods of sloppiness and laziness and he had begun to take it personal. As if his leadership style somehow reflected his own personal fears. He struggled to not become defensive about this, to stay true to the principles of leadership and management he had read about in so many books or seminar handouts over the last three years. But perhaps his fatal flaws were too much to overcome. Perhaps the chasms in his psyche that he had tried to fill in with ideas and habits like caulk along the cracked edges of a window seal that keeps the cold draft at bay needed to be replaced in full.

He was slipping now. Growing tired from the strain of pitching the rising water from the floor yet starting to punch at the air to see if he could land a blow. And Shane still keeping things from him. Important things like "I got a call from Sheila Vallejo about that thing we talked about last month."

"This guy is seriously starting to piss me off," Samuel thought to himself as he hung up the phone.

When Theresa had approved the statement he'd written he got Robinson on the phone again.

"Bill, I'm not allowed to take questions but we do have a comment we'll give you for the story you are doing if that is acceptable."

Robinson, likely smiling on the other end of the phone as he thought how naïve the other guy must be, told him to hang on while he got a note file open.

"Sure, I'm ready now," Robinson said.

Samuel read the three or four sentences he'd put together about how even though it was tough to run two daily newspapers with such a young staff that they were growing everyday and dedicated to putting out the best local news report possible.

After he was sure Robinson had it word for word he hung up certain that he had landed a right cross to keep the jabs at bay.

Since he'd moved from surviving at all costs to fighting back he was somewhat proud of his well crafted phrases. He had acknowledged that a mistake was made by rookie reporters, sort of a way to absorb what he felt was a glancing blow from Vallejo and Robinson jabbing him with a staff failure. But he landed his own right cross with "best local news report" and stuck that right on Robinson's chin. He hoped that the veteran newsman on the other end of the line felt the sting of his energetic reply.

Amidst these thoughts he still felt uneasy about not calling up his own chain of command.

"I still think we need to call Carl or Donna," he said to her as she rose to go back to her office.

Theresa stopped suddenly and placed a finger in the air in her firm yet playful manner that he knew meant that she'd had enough of his uncertainty.

"Samuel I told you that if anyone is to call Carl it will be me. There is no sense in us bothering them with issues we can handle ourselves. If there is any fallout from this I will take it. You stay focused and get this staff moving toward the goal again."

His instincts told him that she was wrong and that the people up the chain of command would want to know about this but there she stood with her index finger planted firmly in the air in front of his chest with her lips pursed and her brow furrowed and plainly telling him to stop.

And he did.

FIVE

Samuel had not pushed Shane to hand over his envelope before entering the conference room, opting instead to lean on Michael's malleable will in order to get an idea of what was going on. As Shane passed his envelope across the long conference table he took it in his hand thinking it would be an appeal for his friend to have a second chance.

So when he pulled out the piece of paper inside and read the familiar words he had just read in Michael's note he was stunned.

He got through the first part about needing to acknowledge a mistake and through the second part that contained a list of dates and when he got to the apology at the end he slapped the letter down on the table.

"You guys are fucking killing me," Samuel said out loud as he passed the paper over to Carla who sat silently to his right. "You both know this is totally unacceptable. I can't believe this is happening. Give me one reason why I should not fire you both this instant?"

Shane shifted in his chair as Michael looked even more steadily at his hands clasped together on the table in front of him. His head seemed to move lower toward his clenched hands. Shane sunk further into his chair like a hot air balloon deflating before a crimson sunset after briefly flying across the treetops and looking down from the heights of personal achievement.

"You guys are killing me," Samuel said again. Michael spoke first.

"I know it's a very big fuck up but all I can say is that I know I was wrong. It's against everything I've learned and worked for and if I had it to do over again I wouldn't do it and if given the chance to continue working here I will make up for it to the best of my ability."

Which was all good and well, he thought, but the industry will have zero tolerance for this. But at that moment there was something else at work inside of him. Samuel watched the shame flow across Michael's face like a storm that sweeps across a field of grain, moving steadily until it overtakes the entire view. Michael looked helpless, like he wanted to shrink away to nothing and disappear. He liked Michael. Michael had worked hard for him. Michael had listened to his suggestions and treated him with a refreshing level of respect.

He remembered how Michael brought not one but both of his parents to his job interview and how his father hovered over Michael afterward, standing in the doorway to Samuel's office like a father would size up a suitor for his one and only daughter. At the time, back in January, he found it strange that a recent graduate from the UNC School of Journalism would need to bring his parents up from Charlotte to Small City to attend his job interview. Samuel's heart then was still the heart of a man yet to endure the transformation that fatherhood brings. And so he could not understand what bonded Michael and his father so tightly.

But all that changed a few months later.

Samuel's wife had called him on the phone in early August just before the light shifts and summer begins to recede and that first hint of fresh air blows through the trees as the pulsating cries of the cicadas swirl from every direction. He was in his office adjusting to his new role as commander in chief just after that fascist ass-hole of a managing editor had been fired for plagiarizing a political cartoon in a weak effort to poke a local politician in the eye. Things moved along smoothly in the days and weeks after the transition, as if the staff's energy had been pent up under the burdensome atmosphere and was now flowing at will. He picked up the receiver not expecting it to mean much. But he could tell by her voice that she had something to say. After a few moments her voice broke and she said the words that changed his life.

"I'm pregnant."

For a lot of men those words are either easy to hear because they don't much care what comes next or they are frightening because they loathe responsibility. For him it was neither. It was the culmination of a journey that he began more than eight years before. It was the pinnacle he had sought to reach when he first looked up from the depths of his hole, when he first saw that sliver of light from the back of his hollow cave and decided that he would fight.

So now it wasn't as simple as the sexual act that brought egg and sperm together to morph into the fetus that grew strong, he was certain, in his young wife's body. No, that oft repeated act paled in comparison to the triumph of his will over his nature. He was 34 and had been to the lowest hell of isolation and turned around and walked steadily forward from that point, through that initial valley of despair to begin climbing the plain that lead to the vista from which he first looked back on the wreckage of youth and first thought he could go further toward that mountain in front of him—the one with the snowy peak where he was certain the cool stillness of achievement would reward him.

Within a few weeks they began looking for a house to buy. Up till now they were content in a small rental in a not so great neighborhood because she was attending graduate classes in Big City and he worked the evening shift and in their free time they hit the road and made use of Mr. Eisenhower's highway system. They had not intended to stay in Small City for more than two years but when Mr. Fascist Dictator was fired and Samuel found himself on the front lines, tempted by the allure of higher pay and increased power, he fell into the trap he so wanted to avoid and chased the temptation. He still believed then that he could mold the newsroom to his will and show signs of ability and then move to a larger paper and repeat the process.

But as August turned to September and the crisp air of fall washed over them so too did a sense of nostalgia and a desire for stability. They had been married four years now and had moved twice in that time. And Small City, even with all its 21st century problems and with its feet cemented in past achievements amidst the rise of the sunbelt economy, was a tolerable place for two people in their prime. His pay was steady and she made connections at the local Baptist church she attended on Sundays and was hired to teach at a small college in the county on a part-time basis. She would finish her graduate work next semester, right about the time the baby was due. And so as they lay awake in bed at night and talked of young love with its boundless hope—or chatted over a meal at one of those designer restaurant chains that serve the same menu of sandwiches, ribs and fried nothing—the idea of stability seemed appealing.

He certainly could not bring a child into the world in the rental house. Certainly not his child and certainly not in this neighborhood. They found a small bungalow for sale in an older neighborhood that had colonials and ranches and countless smaller houses and seemed a place they could pass a few years. The economy was strong and they could hold the house for three, four or five years and then sell, if not at a profit, then at a price that would allow them to live rent free for the duration.

That winter passed and he remained watchful of his wife's condition and settled in on the couch to watch basketball in the evenings, taking the occasional phone call from Charles or Carla back at the office about a reporter's story or a content decision for the front page. But the staff was better than it had ever been. Charles was as talented as anyone he had ever seen at laying out pages. He created crisp, well balanced fronts and handled the inside page volume with ease. It was, he thought, the best hire he had made in three years because as Charles took that pressure on it alleviated four or five others to focus on creating stories and other content. That in turn gave Charles better material to make even more appealing packages.

He had leaned on Carla as well to take on more management of the staff and she was growing into the role. There were still the occasional ruffled feathers from some of the young reporters especially who resented Carla's lack of pedigree. She had no college degree and had come into the company before the two dailies merged.

She was a bright young woman who went straight into the textile mill from high school about 10 years ago. But a dwindling manufacturing sector hung on the horizon and she was aware of the shifts in technology and so she shifted over to the reception desk at the paper in the town about 10 miles from the main office in Small City. Because of her roots deep in the fabric of the community, her tough as nails work ethic and maybe just a little touch of servile flattery, she quickly positioned herself in a reporter's chair and then moved to the layout desk. As the company combined properties, all these skills she rode like a wave amidst the torrent of change until she found herself still standing as the wave settled along the shore.

When Samuel arrived at the Small City Review she was the sole page designer and without her constancy he would not have survived the first two months on the job. They joked now about how she didn't think he would last the first week and even once told him the staff had placed bets on how many days he would last.

"I could not have done it without you," Samuel told her in one of their first conversations after the dictator was sacked and the atmosphere began to improve.

It was because of this that he supported her without fail each and every time some recent college graduate tried to turn up their nose at her ideas or her being in general.

By the time March rolled in like a lion, his wife seemed like she would burst at the seams. He was driving her twice a week in the evenings to her classes in Big City. He would go to the coffee shop on Tate Street around the corner from campus and read books about Frank Zappa or Led Zeppelin or the French Revolution to pass the time but his heart and mind were never far from that baby—a boy they had been told weeks ago—that was coming. He did his best to keep calm and bear whatever part of her burden that he could but she was a worker and intent on doing as much as possible. The time passed effortlessly for him. She seemed not too bothered by the life growing inside of her and rarely complained. Sickness never came, her health was strong and checkups came and went without incident.

But almost immediately after the birth the problems began. In the first few days it was high levels of bile the baby was unable to process and as his bilirubin count remained high he was kept inside a lighted incubator with a tiny black mask on his face that the child fought with great effort. After three days they took the baby home but the tension mounted each time he was due for a feeding. Samuel would go to a far corner of the house to give the new mother her space but he could hear the cries and feel the tension through the walls and down the halls to the place where he sat listening.

After a few days at home a nurse came to visit as part of a mandatory state program for new mothers. Her eyes grew as big as pineapples when she took the new mother's blood pressure and she arranged an immediate visit to the ob-gyn who diagnosed eclampsia and pre-scribed some medications.

"It's rare to see this postpartum," he said into his digital recorder as he left notes for himself but not once did any of them consider this might impact the mother's milk. She continued to struggle and he helped as he could but it was obvious to him after a week that some-thing was not working. He tried to talk her into using formula but it appeared to him as if she was dialed into the notion that a real woman breastfeed her child. But after the first week he noticed his son's skin began to sag and his face looked gaunt. On Monday he called the pediatrician and expressed his concern and that after-noon took the baby to have blood work done. When the nurse failed after three attempts to draw blood from the baby who not once woke up, she left the office and came back in a few minutes.

"Dr. Scott would like to speak to you on the phone," she said.

The doctor's voice was reserved as he instructed him to call his wife and have her pack a small bag and to take the baby directly to the emergency room at the pediatric hospital one hour away.

"I will call them and they will be expecting you," he said.

He was in a foreign world now. Failure to thrive, eclampsia, dehydration were all words he had not once considered before and as he drove the hour to the hos-pital he didn't once think the baby could die.

As the doctors in varying lab coats of green and white and blue came and went and hovered over the lifeless child that now lay in the tiny bed in a small area no wider than six feet it dawned on him that the baby could die. He was pacing just outside of the child's unit in the ER when the first hint of death crept over him and he felt as if he could fall into the floor that moment.

After so much waiting, so much persistence in his life at birth control, so much focus on doing it the right way, when he was emotionally ready and had the money to support another life for the duration, there was no way he could begin to accept that the baby could die. The child, with tiny eyes shut and limp arms and fingers, had opened a joy in his heart he had never known. He couldn't die. Not now. He rubbed his hands from his forehead and across his eyes to his chin where he let them rest as he understood the gravity of the condition. The grim, focused faces of the doctors that came and went let him know they were in deep trouble. He had to keep it together. His wife sat motionless and seemingly dazed in a thin plastic chair at the foot of the bed. He asked her if she had brought the medications she was supposed to take for her spiked blood pressure and to help her body process the toxicity left by the pregnancy. She had. And so he continued to watch the baby, now with a large needle piercing his fontanel providing critical nutrients that would determine life or death.

The hours passed slowly. He took phone calls from his mother, his aunt, his sister, unable to answer their frantic concerns.

"I don't know," he would say to them. "Just pray."

Soon they were following a male nurse as he pushed a cart bearing the child's bed through the ER and to an elevator that took them to the pediatric ICU. A step in the right direction he thought but the baby's eyes had not opened and the needle was still in place.

It would remain this way for two days until the emergency doctor who was reluctant to provide forward looking statements passed the baton to the pediatrician who specialized in neurology. She provided a much clearer picture. The needle would remain in the child's head for a day or two more and if his statistics improved they would move to controlled feeding. If after two more days he continued to thrive then the parents could begin feeding him.

Later he would kick himself over and over when he realized just how much milk the child had needed and for not monitoring his wife closer. But her mother had been with her for several days and if he was ever to trust something so important to other people then surely he could trust his wife and her mother to feed their newborn son.

But now he did know. And now the question of breast milk or formula was settled, if in the most difficult fashion possible, with incredible heartache and terror at the sight of something he loved so much that was so fragile and helpless yet fighting through the suffering to thrive.

As Samuel watched Michael struggle with the paralysis of shame he again felt something he hadn't known before that time he watched his son fight for life. He felt sorry for Michael. He felt a type of fatherly compassion for someone he perhaps even loved like his own son and wanted to watch him succeed and grow into something strong that reflected his own effort. Maybe he saw in Michael a future vision of his own son fighting again with overwhelming obstacles and failure and trying to stay upright or get up and walk. And really what was Michael besides an infant reporter with less than eight months on the job training. And hadn't they told him at corporate to just do the best he could with what he had to work with and that if failure occurred to learn from it and turn it into a growth process and don't repeat the same mistake again.

But Samuel was tired now. He was worn down still by the guilt at having let his own son fall so close to the arms of death. And perhaps even now it was uncertain if his son faced lifelong developmental challenges because of the dehydration. And wasn't it his own fault for not being more forceful and following his instincts that screamed to him each time the baby cried and the mother sighed in exasperation and the feeding time would pass again without much in the way of sustenance? Could he make up for that now by giving Michael a second chance even though he knew that journalistic ethics demanded his career be cut off immediately? And wasn't that like death for Michael's future? Had his future even had a chance to get started, much like his own son's four month experience?

His mind was clouded now and emotion began to overtake his instincts. Maybe he should call Arthur or Joe up in Fredericksville and ask them for advice. But he knew what the answer would be and might as well fire Michael and Shane now if he was even going to bother with making that call.

"How many people know about this," Samuel asked without realizing his mouth spoke.

Michael said that while in Chapel Hill over the July Fourth weekend and driving back from the bar his friend saw the Small City Review on the floorboard and wanted to look at some of Michael's work. The friend noticed a third friend pictured in the man on the street profile and knew that the person had never been anywhere near Small City. He pressed Michael on this issue and Michael told them that he'd taken the photo from Facebook to make a deadline he missed. He claimed to have called the friend and they said it was ok to use their picture.

The friend in the car objected to the arrangement and felt it was against the ethics of journalism to use a far away friend to meet a local deadline and so made Michael promise that he would confess to his editor and take whatever punishment was handed down.

"And this friend will be satisfied with what discipline I hand down?" Samuel asked.

Both Michael and Shane said that the friend had only demanded that they confess and that there was no further threat. He paused and let his mind process the various angles. If he asked for advice from outside he would surely have to fire both of them. He did not want to do that. The combination of fatherly love for Michael's naiveté and his reluctance to have to start over again and repeat the hiring process were foremost in mind. He didn't speak these words but as he sat in his cushioned chair and fretted over the situation and looked across the conference table at these two hapless fellows, compassion washed over him. But he was also angry. He was furious. He was ashamed and knew that the institutional mediocrity and lingering laziness he inherited when he came to this newsroom were still all too common.

Even after three years of daily effort to instill in his staff the type of pride and effort that Carla and Charles were showing, this disinclination to achieve lingered like a cancer in the minds and spirit of some staff members.

At that particular moment he resigned himself to defeat at the hands of whatever it was that gripped the building and the people that worked there. He couldn't defeat it by himself. And why sacrifice these two to an ethic of higher standards when throughout the building in each and every department sorriness, laziness and rule breaking were tolerated.

"I need to be certain that no one else knows about this," Samuel said. "I have a wife and an infant and a mortgage and I'll be damned if I am going to throw all of that away at this very moment just to give you two a second chance."

Michael assured him that his friend would not betray his trust and that he only demanded to hear from Michael that he'd confessed and been punished. He had told Shane because the friend knew Shane as well and Michael had actually gotten the idea to take a photo from Facebook from Shane because he'd noticed Shane doing it for about a month in May before he left to go to the fellowship at the D.C. bureau. While Shane was away Michael thought he could slip in a few photos and be done with it.

Shane said that he had not spoken of it to anyone but that he felt shameful and couldn't let Michael confess without also himself confessing and receiving his just reward.

Wisdom knows that the easiest path is the fool's path. But when a man is tired and worn down by frustration and fear and in the earliest days of understanding love for the first time in his 34 years he is not yet possessed of wisdom. And so the fool's path seems smooth and the fool can see a way to walk away from the crisis and toward the goal he has for himself.

And you would have to be a fool to believe two infants who would lie to their best friend if it saved them from shame.

A fool is certainly what Samuel was when he told them that in no uncertain terms if he discovered they had done anything that even hinted of laziness let alone fabrication in a bylined story or news item that he would fire them on the spot. They both assured him that they had only cheated on the man on the street photo because they did not want to do it because they felt it was busy work for the ad department.

A fool is what he was when he told them to both go back to work and that he would devise an appropriate punishment that would most likely involve the two of them being responsible for the man on the street photo for the next six months in addition to all their other duties.

That seemed like the easiest path. In shock and disbelief, having been worn down by the mediocrity meandering through his workplace, and with his heart and mind not far from the infant struggling to move ahead after coming back from the edge of death itself, he felt justified to send these two infants back to work and let them try to grow into men.

SIX

Theresa leaves his office and he tries to focus on the work in front of him. It's 3:30 in the afternoon and it's obvious he will not clear the pile by himself. Carla and Charles are in the outer office now and as he often does he phones Charles and asks him to fill the editorial page for him with some wire copy.

He wants to find a way to write an op-ed piece each day but the combination of mundane tasks and the stream of crisis-ness that never seems to end often get the better of him.

He wonders how many people know about the impending story but he decides to keep it to himself for now. Try and finish the day, he thinks. Get the papers out. Remember it's like his former editor Joe told him; that the best thing about working in the newspaper business is that if you fuck up you get to do it all again tomorrow. So let's get through this crisis and refocus the energy where it belongs: on journalism.

He's still responsible for a few dozen decisions this afternoon despite the swirl of uncertainty moving around him as he worries about what the Big City Daily News will write in their paper tomorrow. The buzz in the newsroom grows as four o'clock comes around. The sports guys and the photographer are here now, along with Charles and Carla. It's his favorite part of the day when the evening folks arrive as the day side staff is nearing the finish line and the combination of fresh energy and hustle electrifies the newsroom.

Since it's the 26th day of July and he has monthly readership reports to submit on the management tracking software he calls for Dana the news clerk to ask if she's finished compiling the in-house promo stats and the staff byline tally. It will be ready in the morning she says and so he moves on to something else. There are only two stories in the daily budget folder on the computer and he read those before lunch because they were turned in late last night by the features reporter and are scheduled to run in the people section over the next couple of days.

It's the middle of summer, about three weeks before school starts, and two of his six reporters are on vacation. Most news junkies know late July and into August are slow news periods. It's the time of year when pop culture frenzies take the nation by storm or off the wall people stories spread across the wires as editors from Detroit down to Houston and sea to shining sea thirst for fresh copy to make a page and keep circulation numbers off the floor. In newsrooms across America editors are waiting to pounce on that one story that will be the slow news phenomenon of the summer. As for now they can only wait like a loaded spring, ready to release the pent up tension of relevance as they attempt to regain their reader's attention away from light summer reading and escapist vacation literature.

Locally things are slow as well. It's an election off year and so local politics are at a lull. They've beaten the "collapse of the local economy" theme into the ground and he's challenged his staff to focus on solution oriented pieces. They've analyzed trends and data sets and stats and figures from a myriad of budgets and comprehensive test score reports to give readers a broader picture of county government and local schools. The staff even worked well together last month in producing their first team project—an analysis of plea bargains and dismissals by the local district attorney and the nature of repeat offenders involved with local crime.

He's used the time to school some of the news staff on business trend stories and real estate, teaching them how to use new online tools to research property records and business filings, how to look up corporate information with the state office and use that information to cross reference local property tax records. There are environmental issues to dig into, coal powered electric generating steam stations on rivers that supply municipal water sources. There are developers clear cutting large swaths of the county leaving a blighted landscape not to mention the increased sediment runoff that chokes small tributaries and creeks that feed the three major rivers snaking across the county.

Plenty to do, he thinks to himself, if I can just get them to think outside the box and plan.

He's seen Michael cross the floor of the newsroom, having returned from the city council meeting. I'll give him a few minutes to get settled in, he thinks, and then Rachel the intern from the UNC School of Journalism appears at his door. She's a breath of fresh air, so quiet and dedicated that he almost forgets she is here at times, but she's got talent for miles and surprises him on a regular basis with the stories she digs up.

"Do you have a minute to read my Duke Power story?" she asks.

"Yes, Rachel, come on in," he gestures to the two chairs up against the wall across from his desk.

Duke Power, a major regional electric company, has two power plants in the county. One is on the far western side of the county on Belews Lake, a man made reservoir that supplies water to the coal-fired steam station. Rachel sorted through federal databases and permit applications to paint a picture of upgrades and improved processes at the plant that are part of the new "clean coal" movement. Her research got the company to put out a press release about a new scrubber technology they installed on the two large smokestacks that dominate the horizon for miles around the lake. It's a good piece of research and shows her promise as a reporter. She's from a prominent family of lawyers in a nearby city and came to the staff via the university's internship program that he happily signed the paper up for last year after hiring Shane Vallow.

It's a 40-inch story complete with a few photos from her recent visit to interview the plant manager. It's a good story, but maybe a bit too dry and reading too much like a press release. They discuss how to make her copy more active and project a sense of place. He thumbs through the two-inch folder of writing and reporting tip sheets he's collected over the years and hands her a copy of "Writing Copy that Sings" by Chip Scanlan, one of his favorite tipsters.

They discuss her writing and he thanks her for the solid effort she's giving. She smiles and gets up to leave and he thinks that for a rising junior in college she is damn sharp. He's certain she'll end up at the New York Times or a major wire service like Reuters or Bloomberg. He's happy to send staffers up the ladder to bigger opportunities. That's what he wants. It's what he did and he's thankful for the ones who helped him along the way. But his three years as an editor have been enough and he's tired of the revolving door. Not enough writing opportunities for him now. If he can get through this current crisis he'll get that resume out and polish that clip file until he can move up the ladder himself.

He's thirsty and the large water jug he brings to work each day is almost empty so he rises to go to the break room for a Coke. The newsroom is humming with the snap-punch of keystrokes and the tension of concentration. Dana is putting the finishing touches on her data entry so she can shut down and make room for the proofreader who comes in at 5pm. Charles and Carla trade notes over the layout mockup as Carla assigns him inside pages to knock out before their dinner break in a few hours after which they will put the front pages together. The photographer, Ross, scans photos and color corrects files for Charles to anchor the front section so that when a potential reader sees a copy in the newsstand they won't hesitate to drop two quarters.

For an instant he almost forgets that the Big City Daily News is about to take the reputation of his newsroom out at the knees. He's too busy feeling the buzz of energy pulsating from this small room where eight to 10 people are moving with a growing sense of effort and dedication to quality. He can almost feel a sense of accomplishment at having guided the news staff this far – from rank incompetence made worse by sloth to a place that in just the right light resembled professional-ism. Empowerment does work, he thinks to himself as he exits the far end of the newsroom and steps along the hallway to the break room. Up ahead he sees the sports editor, Steve, looking languidly through the offerings of the snack machine for something to abate his appetite.

"Steve-O what looks good?" he asks.

"Same old stuff. Cheap thrills and empty calories."

He laughs. Steve is a riot. A veritable encyclopedia of one liners from Seinfeld. Samuel puts a dollar in the drink machine and punches the button for a Coke. The can filters through the machine's guts and falls with a sudden thud to the bin where he reaches down and grabs it up. He wipes off the mouth piece before snapping the top and taking a sip. The cold smacks the back of his throat before filtering with effervescence into his chest and down to his stomach.

Steve still looks over the machine as he pauses. Steve makes a selection for Bugles and moves to the Coke machine.

"Look, I need to tell you about something that is going down tomorrow," Samuel says. Steve's been a big part of the success here. It was Carla and Steve that agreed to handle their tasks efficiently and without much super-vision that allowed him to focus on the new set up with the reporters and focus on his op-ed goals when he wasn't neck deep in corporate or personnel paperwork. He likes Steve. Steve has a dry wit and a can do attitude and doesn't get ruffled when he doesn't get his way.

"You heard of Facebook?" he asks Steve.

"Yea isn't that that online yearbook college kids are using now?" Steve replies.

"Something like that I think," Samuel says. "I never gave it much thought until last month. I'm just gonna tell you straight. Shane and Michael took some pictures off of Facebook of their friends and submitted them for man on the street photos."

Steve winces and forms his lips into an "O" as he pulls his eyebrows together for a second. He's pulling apart the bag of Bugles and relaxes his face and shoulders a moment after making the expression.

"Yea, I know," Samuel says. "I can't believe after all the times we've gone over how simple it is and how important it is to make deadlines we are still talking about this."

He sips his Coke as Steve sets his bag of Bugles on the large round plastic table next to the four-pane glass window in the corner of the room. Steve picks up his Sprite.

"Anyway it seems that Michael was in Chapel Hill over the July 4th break and one of their friends noticed the pictures and questioned it. Michael and Shane came to me and Carla about it about three weeks ago. I blew up at them but I decided it was a juvenile error and not something they should be fired over."

Steve raises his shoulders as he turns one palm over while raising an eyebrow and pursing his lips in that deadpan "What can you do" gesture perfected in mob movies and New York sitcoms.

"Seriously," Samuel continues as Steve turns the bag of Bugles up and tosses the last few crumbs into his mouth. Steve crumples the bag and tosses it to the black utility trash can between the drink and snack machine. "I mean I knew it was 'fire them then or roll the dice and keep going'. Apparently the Big City Daily News got a hold of it. I assume some of their friends from Chapel Hill work there. I think one is interning there this summer. So they are doing a story on it that will publish tomorrow."

Steve silently mouths "Holy Shit" in a slow enunciated fashion while opening his eyes as wide as possible.

"I wanted to tell you so you didn't get hit with it from left field tomorrow. I think tomorrow is going to be one of the worst days of my life. I'm not sure if I'll survive the day or not," Samuel says.

"Well how bad can it be, Sam? I mean it's just an advertorial busy work item. Everybody knows it's crap that has nothing to do with reporting," Steve says.

"True, but we've been outperforming their bureau and making an aggressive push for readership for about six months now. It's probably a hit to damage us and put us back in the box."

Steve nods.

"Well if anybody asks you can tell them that they came to me earlier this month and admitted to making mistakes. I disciplined them accordingly and documented it as a personnel matter as I would anyone else who made a bad decision."

He sips his Coke and looks apologetically at Steve.

"I'm sorry if it embarrasses you, Steve. I know how people like to make fun of the paper's reputation. But we've been moving in the right direction and I hope we can continue that momentum after tomorrow."

"I think we can, Sam. I wouldn't worry about it too much."

"I hope you are right. But I want you to know, no matter what happens, that I appreciate your effort and all you've done to help us get to this point."

"You'll be fine, Sam. Don't sweat it too hard. Say, how is the baby?"

"He's coming along fine now, thanks. He's gaining weight steadily and meeting all his developmental goals. I think we are out of the woods. You know, I never knew just how fragile life is until the delivery and those first few days. It's amazing that any of us are here."

He turns and heads back to the newsroom as Steve surveys the snack machine again. Michael stands outside of his office with an anxious look.

"Your story ready, Michael?"

"Yes. Do you have time to read it now?"

"I think so my good man. Let's see what you have."

He takes his seat behind the computer monitor and places the Coke can on the far left of his desk. He pulls up the file system and opens Michael's story. It's a straight news story from the council meeting about the city voting to give a low interest loan to the current owners of the dilapidated mall in the center of town so they can resurface the parking lot, paint the exterior and make a few infrastructure improvements. The place has been in decline for more than a decade and is on the verge of becoming an eyesore. Michael's copy conveys the urgency of the city's need to improve the commercial climate. It's complete with three sources – a mall representative, the city manager and the chamber of commerce director – and hard financial and foot traffic details. They briefly discuss the lede sentence and whittle it down to 31 words before workshopping the headline.

Michael holds the council agenda booklet in his hand and when Samuel's finished reading the story, Michael hands the book over to him. He's trained Michael on how to mine the agenda packet for stories to carry him through the weeks in between meetings, tackling the big item from the meeting itself on the same day and parsing others out in between breaking news and feature reporting on businesses. Michael has marked several items that seem worthwhile—a street widening and repaving project that will require utilities to be moved and an item about minority recruitment in the police department—and he's pleased to see Michael's reporting senses maturing.

"Very good, Michael. You are doing well. That was a sharp, tight story. Keep focusing on compacting the lede as you maintain the crispness of the story itself."

"Thanks, Samuel. I think this analyzing the agenda is helping me to stay focused throughout the month."

"Well, it's standard procedure and will serve you well when you move to a bigger shop."

He pauses, not wanting to address the lingering crisis that hovers just off the center of their conversation.

"Michael has Sheila Vallejo called you today?" Samuel asks.

Michael turns grim and a ruddiness creeps over his face. "Yes, she's called me like five times since this morning. She's really crossed the line into harassment I think."

"And what did she want?"

"She wants me to comment on the quotes of course and I told her I couldn't make a comment because it was a personnel matter."

"And she's called you several more times?"

Michael nods. "I knew it was a bad fuck up when it happened but I can't believe they're going to make a big story out of it now." His face is red now and the tension shows as he's moved to the edge of the chair, with his pen atop the council agenda packet held in place by one hand as the other hand lies clinched upon his knee.

Braced by the confidence Theresa and then Steve exuded, he's believing now that he can weather the storm and that Theresa will run interference for whatever fallout from the story comes his way tomorrow. Michael's a steady performer and a good young reporter and so he wants to help maintain his confidence.

"I think tomorrow will be a rough day but if you can stay focused and produce a story or two I think it will help. They will hit us in the gut but we are in control of our own reaction. If we get knocked off kilter they will have won. But if we stay focused and absorb whatever blow they deliver and continue to grow, each of us in the way that is required, then I think we can take the lick and move on. Does that make sense to you?"

"Yes, it does, but I'm just still very sorry for putting you through this."

"I believe you and I want you to understand that I see your effort and I appreciate the hard work you've put in," Samuel says. "Like last week when you went to the accident site late at night after you had worked your shift already for the day. That's the type of dedication and effort that gets you to where you want to be. Maybe you use that sting of failure and the tension that comes each time you feel the shame and use it to push yourself to the highest level of achievement."

"Thanks, Samuel. It means a lot to me to have you believe in me after what happened."

"We all fail. I've failed," Samuel says. "We'll both probably fail again but just remember to get back up."

Michael stands and is moving to the door. He feels that odd sense of fatherly concern for Michael as he watches him leave and he thinks for a moment again that everything will work out for them both. He moves Michael's story file from the "first read" bin to the "second read" bin where Carla will read over it before moving it to "ready for page". He's going over the list of files in the pipeline when Carla comes to the door.

"You ready to go over the budget?"

He nods and she enters. "Go ahead and close the door if you would," he says to her and she does so before taking the seat next to his desk.

He rubs his hands across his face and picks up the Coke, draining the last few sips before tossing the can into the trash.

"Is something going on?" she asks. "I noticed Steve looked a bit concerned after you talked to him in the break room and Michael looks worried as well. And you've got that look that lets me know you are wrestling with something ... -

He cuts her off in mid-sentence.

"Well you know we never get more than a couple of weeks in between crises here."

"What's going on?"

"Well wouldn't you know that Sheila Vallejo from the Big City Daily News called and they are running a story tomorrow about the man on the street quotes."

"No way," she says. "How did they find out about it?"

"Well it seems that whomever Shane and Michael trusted to keep it to themselves couldn't and so there is an intern at the Big City paper and they know about it and they've contacted one or more of the people photo'd and they've called Michael and Shane several times to-day and they left me a message as well. Theresa says not to worry about it. To focus on getting the papers out and she will handle the fallout but I'm concerned that we should call Carl or Arthur at the regional office for advice. But she shut me down and said not to, so what can I do about it?"

"How big of a story do you think they'll do?"

He sighs long as he looks up at the Dali print, at the butterfly and the rich colors and the deep blue of the background sky. He wants to crawl into the painting and run screaming across the dry colors and find a place to hide off in the horizon.

"Oh I imagine if they have Sheila calling around and have talked to two of the people photo'd, and with her being a features writer, that they will turn it into a news feature with a quirky head and a storytelling narrative that makes us all look like dumbasses. We'll be hit hard with it I'm sure."

Carla's looking at him but she's leaned back in the chair with her elbow propped on the armrest and her fingertips pressed against the side of her head.

"I still think you did the right thing. Like I told you that day I was proud of you, real proud that you didn't blow up at them and throw them out of the building in an emotional reaction. I know you've been through a lot recently but I thought, and still think, you showed good leadership in the way you handled that."

"It kills me that we've put together such a strong team and now we are having to deal with this of all things, over a –" he pauses so as not to drop the f-bomb he normally would since he knows Carla is a church goer and he's still trying to solidify their personal respect "– over a silly little thing like the man on the street photo. Of all the things."

"Well you can't hold their hand on every detail, Sam. And they seem to have responded well. The papers have looked great lately."

"Yea you and Charles are doing a great job on the fronts. So what do we have for tomorrow?"

They discuss the details of the top stories and feature items to split between the two papers and envision two separate design schemes for the fronts. The goal is to have the papers appear completely different so that if the two are side by side a reader might want to buy both. And with that done again Carla is gathering up her notes and preparing to leave.

"I'm going to go on home. If you need anything just call me," Samuel says. "If anybody has a question or concern about the Big City story, have them call me or just tell them that we handled the mistakes as we would anyone else's and disciplined them according to policy for any personnel matter. I don't know what else to do at this point."

"You've done all you can in forgiving them and giving them a chance to make up for it. The rest is up to them, Sam. Go on home. We've got plenty for the papers to-morrow."

Her words reassured him again that tomorrow was survivable. He'd shown forgiveness to two very young men, fresh out of college and working for the first time.

Was it his fault that the university system failed to teach work ethic along with intellectual rigor and methodology? Could he control the fact that the Millennials, as Shane and Michael's generation was known, carried a deep sense of entitlement that dwarfed the habits of work and diligence. How was he to know he would have to teach 22 year olds fresh from the finest university in the state how to be rather than to seem?

He relied on the reputation for excellence *inherent* in the words "University of North Carolina at Chapel Hill" when he first hired Amy and then expanded the connection by hiring Shane and Michael. Not once did he imagine that part of that package would be a lazy sense of entitlement that would etiolate the rich reputation of that storied institution. He just shook his head another time as he crossed the small parking lot to his car after passing under the flagpole. Looking up to the North Carolina flag blowing just beneath the American flag he felt again the pride and dignity experienced on those first days working here when he realized how far he had come. To be back at home in North Carolina and to be a professional that his family could be proud of lifted his spirits and that of his relatives and anyone who knew what depths he fought back from just a few years before.

If he knew what Sheila Vallejo at that very moment had written, what story she turned into her editor, who in turn moved it along the file system at the Big City Daily News from the news editor to the managing editor to the copy editor who placed it on the page of the local section that ran in the outlying counties of their coverage area and later the metro editor who slated it to run on the bottom right of the front section of the city edition, then Samuel would have not once returned to the office. Once he was in his car driving down Vance Street toward the sprawling working class neighborhood in which he'd purchased a small bungalow home where his wife and infant son now at this moment waited for him he'd write a letter of resignation and email it straight to Carl at the regional office.

But ignorance is bliss and those closest to him in the management structure at the paper implied that a fatherly compassion was appropriate for the scope of the wrong committed by Michael and Shane. With the opportunity that comes with forgiveness conveyed to them, both young staffers hustled and sweated to earn their reputation back. Surely everyone would see that. His magnanimity would be applauded, well if not applauded at least recognized, and amidst the laughter and ridicule that surely would come with tomorrow's story he would retain the high moral ground. He would take their best shot and make the most of it by pushing the staff to newer heights and greater standards of success.

SEVEN

His mind bops to electric Miles as he sweeps down the large hill in his small car along the street that leads to the house he bought back in the winter. It's fun to listen to the big groove of the electric bass beneath the attenuated horn. And for those few small minutes he's lost all his troubles, focused solely on the road before him as the jazz reverberates within the car and he thinks again that he's glad he bought the Corolla with the JBL speakers. Past the park off to his right in the nadir of the road and up the hill where he can see the modest home up on the crest, just beyond the stop sign. The aging maple tree with its butchered shape looms before him. "I need to cut that thing down soon," he thinks as he glides across the intersection before pulling left into the double-wide concrete driveway just past the large brown mailbox.

He checks himself for a moment, something he's learned to do to improve the health of his domestic life. By leaving the stress of the office in the car he can have a fresh start with her and give back some of the joy and comfort she gives him. Early on he could feel himself following his father's footsteps and barking at her over something trivial at home as he tried to filter the stress of the day. Too many petty arguments later he found a way to exhale the clutter of the office life and let it drift off before he opened the door to what was really important.

Beyond the 12-pane glass door that opens into the sun porch on the right side of the house he walks into the front den, lit by the soft afternoon light of late summer and filtered through the blinds and windows across the southern facing front side of the house. She's playing with their son who giggles beneath a fabric mobile from which hang small pillowed animals, bells on a chain and a plastic mirror.

"There's your daddy," she says and the baby giggles and swings at the monkey and kicks at the giraffe and she helps him roll over to his stomach. He looks up at the man standing, backlit by the late afternoon sun, towering like a minaret among the low lying furniture. Samuel bends down to pick the boy up and cuddles him in his arms before holding him up in the air, arms extended as they both laugh.

After kissing him on the cheek he hands the baby back to his mother and moves down the hallway to the back bedroom where he changes into his house clothes, as he calls them, which in late July consist of some basketball shorts and a loose tee-shirt. Today he chooses the black Fishbone holdover from a decade earlier. The front side reads "if you give a monkey a brain ..." with "he'll swear he is the center of the universe ..." across the back.

Back in the living room she's standing now and moves to him. He embraces her and feels the warmth of her curves against his body. They exchange the soft kiss of familiar love.

"How was your day?" she asks him as she does most days, never certain if he's going to share an engaging story or explode with the tension of middle management.

He goes right to it.

"Big City Daily News is doing a story about the made up quotes for man on the street. They called our office all day trying to get us to make a comment. I think the story will run tomorrow."

"Oh no," she says with a furrowed brow. "Is that going to be bad?"

He's pulled away from her now and is standing before the three large bay windows that look out to the maple tree in the yard that blocks a good portion of his view down the street. Smaller clapboard and vinyl siding homes run the length of the street and down the avenue toward the park. It's as if the planned section of the neighborhood stopped on his corner and they later came through and stuffed the land with as many small homes as could fit. He's glad the tree blocks the view but it will have to go soon. Several thick branches have been ripped into by the electric company over the years and one half of the main runner has been sliced away so the tree grows oddly on one side and maintains a damaged vacancy on the other.

"It's not going to be good. I don't know why I bother anymore. You know how I've said over the years that I feel like I'm bailing out the Titanic with a small pail?"

She's moved beside him again, holding the baby, bouncing it on her hips, curved just so for an infant to rest. She raises a free hand to place on his shoulder.

"You know, if I'm not dealing with Romper Room non-sense from a bunch of 20-somethings and their petty drama then it's some off the wall juxtaposition of ethics or interest not even Nostradamus could predict. I can't deal with it much more. I'm sick of it actually," Samuel says.

He pauses for a minute to enjoy the sunlight as it gleams across the tops of glowing trees with leaves stretched out to soak up the radiance. He wants to leave. He wants to get back in the car and take Lisa and the baby and drive away and never come back. But he's not an escape artist.

"Theresa seems to think we will get through it ok. She seems almost too sure of herself actually. I asked her three times to call up to the regional office or to let me call Donna at corporate for some advice but she said absolutely not. I think she wants them to think she can deal with everything that comes her way but I'm afraid she's wrong. Or that she doesn't see how bad this will look from a journalism standpoint."

He's turned back to her. The baby plays with the loose ends of her honey brown hair that lies softly across her shoulders.

"You know with Steven Glass and Jayson Blair and what happened with Bob in Fredericksville and with Harlan here ... I don't think she understands the potential this has to go national or get picked up by the wires. I mean it's the Big City Daily News. The wires are sure to pick up on it. So I don't know."

It's just after six now and between the two of them they know nothing they say tonight can alter what comes next. She puts the baby in his playpen and the boy busies himself with the soft fabric of a play base-ball lying among the furry lion and the brown puppy doll with the floppy red ears. She moves to the kitchen to prepare their evening meal and he begins working the lock in his mind, certain there is a solution to the problem.

He's not one to stop trying until he finds the answer. After all, he is a trained reporter. And as his mind mulls the situation he remembers the j-school professor in Chapel Hill. He's an expert in small newspapers—the guru actually of the state press clique—and has been working in the business since the early 70s. He moves to the computer and runs a Google search for "Jack Laughter" and his university bio comes up. He looks at his watch. "Six eleven." No tenured professor at the University of North Carolina at Chapel Hill is going to be in the office at that time but he dials the number on his small Nokia cell phone anyway. With his neck craned to the side holding the phone to his ear he's already typing in "Orange County property tax records" into Google and as the phone rings for the twelfth time the search results are coming up on the screen so he cuts the phone off and sets it on the desk.

He finds Laughter's address and runs his name + street address after typing "phonebook:" into Google and a White Page search result comes back with a phone number for that street address.

He punches the number into his cell, stands up and walks outside before pushing send. Outside the sun is behind the semi-circular crowns of the maple trees in his neighbor's yard and sinking beyond the towering oaks growing along the street as it runs down the hill toward the park. He leans against the side of his car as the phone rings a third time.

Suddenly a voice answers.

"Hello," a man says.

"Hi, uh, is this Professor Laughter from the School of Journalism?"

"Yes."

"Hi sir. My name is Samuel Ashton and I'm the editor of a small paper near Big City. I wondered if you had a few minutes to help me with a problem I have."

"Well sure, Samuel. What's up?"

He goes through the condensed version of the story the best he knows how, trying to use the inverted pyramid as opposed to the Wall Street Journal story form.

There's an advertorial man on the street item we have to fill each day. The staff won't take it seriously and keep missing the deadlines. I tried two or three ways to make it easy for them but settled on an annual schedule and told them to adhere to it. They still missed the deadlines so I threatened to write up the next person who missed it. We had a baby in the spring. I missed two or three weeks of work because we had a small crisis. Two of the staff are recent hires from your program. Shane Vallow and Michael Profaci. They came to me earlier this month and confessed to taking photos of classmates from Carolina off of Facebook and turning them in for their slot.

Profaci was in Chapel Hill around the Fourth of July and another classmate saw the photos in a newspaper in his back seat. Long story short, a classmate interning at the Big City Daily News told her editors there about it and they are running a story tomorrow about it.

"At the time I counseled Shane and Michael and went over the question of whether they had fabricated anything for a bylined article or news assignment and I'm confident they did not. I think it was just a case of laziness and it bit them."

"I remember Vallow from the Daily Tar Heel," Laughter says. "I don't remember Profaci but Vallow certainly knows better than that."

"I, uh, I know. I can't believe it myself. What makes it worse, and this is my problem, my publisher has forbidden me from going up the chain of command to ask for advice. I'm a new manager, baptism by fire and all, and I usually turn to my friend Arthur in Danville or Joe in Fredericksville where I used to work, for leadership advice. But she's forbidden me."

"Well, that's certainly a problem. What's her reasoning?"

"She's only been here about eight months herself and I think she wants to show them she's got things under control. It's been a tough transition because we were without a publisher for about a year. I was without a top editor for about six months before that. So for about 18 months we had a leadership vacuum and a lot of people in mid management got too big for their britches and so she's had to fight to get everyone back in their right place."

"That doesn't seem like a rationale for keeping you from seeking ethical advice."

"I agree and it concerns me. But my bigger concern is did I make the right decision? I mean, am I going to get crucified by my peers in the morning when this story comes out? Was I justified in not firing them?"

"I can see both sides," Laughter says. "On the one hand we can't tolerate fabrication or plagiarism but on the other hand was this journalism or not? And with them both being on the job less than a year you can't be expected to predict every mistake they might make and prevent it from happening. I mean, it's akin to on the job training." The professor pauses. "No, I think you're within the bounds of ethics to counsel them and prevent it from happening again, so long as it's not occurred in a news item."

"I still just can't believe they did this. Of all the things possible under the sun I would never have expected this type of thing from a Carolina graduate," Samuel says.

There hangs an uneasy silence as he looks to the distance and the baby blue sky is now tinged with the incandescent orange of evening.

"No I agree," the professor says. "It's certainly a unique situation and I'm sorry that this is happening to you. We'll double our efforts on this end."

He slides the phone into his pocket and rubs his face as if trying to shake himself awake from what has to be one of those epic dreams you have sometimes. But he looks up to the sky and watches as pale clouds float on the horizon and the faintness of real light still burns beneath them as they hang above the amber glow. The only thing to do now is to wait and react tomorrow to whatever fallout comes his way.

He feels the potential for opportunity rise in him again, as it does often when his eyes linger across a creeping sunset. It's not the fade so much as the knowing that it comes back. That even if it's dark where you are now people are moving to the buoyant possibility elsewhere and that your time is coming back around again.

EIGHT

He rose in the openness of the morning with the last energy of a man who can sense doom but is too stubborn to surrender. Push on! Push on! Live strong and never give up! And in that sense he acted out the only role that was open for him. He felt strong enough to confront the day. He'd been attacked before, quite often actually, and was strengthened by the experience. Now possessed with the resolve to survive he pulled the car away from his house and retraced the path to the office. No CD this morning. No NPR news talk. His hands steeled about the steering wheel he pressed on in focused silence.

He would need focus and silence to get through this day and felt readily prepared to listen and acknowledge, to confirm and accept. If he guided himself with poise then perhaps that would be what people came away from this day with—the sense of a young man in a trying situation doing his best with what skills he possessed.

The late July morning sky hung powder white over the roadway as the heat of the day began to build. By 10 am it might be a clear day. By 4 pm the projected high of 98 degrees would oppress the deepest southerner. Perhaps an afternoon storm would drive the heat away, leaving a fresh evening as a reward for diligence.

Driving up the long, slow slope of the street up to his office he recalled Michael's story from yesterday— the story about the road widening project. This was the street in question, a narrow two lane strip off of the main highway leading west out of town, tailing off just beyond the first main housing block outside of the commercial district before snaking its way in a westerly direction and crossing the four-lane bypass that tracks a semicircle around the edge of the city. The office was 75 yards just this side of the intersection. A Hardees, a drug store, a bank and a convenience store with a gas station occupied the four corners of the intersection and this pulled a large volume of foot traffic along the edge of the street. It was an unsafe place for pedestrians, especially at night, and especially for the less than cautious folk who ambled along with no heed of the rules of the road. He'd almost hit someone walking on several occasions in his first year at the paper, when he still worked the swing shift in the evening.

The project called for the two lanes to be widened, with an added turn lane and sidewalks on both sides of the street. He'd written an editorial praising the project just last week and now was spinning in his mind an idea to track the project over the coming months. Perhaps a photo collection like a time lapse film strip showing the evolution of the construction would give Michael and the news photographer, Ross, a project to work on and help Michael move beyond today's sledgehammer. The photo content would give Charles ample design elements to work with. He'd almost envisioned the awards reception at next year's state press awards ceremony when he crested the hill and saw the TV van in the parking lot of the newspaper.

The building had two main entrances on the front and a service road ran the length of the building on the left side. He often turned onto the service road to head toward the back of the parking lot in order to park near the employee's entrance by the loading docks. He rounded the median between the service road and the parking lot thinking he should just keep going and pull back out onto the road and go back home. But he'd fought back from worse than this. "

"I can do this," he said to himself.

The van was from a station across the border in Virginia. They were based in Fredericksville, about 70 miles up the highway that ran through town, but had a bureau 20 miles away just across the border in Danville. Similar to the competitive market situation between the company that owned the Small City Review and the company that owned the Big City Daily News, this ABC affiliate competed in three markets with his company. Southeastern Media Holding Company, the firm he worked for, owned both newspaper and television stations in 45 markets, primarily in the southeast with a few television stations across the Midwest and the Plains. When he worked in Fredericksville he went toe to toe with the staff from this affiliate, winning more often than losing.

A deadly silence gripped the building when he stepped into the warehouse where just yesterday a festive staff cookout occurred, before Sheila Vallejo's phone call shattered the tiny piece of certainty he'd carved out for himself. Through the heavy industrial door separating the warehouse from the back hallway of the office building he moved down the hall to one of the entrances into the newsroom. The second hand on the clock swept across its two partners, one resting just before nine while the larger one closed in on 10.

"It's awfully early for a news crew to be here from Danville," he thought to himself as he crossed the carpeted newsroom, vacant except for Dana who worked at her desk. She looked up at him as he neared.

"There's a reporter from News 13 outside and we've had four phone calls from TV and radio stations since I got here at 8:30," she said. "What in the world is going on?"

He took the message slips from her. Fox8. News12. Channel 2. Talk 101 FM.

"No rest for the wicked," he said. Which did not comfort her.

"Why are all these people calling?"

"Look, Dana. It's ok. It's going to be a long, hard day but I will deal with it. What's happened is that Shane and Michael did something lazy. They turned in photos of their friends from UNC as man on the street instead of going out and taking a photo of somebody here in town. Big City Daily News heard about it and they did a story on it this morning."

Her mouth hung open as the color in her face moved to resonate with the deep rose colored blush she'd dusted her cheek with that morning.

"They did a story about that? But why would that interest them?"

"Dana, it's complicated, but basically for two reasons. It reeks of a possible ethical violation and it makes us look bad ..." the ringing of the phone cut him off. She looked at the phone with a tense trepidation. "Just answer it as you normally do and take a message. Just do the best you can and we'll get through it together."

She turned back to her desk and took a seat. He stepped into his office and no sooner sat down than the front desk receptionist was standing over him. "John Allen from News 13 is here to see you," Ella said. She wore a look of consternation.

"Ella, could you close the door for a second?" he asked her. She agreed and stepped in front of the closed door. Ella was an older black woman. Gentle and kind—a grandmother to many and mother to three, including a flight officer in the Air Force who currently flew on Air Force One. She'd been nothing short of graceful to him and on several occasions helped him steer clear of local pitfalls and an occasional viper intent on biting him.

"Ella, it is going to be a long, tough day. I guess you've seen the Big City paper?" She nodded. "Well, Theresa is not here today and I am going to have to focus on keeping the staff moving forward. I need your help if I am going to make it through the day."

"Well Samuel you can't just ignore these people and the phone has been ringing off the hook all morning."

"I'm sure it has, but will you help me, Ella? I can't handle all of what is surely to come today."

She nods. "What would you like to do?"

"I think procedure is what we need to focus on. I'm sure there will be a hundred calls today. So I think what we should do is that if it is not a staff member or someone from the company then please just put them straight to my voicemail or ask to take a message. Tell them I am tied up in meetings, because once I hear from corporate then I will be tied up I'm sure. So, you don't have to argue or make excuses or even explain anything. Just say he is tied up in meetings and offer voicemail or to take a message. If you can do that for me I will be grateful."

She smiles softly. "I can do that for you Samuel. What about those two boys?"

"Well, I'll tell you like I would tell anyone. They made a mistake. They approached me about it several weeks ago and I counseled them and disciplined them as I would any employee who made a mistake. I don't know what else to say about it. It wasn't good enough for people who don't understand the full picture of what happened so they decided to attack us with it. But I think we will be better for it."

Ella points with her thumb over her shoulder. "And what about Mr. Allen?"

"If you could just tell him I will not speak with him and that if he wants a comment he will have to call corporate in Richmond. Give him their number if he wants it."

She opens the door to leave.

"Oh and Ella, can you please bring me the copy of the Big City paper when you get the chance."

He's proud of himself now. Calm. Poised. Professional. Yet in his naiveté he is ignorant of the speed at which information is moving through CAT4 cable line and being beamed by communication satellites and coursing its way from the server at the Big City Daily News where the night wire editor first uploaded the item slugged "Newspaper quotes people it didn't interview" just after midnight. In the ensuing eight hours the story has spread forward five time zones to London where the papers there have printed it in their "News from America" columns and populated their websites with the quirky item about the hick editor who won't answer questions. He hasn't even seen the story yet—Ella is now moving back down the hall with a copy—but as dawn broke in New York City and Boston and Washington, D.C. a few hours back the item fought its way to the top of several wire columns on internal news servers and sleepy eyed interactive media and morning side editors have clicked and copied and pasted the story so that it sits atop fresh news lists from Miami to Maine.

Editors and reporters up and down the east coast are livid that one more charlatan somewhere in the hinterland dares to besmirch the holy frock of journalism with his situational ethics.

Ella enters the office and hands him the paper along with a card from John Allen, the reporter from News13. "He left," is all she says while handing him the two items. He mouths "Thank you" and exchanges a smile with her as she turns to leave. Down the front hall he can hear the phone ringing steadily and he sees the message light on the telephone receiver on his desk blinking.

He scans the front page of the Big City Daily News and then opens the top half of the fold and pulls the local section. He's got the headline in his eye before the bottom half of the paper is free.

"Emma Sampson knows the kind of music she likes so imagine her surprise when she learned she'd been featured in a newspaper she's never heard of talking about her favorite artists." So began the story, confirming his worst case scenario. "Sampson, 22, and an intern at a Robinson Media Corp. newspaper in Salisbury graduated from the UNC School of Journalism with two reporters who work for the Small City Review. She was featured in the May 12 edition of the paper in a small daily feature that runs on the front page called "Two Cents Worth." The problem is she has never been to Small City. Nor, claims Sampson, was she ever interviewed by the paper or asked for permission to be featured."

"Sampson is one of four people featured in the newspaper's daily man-on-the-street item who attended college with Shane Vallow and Michael Profaci, reporters at the Small City Review."

"Sampson's photo appears to have been lifted from TheFacebook.com, a college social networking site. Vallow and Profaci list Sampson as a friend along with the other three people who claim to have never been contacted by the paper prior to their photo appearing."

"Neither publisher Theresa Courts or editor Samuel Ashton would answer questions when contacted by the Big City Daily News."

"Sampson claims to have received "a professional apology" from Vallow for using her photo and her name."

"Vallow had no comment Tuesday, except to say that staffers had been told not to talk to the Big City Daily News."

"There's plenty I would like to say if I didn't think I would get fired for saying them," Vallow said.

The story continued to describe the paper as being owned by Southeastern Media Holdings and quoted two more people whose name and photo Vallow submitted as opposed to completing the assignment.

Sampson's money shot was a defense of the university newspaper, The Daily Tar Heel.

"Sampson said she was sad to think how the reporter's actions reflected on the Daily Tar Heel, which taught reporters "the difference between what is ethical and what is not."

Another former classmate was quoted as saying "That bothers me a great deal because these were two guys I really respected."

Vallejo most likely wore a delightful smile when she penned the closing sentence. In addition to being let down by the ethical taint brought about by Vallow being unable to complete a routine assignment and feeling the need to rip her photo from the Internet, he got her favorite style of music wrong. She had been quoted as favoring The Breeders over everyone else.

"I'm more of a jam band type girl," she said.

NINE

Before the chaos of the universe took shape at creation an endless number of tangents caressed each other in darkness, not quite ever fully aware of the possible shapes or patterns made by viewing the process from a removed vantage point. Life exists amidst the released energy of these interactions. The pulsations of the seemingly random hold meaning within the context of the monad. Dark green can be blue for some poets. Stability can be imprisonment for energy coiled with the force of creativity.

And compassion can be willful concealment when the events that form the cloud are viewed from the pure atmosphere of the sky as opposed to the cluttered dust of the everyday.

He put the paper on the desk, his instinct confirmed once again. Vallejo did a bang up job with the conversational story introduction and the way she tied the end to the beginning was a masterful stroke. He was impressed, even if devastated to be the tangent the story hung on.

But two things stood out to him. The first was Vallow's comment about having plenty to say "if I didn't think I would get fired for saying them." What was that about? And second the main source in the story, Emma Sampson, said she was never contacted by anyone from the paper. She's quoted as saying Shane Vallow apologized to her "for using her picture and name."

But Shane told him to his face that he'd gotten permission from the friends he used and that he only took the photos from the internet. Now Sampson's revelation casts Shane in a devastating lie.

The phone was ringing down the hall again. In another second his desk phone rang. With some trepidation he picked it up.

"Hello?"

"Samuel, this is David Quinn over at the Journal. How you holding up man?"

The managing editor at the newspaper in Winston-Salem, David Quinn encouraged him to apply for an assistant metro-editor spot at the Journal just a couple of months ago. He'd been impressed with Samuel's ability to manage the cauldron at Small City after Harlan Stevens had been fired and the publisher left for Georgia, leaving him there alone, a second year manager in a low-performing environment.

It had been his life's dream to work at the Winston-Salem Journal since he was a child and then a teenager reading the paper everyday in the afternoon when he came home from school. He'd grown beyond the sports section and the comic pages when he was about 12, after some national or international story he'd seen on the TV caught his interest. The pages of the front news section and then the editorial pages especially were a window for him into the larger world. It brought the world into a focused reality and made faraway places more than just spaces on a map in between lines that had no real logic to them but separated places with names like Syria, Tibet or Belize into identifiable categories.

He'd read every story, everyday, and his ability to retain information like a sponge was a large boost to his persona, accelerating him beyond his provincial roots while keeping him from being a pedantic conversationalist.

Even the publisher at the Journal had pulled him aside at a division meeting back in the winter and encouraged him to apply.

But he'd politely turned them down, not even both-ering to apply, for reasons not clear to anyone outside of his head. There were just too many possible tangents that could collide. There was a sidewalk and a police officer and a confused younger man, stifled by the un-certainty of stability who uncoiled his energy. He'd used the baby and the newly purchased house as an excuse, saying he couldn't go back to working the night shift and leave his wife at home alone.

It was a reasonable excuse but not reason enough for a man to turn down an opportunity to achieve a life-long dream.

"God David it is good to hear your voice. I'm in a complete mess over here."

"Well what's going on? Why didn't you call me yester-day before this story came out?"

"I wanted to, believe me. But Theresa forbid me from reaching out to you or Joe or Arthur. I asked her three times and even told her I wanted to call Donna up in Richmond but she ordered me not to and said she would be the one to call outside if she felt the need."

"You mean Donna doesn't know about this?"

"No, I haven't told her."

"Listen, Samuel, I don't know what your publisher is thinking but you better call Donna right now. She's going to go ballistic when she hears about this and it better come from you. This will be on Romenesko by lunch if it isn't already."

"Well Theresa isn't here today, they have a publisher's meeting in Concord ..." David cut him off.

"Samuel, it's too late for that. Forget what your publisher said. You answer to Donna on the news side and you need to hang up and call her. Look man, take care of yourself. Call me later if you need to talk."

He hung up the phone and went to look up Donna's number on the internal company website. His phone rang before he could type her name in the search field. It might be David again so he picked it up.

"Samuel this is Tom Holmes from the AP bureau in Raleigh and I wondered if I could ask you a few questions about this ..." He cut Holmes off.

"Tom, I tell you it's a rough time right now. I've got a nightmare on my hands and I'm just about to call my company vice-president for direction so I think you can understand if I tell you I don't have the leeway to talk right now."

"Well it's a national, if not global story by now and I think you're going to want to ..."

"Look Tom, I respect the AP a great deal. I know what the AP stands for. If I'm given the opportunity to speak outside the company I will call you first. How about that."

Satisfied, Holmes left his number and since he'd by now found Donna's number in the company directory he punched her number into the keypad, took a deep breath and exhaled.

"Donna Turner," she answered on the second ring.

"Donna, this is Samuel Ashton down in Small City."

"Hey Samuel, how's it going this morning?" She was oblivious to the infamous news feature about the hick editor who would not answer questions that was coursing its way through the global alliance of wire services beamed via satellite across continents and industry specific websites published instantaneously with a paste and a click.

In another moment her voice steeled. Her teeth clenched. He could see her scowl coming straight through the telephone line and prop itself before him on the desk where he now looked at romenesko.com and saw his name featured on the lead-in to the item from Big City.

"Samuel, you know we don't just make it up!" she said bitterly. "Why on earth did you not call me yesterday. We don't let our competitors air our dirty laundry!"

She was angrily rebuking him. She'd been the editor of the largest newspaper in the company, the paper in Tampa, before becoming vice-president for news after her predecessor moved up the corporate chain. She was tough and fair and up until this very moment had been nothing short of fawning over his job of handling the situation in Small City. Once on a conference call with other editors she complimented him on a point he'd made about managing the flow of mandatory paperwork up to corporate. After the call Quinn from Winston had emailed him saying jokingly "we'll all be working for you in a few years."

Those days seemed as ancient as the creation story now as Turner bit into him.

"Theresa ordered me not to call anyone over her head. I asked her three times to call you or Joe or Arthur and she forbid it."

"Where is she now?"

"She's on the way to the publisher's conference in Concord. I'm here by myself. The phone is ringing off the hook. I've got messages from three TV stations and the AP in Raleigh wants a comment."

"You don't talk!" she yells into the phone. "You've talked enough already. Jesus. This is on Romenekso now. You don't talk anymore. To anyone. Until you hear from me. Is that clear?"

"Yes, Donna. I'm sorry."

"Where are Shane and Michael?"

He looked at his watch. It was 9:20 a.m.

"Shane is filling in at the other office. Michael isn't here yet."

There is a long silence.

"There's a lot he'd like to say? Well what would he like to say? C'mon Sam. Aren't your people trained better than this? We don't make comments to our competitors."

"I know Donna. I've gone over that with them twice. Just like I've gone over this man on the street assignment with the staff several times."

"And we just gave him the D.C. fellowship. What an ungrateful little twerp! These guys are toast."

"Am I toast too Donna?"

She pauses.

"No Samuel. I don't think so. But we've got to get a handle on this. I can't believe Theresa told you not to call. You should have run an apology in the paper today to get ahead of this piece in the Big City Paper."

"I mentioned that to her as well, Donna. She said no. And she said for me not to call anyone."

"I can't believe this," she says. "Hold on." He hears commotion, muffled voices, shuffling paper.

"Samuel, Troy is standing here and says he's gotten three calls for comment in the last five minutes. You don't talk to anyone, you understand. Anyone calls you say you can't comment and refer them to me. Is that clear?"

"Yes, Donna."

"I'll call you back."

The words "they're toast" hung on his mind as he placed the receiver in its cradle and tried to catch his breath. If that was her instant reaction to the story then he was in deep trouble. But he's not giving up now. His memory recalls Shane's apparent lie. He'd claimed to have asked his friends the question and for their permission and only taken their photo from TheFacebook.com but in the story Emma Sampson claimed otherwise.

She'd been featured in the May 12 edition. He pulled out the assignment calendar from the folder in his desk labeled "Floating assignments." Shane had been on deck for the week of May 12. Samuel'd been home from

Brenner with the baby for 10 days on May 12. Shane's fellowship award was announced a month earlier and he'd gone to DC for a month beginning June 1.

His heart sank. He'd end up firing Shane today after all and maybe even getting fired himself. For now though, he was concerned about the lie Shane told him to his face.

He picked up the phone again and dialed the number for the other office. The receptionist picked up and he asked her if Shane was there.

"He sure is, Samuel. One moment."

The tension of silence and then Shane picks up.

"Shane, have you read this story this morning in the Big City Daily News?"

"Yes I've read it."

"Didn't I tell you not to talk to her?"

"I told her three times I didn't want to talk to her. The fourth time she called she kept pushing and pushing and so I said that there was plenty I'd like to say but I figured I would get fired for saying anything. I can't believe she printed that."

"Well, Shane, she was fishing for anything but that's not my biggest problem actually."

"No, I guess not."

"You told me that you'd spoken to your friends and that they answered the questions and that you only took their photo from the internet didn't you?"

"Yea, I did, Samuel."

278 ~ JEFF SYKES

"And that's now what your friend Emma says in the story is it?"

"No, it's not."

"I think I am smart enough to figure out that means you lied to me. You lied to me to my face at the very moment I was trying to forgive you."

Silence.

"I know, Sam. I'm sorry. I'm so sorry I don't know what to say about it."

He could feel Shane's body sinking like a sandcastle on the shore after it's been pummeled by the tide. Anger rose in him. He could choke Shane with one hand while he held the phone in the other if the boy had been within reach at that very moment. But the urge subsided. He looked at the black and white printer paper photo of his son crawling on the floor and struggling to lift his head. There was another of him lying on his back playing with a stuffed toy suspended from a mobile over his head. His wife had emailed them last week and he'd printed them out and showed them around the office.

That fatherly pity rose in him again. He chose not to scream at Shane in the way Donna had rebuked him just moments ago. He continued in a cool, almost detached voice.

"Shane, I am suspending you immediately until further notice. I'm not sure what's going to happen. I think we'll all lose our jobs by the end of the day, but right now I am suspending you until I can figure out what's going on."

"I understand," Shane said.

"Just go home or whatever you want to do but don't come here and please don't talk to any other media about this."

"I'm sorry, Samuel. I never meant to hurt you."

"I know. It's a no win situation. I knew that when I took the chance."

"Sam, I want you to know something."

"What's that?"

"No one's ever stood up for me the way you did the day you chose not to fire me. I've never had anyone show that kind of faith in me and I admire you for it. I'm sorry I hurt you."

"Don't worry about it, Shane. You're a good kid. You've worked hard for me and I'm thankful for that. I'm sorry this has happened to you. I don't know why you did this but I want you to know that I've made mistakes a thousand times worse than this and you need to accept the failure and move on. Just go somewhere, no matter how small, and try to start over."

"Are they going to fire me?"

"I can't lie to you. I think probably so. If I was in your position I would resign now. Just type up a letter and bring it to Audrey in HR and give her your key. Just walk away and go start over."

Shane thanked him again and he could hear a tear swelling in the young man's voice. He told Shane it would be ok and to take care of himself. Hollow, functionless words spoken from the comfort of habit. He searched for a few seconds of peace after hanging up the phone. A pang of sadness at the shame Shane brought to himself and then a sense of the dizzying randomness of the series of events since the two reporters who represented the hope for achievement and a stronger reputation confronted him with their failure.

Again his eyes were drawn to the printer paper photo of his newborn son playing on the floor at home. The elegant smile and bright, playful eyes full of life and energy. The child awakened a place in his soul he'd not known before. A father's love for a son completed the circuit in his understanding, amplifying all those wasted moments of his past with a larger sense of regret.

And what of responsibility? It was the very thing he emphasized to Shane and Michael at the time of their confession, as they begged for forgiveness and a chance at redemption.

"I've got a wife and a baby and a mortgage and I can't throw that away to protect the two of you," were his exact words. His instincts acting as prophecy yet again.

The ringing phone shattered his moment of solace. This time it was the cell phone attached to a clip on his belt. He unhooked the small, egg-shaped phone and looked at the screen. It was Theresa.

"Hey boss," he said, attempting to feign an upbeat mindset.

"Samuel, what's going on? Carl called me and told me to turn around and head back to the office. I'm an hour down the road already."

For a moment he was tempted to lay into her. To rip apart her hee-haw leadership, her utter lack of understanding of the context the journalistic community operated in. Her ignorance of the dual pressures of credibility and digital competition for readership.

"We're on Romenesko. The top story. We're at the top of the AP wire in several columns. I've got messages here from TV and print media up and down the east coast."

"What is Roman, whatever it is you said?"

"Romenesko. Jim Romenesko is a blogger for Poynter. He writes an industry insider column twice a day that's read by every editor in the country and about 90 percent of the reporters."

Silence on the line except for the dull roar of the passing roadway that he can hear on his end of the line as she makes her way back to the office.

"Well what does he say?"

"He says the same thing everyone is saying. That the editor, Samuel Ashton, refuses to answer questions about the fabrication. That's all anyone is focused on, the fact that I refuse to answer questions. I've got requests here from the AP, Editor and Publisher, the Washington Post, not to mention Fox8, News 2 and Channel 12. Oh, and that ABC affiliate up in Fredericksville had a reporter here before 9 am."

"Lord have mercy," she said. "Have you heard from anyone at corporate?"

"Yes. David Quinn called just after 9. He'd read the story and said I had better call Donna Turner asap

because she'd be livid if she heard about this from anyone besides us."

"And what did she say?"

"Well, she said we were toast and that we shouldn't let
our competition air our dirty laundry without speaking
first and she ordered me not to talk to any of the several
media sources who are calling non-stop here."

"Lord Jesus," she said. More dull roaring of the roadway across the deadness of the cell connection.

She continued.

"Well, Sam, I'll be there in about an hour and we will
handle it together. Just hang on and till I get there."

He encourages her to drive carefully as they end their
exchange. He notices via the clock on his cell phone
that it's now 9:38 am. He's passed less than an hour
at the office and feels he's aged a decade. The news of
his incompetence is spreading like a wildfire across the
Midwest now as editors in Indianapolis, Madison and St.
Louis notice the industry item about an ethical breach
and with a cringe of tightness feel the urge to post the
story on their nascent web presence. A few dozen blog-
gers, after noticing the item on Romenesko, and reveling
in the certainty of their situation, opine about his shortcomings for a few hundred words and then click "post"
on their management system after hotlinking to the
Romenesko item in their body copy.

While the confines of his office serve as an eye wall
cutting him off from the topical fury that rages about
him, the storm gathers strength as the 10 o'clock hour

approaches. He's looking at his email inbox now. There's a note of comfort from the pastor of the small church he began attending in June. He'd not been to a church in 15 years but his heart seemed to grow a few sizes in the weeks after his son came home from the children's intensive care unit and in a spirit of thankfulness he thought that maybe he should give church a chance. There's a note from Jack Laughter, the UNC journalism professor he spoke to on the phone last night. He says that he still thinks it was acceptable not to fire the two cubs but that it was a major mistake not to acknowledge the gaffe in print and that "your publisher is dead wrong" to not let you explain your line of thinking.

Further down the list repeat a dozen or more messages with the subject line "Requesting interview" or "Please call our station". There's a note from a local antagonist "Scandal at the Small City Review" that consists of a link to the Big City News website where they have posted the story. The antagonist, a local political wannabe, has cc'd 200 local and state contacts, as if the ants gnawing at his ankles could do more damage than the vultures circling overhead.

But about 85 messages from the top he sees a name that catches his attention for taking his breath away. The subject line reads "Hey Samuel!" and it's from Steve Hooker. He's not talked to Steve Hooker since the week before Samuel attacked a police officer about eight years ago while high on some really pure cocaine.

"Hey Samuel! It's Steve Hooker from your days back at the finance office. Man it looks like you've really done a lot with your life since those days. I am so proud of you. Your family must be so proud at how far you have come. Do you remember Ken McKay? He emailed me this morning with a photo of you asking if I thought you were the same guy we used to know. I told him I had no doubts it was you since we went to the same high school and later worked together every day for three years. Steve is a reporter now in Nashville. I guess you remember he used to work at the Journal in Winston-Salem."

He knew the name well. Ken McKay was on the staff of the Winston-Salem Journal when Samuel uncoiled his energy about eight years ago while high on some really pure cocaine. McKay covered his arrest and court proceedings. McKay penned the articles that ran about him above the fold on the front page. McKay had worked under David Quinn, who was the city editor at the Journal back then. He'd always thought Quinn would remember him at some point. He was sure McKay would remind him now, if he hadn't already done so.

Perhaps fear, but more likely sadness, gripped him now. Because he knew it was over. Memories pulsated behind his eyes as he stared at his son's face. What a beautiful, now healthy and smiling four-month old boy. Ten years ago when he was dead inside and clinging to stimulants to connect him to reality he couldn't have imagined having a love like this. His mind sifted through the process of evolution. Despair and desperation. Broken and bruised. Ten months in jail for assaulting a cop. Solitary confinement but sober for the first time since he was 15. Desperate months of shame when he got out. Having to face his mother, his grandmother, the disappointment in his father's eyes. The continuing despair and shame until his aunt told him about the rehabilitation program that paid for him to finish his college degree.

The breathless flurry of joy that came with second opportunity. The sober success of achievement. Chasing his dream to become a reporter. Rising to become news editor of the college paper. Meeting the girl with the wry smile and the honey brown hair who now was at home with their little son who's been to the edge of death and back again in sixteen weeks but could possibly carry the scar of permanent disability. Graduating with honors and getting hired a week before classes ended to become a real live reporter at a daily newspaper in Morganton, which meant he was only two hours by car from her while she finished her last year of study.

Being promoted to the larger paper in Fredericksville. Winning the notoriety of his coworkers and the state press association. An unbroken chain of success since he'd cleared his mind of the dope that held him down. But then he betrayed his instincts and came here. To this place that felt like stifling death from the moment he'd pulled the car off the interstate for that first interview with Harlan Stevens.

And now it was come full circle. The thing he'd feared the most. The thing that pushed him to work so hard and to never stop and look back had never been more than a phone call, an email, a recognized name, a noticed photograph away from overtaking him midstride.

TEN

He was fired two hours later as Carl sat across from him in Theresa's office holding the applications he'd filled out at Morganton, Fredericksville and here at Small City. He never found out what really happened. He'd just assumed that Ken McKay called David Quinn and reminded him about the guy from the finance office who'd attacked the policeman one winter morning in front of Memorial Hospital. Remember how it took three cops and two security guards to subdue him and how we ran the story up the front for several days because he actually was dumb enough to talk to us without getting a lawyer first? Remember how he agreed to an interview while in the county waiting for his trial, remember he ended up pleading guilty and getting ten months, but remember how his brutal honesty and quirky verbal manner gave us the juicy bits we used for a series on the different impact of cocaine on young white males and young black males?

That's how he figured it went because Carl was sitting across from him holding the applications and pointing to the box where it asked if you'd ever been convicted of a crime and he'd checked the "no" box because his probation officer told him before he went off to school on the vocational rehab program to do his best, to never look back, and to do what he had to do to get a job.

He'd paused actually when he first filled out the application. If he checked "yes" he'd never get hired. Not in small town North Carolina. Not in the year 2000 when statewide computer records probably hadn't been integrated yet. Not when they would probably just go to the local courthouse and check his name and since he'd never lived here they'd find nothing. Just this once. He'd get the job and then he'd work like the dickens to earn it. He'd be the best and fulfill his promise and meet that potential his grandmother always told him he had. Even when he was a fat teenager crying in his room alone because the pain of loneliness was too much for him to deal with, she'd tell him even then he was the best and that she loved him and that he could be anything. He'd never believed her. Especially not while his mind was full of dope and alcohol clouded his vision all through his teens and twenties up until the time he hit the cop and got slammed to the sidewalk after they cracked his skull with a titanium baton.

It took that much for them to stop his downward spiral. But once he'd let it all out and let them start piecing him back together he'd managed to get ahead. He couldn't let one box on the third page of a job application stop him.

Carl shook his head and Theresa laid hers on the desk and sobbed actually as Carl made the obvious clear. He told Carl that he understood. He knew it was a cutthroat world and you had to do what you had to do to survive. He was a gambler and had rolled the dice then and last month because that's what you do when you are brave. He'd had enough of living in fear of his shortcomings. He'd lived that way for 25 years and it landed him in the state mental hospital and then in jail. But since then he'd chased the dragon – or was the dragon chasing him – and lived life to the fullest in all its rich variety.

And so when Michael and Shane confessed to him in shame what choice did he have but to counsel them in the confines of his own situational morality and urge them to do better?

Theresa handed him his leather bag after she'd removed the pictures of his wife from his desk and taken down the black and white computer printouts of his son from the poster board next to his desk. He'd be back to get the rest of his belongings next week but asked to take his pictures, the pictures of the love he had in his life, with him as he left.

He drove home in silence with the tears of customary failure welling up in the corner of his eyes. He'd called the girl with the sardonic smile and the honey brown hair and told her he was losing his job. She'd said she was sorry and that she loved him but when he came through the door he couldn't look at her. He could only whimper "I'm sorry babe" in barely legible syntax as he rushed to the back of the house to sit on the edge of the bed.

He cried the kind of tears that a man cries when he's just erased 10 years of hard work and success and landed himself back in the same place he'd started from: broke, shamed, isolated and without means of ascent. He cried sitting on the edge of the bed as his cell phone rang, as emails landed in his inbox at his former office, as newscasters read wire copy about the hick editor who refused to take questions.

He cried for ten minutes but then he was done. He had a son in the other room playing with felt covered animals as he lay on his back and looked up at the multicolored arcs that came together at the apex of the mobile.

The author wishes to thank his family for holding him up when he couldn't stand on his own. Steve Mitchell for his unquestioned friendship and mentoring as I began this writing journey. Kevin Morgan Watson for always being willing to answer a question or give advice. Ray Morrison for sitting next to me at the writer's conference when I was alone and pushing me forward. Brian Clarey for setting the standard for what it means to grind. Jason, Kenny, Eric, Dave and Dale for being the kind of friends a man is thankful for. Most of all, Hannah, for being the love of my life and showing me what it means to be fully alive.

Printed in the USA
CPSIA information can be obtained
at www.ICGtesting.com
CBHW022304210924
14613CB00046B/603